Lord Salvador and the Nectar Brotherhood

Mission to Planet Black Cloud

By E.A. Fantis

Order this book online at www.trafford.com
or email orders@trafford.com

Most Trafford titles are also available at major online book retailers.

afantis@cytanet.com.cy

Note for Librarians: A cataloguing record for this book is available from Library and Archives Canada at www.collectionscanada.ca/amicus/index-e.html

Contributors: Translated from the original Greek by John Vickers.

Printed in Victoria, BC, Canada.

ISBN: 978-1-4251-8982-2 (Soft)
ISBN: 978-1-4251-8983-9 (Hard)
ISBN: 978-1-4251-8984-6 (e-book)

Rev. date 5/18/2009

Trafford PUBLISHING® **www.trafford.com**

North America & international
toll-free: 1 888 232 4444 (USA & Canada)
phone: 250 383 6864 ♦ fax: 250 383 6804 ♦ email: info@trafford.com

The United Kingdom & Europe
phone: +44 (0)1865 487 395 ♦ local rate: 0845 230 9601
facsimile: +44 (0)1865 481 507 ♦ email: info.uk@trafford.com

10 9 8 7 6 5 4 3 2 1

About the Author

Eleftherios (Akis) Fantis was born in Nicosia, Cyprus and studied Law in Moscow (LL.M., Hons) with post-graduate studies in London and Geneva. He has held a number of important political posts, including that of Government Spokesman for the Republic of Cyprus (1988-1993).

As a journalist he has worked on, managed and published several newspapers in Cyprus, Greece and England. He has also presented numerous TV and Radio programmes.

He has written four novels, three books on journalism and sportswriting, a poetry collection and a biography. For many years he has worked as a lecturer in Journalism at Frederick University Cyprus.

This book is dedicated to my family, my wife Athena and my daughters Charoula, Marilia and Louiza.

CHAPTER 1

June 21st was the biggest day of the year for the 'Ark of Hope' orphanage. Another year was coming to an end and the school Sports Day represented the culmination of everything that had gone before. It was always a brilliant fiesta and all of Heliopolis was there.

In the stands, pupils from the first form to the graduating class fought to make an impression, creating a fantastic atmosphere. Divided into classes, dressed identically and with decorum as required by the regulations, they resembled companies of soldiers, all lined up on parade. The vigilant eye of the Head of the orphanage, Master Zarko, surveyed everything. Brandishing his favourite rosewood cane in his right hand, he would give orders, sometimes to his underlings, sometimes to the judges and frequently to the institution's wardens to restore order whenever the youngsters went too far with their shouts and whistles. Around the Head, centre stage, all the official guests were gathered. The aged permanent Mayor of Heliopolis was enjoying a soft drink. Sometimes awake, sometimes asleep, he jumped up with a jolt each time the stadium rocked with cheers.

"Well done, child!" he would exclaim like a cuckoo in a clock, clumsily spilling his drink over those around him. Master Zarko hurried to put things in their place, obliged to grin and apologise to the others, waving his cane up and down, as if bowing. The strict inspectors from the ministry, as official guests at Sports Day, sat one beside the other, expressionless and cold, trying to show their superiority by their unbroken silence. The Chairman of the school board, the powerful Doctor Socrates, his cane under one arm, stroked his curious pointed goatee with satisfaction, relieved that the troubling business of another school year was at an end. The auxiliary staff were still around, ready to carry out Master Zarko's every request, handing out soft drinks and biscuits to the esteemed guests. And right in front of the stage, walking with showy, heavy steps like a robot and with a whistle between his lips, was Mr Takamura, the head warden of the orphanage, ready to restore order with one of his fierce looks – and his whip if necessary.

Behind the main stage, a huge banner proclaimed the Annual Sports Day of the 'Ark of Hope' Orphanage with the institution's famous motto 'Forever Victorious' spelt out in large letters.

On the track it was the usual disorderly picture, with the athletes, judges, helpers and coaches getting in one another's way as they wandered up and down, always with some duty to perform, or at least that was the impression they gave.

The school's two young gym teachers shone in their modern, handsome blue outfits and their behaviour showed everyone in every direction that they had the general run of the sports field.

Monsieur André and Mademoiselle Vivienne – who, as even the very last of the first year pupils knew, were at it with no inhibitions whenever and wherever they fancied – were inseparable lovers, providing the school with all kinds of gossip and tickling the fantasies in the minds of the young boys and girls who lived in the orphanage.

In one corner of the stadium, the athletes were preparing for the final event of the day, which was the long jump. The slim-built Tao Li was the girl pupils' favourite. As a final year student, he knew everyone in the orphanage and, naturally, he and his friends in his gang, the Tigers, were champions when it came to having a good time, breaking the rules and making any girl they fancied fall for their charms.

"Right guys, time for business and we're going for gold… It's in the bag," boasted Tao Li straight after his third jump of 5.83 metres. It was indeed a superb jump for someone of his age and it caused pandemonium among the Tigers and brought applause from the stands. Tao Li smiled with contentment and turned his gaze, full of pride and self-satisfaction, towards the group of girls who were jumping up and down at the edge of the running track, encouraging their team's athletes.

Next to them, the 7th year team were trying to encourage their own athlete before his final jump.

"Come on Jurka, get focused," Johara said to the boy representing her class, "You've got to beat that idiot. Do it for us…"

Jurka Slavik shook his full head of light brown hair and took deep breaths without saying a word. Milo, with his enormous black hands, rubbed his back and waist as he always did for his friend.

"It's not easy but it's not impossible," whispered the big-bodied Milo, in agreement with Johara. "This time you just need to hit the board properly," he added.

"That's right," said little Johara, whose short black hair and nimble body made her look more like a boy than a girl. "Just get focused, man. Do it for all of us. You can do it, Jurka," she told him, staring at him with those beautiful big black eyes of hers. "Show those punks what it means to belong to the Nectar Brotherhood!" she added.

"Off you go now, Jurka. Let's win it!" said Milo in his deep, black voice.

Jurka Slavik merely said, "OK, I'll do my best" and glanced towards the end of the stands. He was searching persistently for something, seemingly indifferent to the advice and admonitions of his friends.

Johara grumbled. "Where are you looking, clumsy boy? She's sitting over there… your… your goddess…"

And then he saw her!

There stood Nefeli, looking like a goddess indeed, her mature body making her stand out in the crowd, surrounded by admirers and girlfriends. Her angelic face shone beneath her rich, wavy, blonde hair and her look had a sweetness that made Jurka tremble as usual.

"She's watching me!" Jurka murmured as their eyes met. Her half-smile filed the light-haired young man with a hitherto unknown shudder of happiness. Nefeli raised her hand coquettishly and threw a carnation onto the sports field in the direction of the athletes. Jurka felt his heart beating hard and he made to grab the flower. But Tao Li was there before him.

"That's for me, idiot! It's the champions who get prizes, not the runners-up…," he said plainly, giving Jurka a sarcastic look. "When you've grown up, we'll talk again, kid…" the arrogant leader of the Tigers gang added before bursting into laughter with the rest of his entourage.

Jurka cursed inwardly and looked back at Nefeli who raised her eyebrows and indicated with a gesture of her hands that there was nothing she could do. The enigmatic half-smile had not disappeared from her lips. Tempers began to rise as Milo moved threateningly towards Tao Li but a voice behind Jurka calmed things down.

"I wish you good luck, Jurka Slavik!"

It was Mrs Benazir, the 7th year teacher who had come to wish her student all the best for his event. Jurka softened at the sight of his favourite teacher.

"Thanks Miss, thanks. I'll do my best. I won't disappoint you," Slavik replied.

Benazir smiled at him and patted him on the back.

"Jurka Slavik, you have the talent. All you need now is to earn yourself a reputation," said the teacher before walking away.

"Next competitor!" As soon as the announcement by André, the gym teacher, was heard, his colleague Vivienne spoke the name of Jurka Slavik over the loudspeakers.

Johara hugged Jurka on one side and Milo did so on the other. The three of them formed a small circle and, as one, they chanted their favourite slogan: "For the Nectar Brotherhood!"

"Jurka!... Jurka!... Jurka!..." echoed around the stadium as the 7th year athlete took up his position at the end of the track and warmed up. The run-up towards the take-off board appeared long and unending. Jurka stood motionless and closed his eyes.

He tried to picture his jump in the darkness, to imagine how he would fly – literally! – beyond the 5.83 metre mark to beat the hated Tao Li and to win Nefeli...

"Lord Salvador of Wisdom, help me to win..." Jurka made his wish as he set off on his most crucial jump.

It was not to be. Tao Li, leader of the Tigers, was not only malicious and unscrupulous by reputation. For him the end always justified the means. He and his cronies were not willing to take any risk, even by the law of averages, of losing and being made fools of by a dumb kid from the 7th form. They had taken measures for any eventuality. Jurka Slavik's jump of 5.75 metres did not allow them to be absolutely certain that he wouldn't be able to make a final jump of more than Tao Li's 5.83 and win. And on the dusty tartan track, who was going to notice the thin white silk thread that the Tigers had installed earlier? Who was going to check the landing area apart from the two gym teacher lovebirds? Since they owed many favours to Tao Li's gang, everything was ready and set up. Jurka Slavik would not complete his final attempt and would thus remain in second place on 5.75 metres. And who would remember the runner-up?

As the athlete began his run towards the take-off board, the entire stadium rose to its feet. Rhythmic chanting and applause accompanied Jurka as he raced towards the jumping area. His footing was perfect and his take-off looked fantastic but, at the very beginning of the landing area, his feet suddenly became entangled in something invisible. Slavik made a clumsy turn in the air and landed untidily in the sand. There was no chance of that being a winning performance – it didn't appear to be more than 5 metres.

For a moment the stadium was silent. Jurka looked in bewilderment at the take-off board but could see nothing unusual. The thin thread had, of course, been removed by Tao Li's friends, and he and his gang were now laughing sarcastically as they made fun of Slavik's supporters.

Milo and Johara ran to the sand pit, screaming angrily. It was more than obvious that there had been foul play. It wasn't possible for someone to trip up in the air!

André, the gym teacher, rushed to stop them.

"What are you two doing in the jumping area? You're not allowed down here!" he told them in a fierce tone that was not to be answered back.

"Monsieur André, something happened. Didn't you see?" said Milo as Johara added sharply: "That's cheating! Someone fixed things against Jurka." The girl with the short black hair added venomously, "And I think we all know who it was!" Her fierce look was aimed in the direction of Tao Li's team which had begun celebrating.

"The motto says 'Forever Victorious' but nobody wins like that!" said Milo in a trembling voice as he hugged Jurka and led him away from the jumping area.

Slavik could not explain what had happened. He had taken off well, his jump had been excellent and then, suddenly, his feet had become tangled up in something. He was absolutely certain of that and he said so to his friends. They would have to lodge an appeal. Meanwhile, those in the stands of the stadium were up in arms. They realised that something underhand had taken place and when they saw Milo and Johara complaining loudly they burst into noise, rhythmically chanting "Jurka - Jurka." Head warden Takamura, constantly blowing his whistle and waving his whip threateningly, ran left and right with the other 'discipline monitors' as they were officially known, issuing vain threats that he would punish anyone who went too far. But the pupils in the stands had exploded with fury and nothing could stop them. Master Zarko had turned a deep red – not only from anger but literally, as the Mayor of Heliopolis had spilt a whole glass of juice over him – and was threatening everyone and everything, waving his cane right and left. The inspectors shook their heads meaningfully while Doctor Socrates, at a loss as to what to do, leaned on his stick and nervously stroked his ridiculous beard.

Vivienne took the microphone and announced that the result of the long jump competition would stand. Tao Li was declared the winner. The whistles intensified, but there was nothing more to be done. The judges' decision was final, particularly since Master Zarko had taken care to pass on the message that they needed to finish the games since there was still the grand reception for the staff and guests to come. He immediately called upon Doctor Socrates to award the cup to the winner and soon Tao Li was strutting around like a cockerel, waving his trophy in the air.

"It's not fair," Jurka said to the two gym teachers and took himself to the edge of the track with Johara and Milo. The big black youth leaned over to his friends and swore revenge. "We can't let this go," he whispered. "They're going to pay a high price for cheating!"

Johara looked upset as Tao Li approached and started to tease and provoke the three of them.

"What's up, champs? Run out of fuel did we?" said the arrogant youth sarcastically as the gang of Tigers behind him started to laugh.

Jurka raised a fist threateningly. "Don't go too far, Tao Li. And just so that you know, winners who cheat don't count in my book..."

"In yours maybe not. But they certainly do in hers," Tao Li replied and, with a wink, he pointed at Nefeli.

The pretty graduate student of the orphanage approached the athletes, all coquettishness, and Jurka once again felt as if he was paralysed. Was she coming over to him? Or to Tao Li?

The school's blonde beauty glanced across at Jurka and the familiar, alluring half-smile formed on her lips once again. Then she turned towards Tao Li who had already taken up a victor's pose, and held out her hand.

"Congratulations Tao Li. Here's to greater things," she said in a whispering, almost melancholy voice, smiling broadly. Jurka felt as if he were lost in a void somewhere. He wanted to breathe but he wasn't getting enough air and his heart was pounding. He felt as if he was choking...

Johara seized him by the arm and brought him back to earth.

"Let's go, man. It's not worth it," she said and both she and Milo hugged Jurka. Slavik just stood there, looking at the Tigers. Now, Nefeli, with Tao Li beside her, surrounded by the punks of the gang, was leaving the stadium with the lightest of doe-like steps. Jurka, rooted to the spot, could only watch his goddess disappear into the distance. Everything around him seemed to be desert as he watched the shapely figure of Nefeli pulling Tao Li and his gang in her wake...

And then, suddenly, there she was rising slowly into the rosy evening sky and following her, like small comets, were Tao Li and the Tigers! And then she was moving further and further away, rising ever higher like a vision in some heavenly painting drawn by a famous old master.

"Lord Salvador of wisdom, what's going on?" Jurka wondered aloud, as a small black cloud suddenly appeared on the horizon and, moving at a steady speed, headed across the clear sky towards Nefeli. The black cloud stopped precisely above the blonde beauty and her followers. From its underside there appeared a crack of light which gradually grew into the shape of a square opening, like a gateway. The half-light slowly took on a dazzling, multicoloured appearance which covered the area, concealing Nefeli, Tao Li and the others. The pretty graduate student was already at the entrance to the gateway when she gave Jurka Slavik an irresistibly sweet look. The enigmatic half-smile disappeared as her hands stretched forward in the air, as if in a final farewell...

What had Jurka Slavik seen? Had she been complaining? Beseeching him? Provoking him? He had no time to think about it since, in the next second, Nefeli had disappeared into the black cloud together with the others. The dazzling light faded as the gateway closed and the black cloud streaked away and disappeared into the unknown, into a vast higher dimension.

Jurka, Milo and Johara stood watching the empty afternoon sky, silent and confused. They could not believe that all this had taken place before their very eyes. They looked around. Nothing was happening in the stadium. Everything had calmed down and the last groups of spectators were leaving under the watchful eyes of the wardens. The stands were emptying rapidly and those who had been in the VIP places had already gone.

"Lord Salvador of wisdom! I want to know what happened..." Jurka shouted but no-one answered. Johara continued to stare at the sky, while an embarrassed Milo rubbed his huge shaven head.

"It wasn't a dream, was it? Tell me it wasn't a dream..." Jurka spoke again and his two friends shook their heads.

"It was definitely not a dream," Johara replied with certainty. "It happened in front of us and we saw it, didn't we?"

Milo agreed. "Only our wise friend Lord Salvador can enlighten us," noted the black giant and Jurka Slavic concurred at once.

"Yes, but that will have to wait until midnight when we have our appointment. Only then will we be able to communicate with Lord Salvador of wisdom," he reminded them.

"I don't know but I reckon we're getting into something here," said Johara. "This story's not going to end without some excitement," she concluded pensively.

"Kiddo, I think things are perfectly clear," said Jurka. "This was an abduction! And I don't think we have a right to stand idly by..."

"Hold on a minute, man!" Milo interrupted. "Tell us how you worked that one out! From what I could see, the babe went with them of her own free will..."

"No, Milo! I saw enough. They've kidnapped her!" declared the light-haired youth, his eyes blazing. "Yes, I'm telling you that Tao Li and his Tigers have kidnapped her. I saw it clearly in Nefeli's helpless look when she waved goodbye. She was begging us, yes that's it, begging us to help her... If you'd rather I put it another way... I can feel it," Jurka added, but Johara disagreed at once.

"I think that what we saw proves that she went willingly. No-one was abducting her and I'm sorry to say this, Jurka, but you can expect just about anything from her, can't you?"

"Yes, but we won't know that until we've made sure. And she's the only one who can clear things up. Anyway, I don't think the Nectar Brotherhood can unthinkingly accept something that may be a criminal act. Who knows what might happen to her? Or even worse, what's happening to her right now as we speak? No, no, we have to act at once, that's what I think," Jurka added.

"Hmm, it seems to me dear Jurka, that you can't hide the fact that Nefeli mesmerises you," commented Johara bitterly.

"No, that's nothing to do with it. We have a duty..." said Slavik, trying to justify himself, but Milo stopped him.

"Come on, man. We saw how you melted down there on the track. Don't try and fool us. And definitely don't try and fool yourself, that's no good..."

Jurka lowered his head. After all, how could he deny it to his friends? As if they didn't know him inside out... What was the point of playing games with them?

"Whatever... His silence says it all. We get it," whispered Johara before reminding the other two that at midnight they would find out what was going on once and for all from Lord Salvador of wisdom.

"OK then," said Jurka. "That's the best way. Rendezvous at midnight in the usual place. Let's be going now. They'll be looking for us."

℘

Peace and quiet reigned in the boarding house at the 'Ark of Hope' orphanage. The party had ended some time before and the wardens had made sure that all the boarders, boys and girls, were in their dormitories at the right time. At 11pm sharp the lights went out and the night bell was rung. Exhausted by the tension and tiredness of the day, the pupils surrendered themselves to sleep without a fight, looking forward to the next day when the school holidays began. Only Jurka and Milo were counting down the minutes as midnight drew near. Outside they could hear every now and then the coughs of the night watchman patrolling the grounds of the orphanage. Jurka gave Milo a gentle nudge.

"Come on, it's time," he whispered to his big-bodied friend who appeared to be flirting with sleep.

Milo stood up, shook his head left and right to recover from his slumbers, moaned and followed Jurka. They knew the way very well. First they climbed out of the corner window on the outside wall of the orphanage and, by walking along the narrow second floor ledge, they reached the corner of the building. There, they grabbed the drainpipe that climbed up the wall and slid down it to the ground. The bushes around the orphanage made for first-rate cover and they ran soundlessly in that direction since the footsteps of the guard could be heard approaching along the narrow pavement which ran like a ring around the whole orphanage. The watchman passed, mechanically looking up and down, right and left, before heading towards the girls' dormitory.

Where was Johara?

The hearts of both boys began to beat hard when, in the bright darkness under the full moon, they spotted the cat-like figure of Johara clinging to the drainpipe and hanging there, as if made of stone, two metres above the ground. The watchman was moving slowly but steadily in her direction. If he saw her it would be disastrous because that would put paid to their plan. Jurka realized that there was no time to lose. They had to do something and to do it at once.

"Find a stone, quick!" he whispered to Milo, "and throw it to the other side, over there onto the gardeners' shed!" Milo didn't waste a second. With one enormous hand he flung the stone in the direction that Jurka had indicated and it landed noisily on the roof of the shed.

The night watchman turned instinctively in the direction of the sudden sound and stretched his head.

"Now what?" they heard him say to himself. Within seconds he had turned in the opposite direction and was running towards the gardeners' shed. The two friends gave a sigh of relief as Johara, already on the ground and now unencumbered, joined her friends in the bushes. From then on, things were much easier as they made their way to Bald Hill.

The famed Bald Hill overlooked not only the area around the orphanage but the whole of Heliopolis. It rose up, like a discarded skull, amid the wooded area, above the trees, orchards and gardens, a smooth, bent stone protruberance. Heaven only knows how mother nature had placed it there.

The three friends of the Nectar Brotherhood soon found themselves at the top of Bald Hill. The light of the full moon bathed the hill in gold and, from the top, down there in the green valley, they could make out sleeping Heliopolis and feel its serenity. On the other side, rising through the trees like dumb monuments, were the impressive stone buildings of their orphanage. The sky sparkled with stars in various patterns and sizes, while the moon, Queen of the night, dominated the infinite, silent sky.

Jurka Slavik, Johara and Milo sat down on the highest point of Bald Hill and, joining hands, formed a small triangle. It was time to communicate with Lord Salvador of wisdom, the mentor and protector of the Nectar Brotherhood. Jurka began gently murmuring the Hymn of the Brotherhood.

"One, two, three
Orphans are we
Shipwrecked on the sea
Of life..."

Johara continued in her delicate voice:

"But we never give up
We always win
Together we fight
And together we sing..."

And Milo, a real tenor, completed the Hymn with the chorus:

"O Brotherhood,
O Brotherhood,
O Nectar Brotherhood!"

Their eyes were fixed on the disc of the moon which now looked very close. Their entreaty sounded like a chanted psalm as all three, with one voice, called upon their protector:

"Lord Salvador
Master of wisdom
And of miracles for good
Visible and invisible,
Lord and Master
Reveal yourself to us
O mentor of the Brotherhood!"

And the miracle happened! The bright disc of the moon began to come alive. Its pale gold colour gradually changed until it had been transformed into a multicoloured circular screen, enclosed within a black frame. Suddenly, the dazzling screen came to life with sound and movement, seemingly within touching distance of the three friends...

A mad party was in full swing! Girls with gorgeous bodies were swaying to music as they danced non-stop, dwarfs were carrying titbits and drinks while others, dressed as servants, were waving fans of ostrich and peacock feathers in an effort to cool the atmosphere. Amid the laughter and all the other sounds, they could just about make out the music by a loud band playing hard rock.

Suddenly Lord Salavador appeared on the screen. He was wearing an enormous navy-style t-shirt with horizontal blue and white stripes which was tucked into ridiculous knee-length trousers revealing white socks in his unlaced trainers. A long, orange waistcoat covered his braces and formed a sort of lizard's tail behind him.

Small and slim, he didn't stop jumping around to the rhythm of the rock music, and he performed somersaults among the half-naked girls and dancing dwarfs. His rainbow-dyed hair waved to the rhythm as he shook his head, while a long earring hanging from one ear banged insistently against his cheek. His nose was painted red, like a clown's, while from his chin hung little bells which made him look like a wild goat. In one hand he held a bottle of wine and, in between jumps and steps, he managed to take one or two sips...

First to recover from the unexpected sight was Jurka.

"Oh my God, Lord Salvador's blind drunk!" he whispered. That that much was obvious, Johara added. They'd made a mistake and were wasting their time. By contrast, Milo appeared to be enjoying the spectacle, clapping along and shaking his massive body to the rhythm of the music.

"How are we going to get through to him now?" Jurka wondered aloud and the other two shrugged their shoulders. Slavik decided to risk it and call on him.

"Ahoy there, Lord Salvador of wisdom!" he greeted him with the ritual phrase.

No reply. Lord Salvador of wisdom continued to perform mad somersaults, all the while enjoying his dancing and drinking.

"Ahoy there, Lord Salvador of wisdom," Jurka repeated. "The Nectar Brotherhood greets you!" he added but, again, nothing changed.

"Damn it!" exploded the young man, seeing that he was getting no reaction.

Fortunately, there came a moment when the music stopped and Lord Salvador, tightly clutching his bottle of drink, dragged himself into a leather armchair bearing a sign that read: "For drunks only". It was an old car seat with ruined upholstery, covered in stains from drink and food. Casters had been fixed to it and on the arms one could clearly see various levers and things that were being used as special driving instruments. Lord Salvador took another swig, belched loudly and pressed a button while pulling the lever on his right. The armchair moved gently back and forth and then started to spin round on the spot before rearing up like a startled stallion. The drunken lord found himself on the floor.

"Oops!" he shrieked and attempted to stand up, staggering from the effects of the drink. Two tall, half-naked, lovely creatures took him by the arms, lifted him up as if playing a game and dumped him back in his chair. Chaos still reigned throughout the scene and now, amid all the voices and shouting, they could also hear songs and crooning.

"There's no point in us waiting, Jurka," said Johara. "Can't you see? It's silly and pointless."

Milo nodded. "Still, I enjoyed the rock music," he admitted, only to find himself at the receiving end of Jurka's comments.

"We didn't come here to enjoy music. We came to find out what happened to Nefeli, didn't we guys?"

"Yes, and what a shame that we're leaving with nothing," teased Johara who, in any case, had major reservations about the whole business.

"So, what do we do? It's your decision, Jurka," said Milo.

At that moment, amid the shouting and the pandemonium, Lord Salvador stood up. With a nod from him, everything grew silent and he suddenly started to sing his Ballad, leaping around and gesturing like a clown.

"My name is Salvador
I'm a lord with shining eyes
All day long I drink and drink
And still they call me wise!"

His crazy, multinational entourage repeated the verse as they danced. Lord Salvador continued his song as he jumped around:

"My name is Salvador
A famous lord am I
All day long I eat and shag
And still they call me wise!"

The others, like a choir, repeated the verse. Lord Salvador then took up a triumphant pose for the chorus:

"Oh yes, I'm wise, I'm wise
In fact I'm second to none
I guard the Good, I punish Bad
I'm Hahanoff's chosen one
I'm loved by rich and poor
I'm the omnipotent Salvador!"

The place roared as the company repeated the chorus and music was again heard from the depths of the hall, which resembled a fairy palace.

"Let's get out of here," Johara proposed coldly. "I can't put up with any more of this stupidity..."

Milo reacted. "Hold on, kiddo. Let's listen to a bit more music and chill out. This is a really cool sight. We might as well enjoy it, don't you think?"

Jurka shook his head. He was on the verge of desperation since everything indicated that their night had been a waste of time. And now, who could say when they'd be able to contact Lord Salvador of wisdom? And when would they find out about Nefeli?

"OK guys, I think we're out of luck tonight. It's obvious that the good Lord has other things to do. And other priorities…" said Jurka bitterly as he took one last, sad look at the multi-coloured, noisy screen of the moon.

"Ahoy there, O Lord Salvador of wisdom…" Slavic murmured in farewell, raising his hand in the direction of the moon. The three members of the Nectar Brotherhood set off gloomily for home.

"Ahoy there to you too, Jurka Slavik!"

The voice came loud and clear, dampening the sound of the music, the stamping of feet and the shouts of the dancers and singers at the mad party.

The three turned back to the screen in surprise. The tiny head of Lord Salvador appeared, like a close-up in an old movie, ringing as he shook his chin up and down to the tempo of the music. His round, sparkling eyes remained fixed on the three friends, while he gasped like a steam engine, trying to recover from his previous wild dancing.

"So, aren't you going to say hello to your friend Lord Salvador?" he insisted, as the three watched on, rooted to the spot. None of them had yet recovered from the unexpected occurrence, nor could they believe that the sozzled little figure could suddenly have regained his senses. Lord Salvador guessed the reason for their perplexity. "Ah, ah, ah! If that's how you're going to be, my friends. I thought you knew me better than that…"

"But you're drunk, Lord Salvador, aren't you?" asked Jurka hesitantly.

Lord Salvador performed a somersault and ended up sprawling awkwardly on the ground. The high-spirited company burst into laughter.

"Now… now… I'm… I'm.. d-d-d-drunk!" The slightly-built lord of wisdom managed to utter the phrase as yet another large belch escaped his lips. "Oops, pardon…" he said and burped once more. Within a second he was upright and on his feet, strutting about.

"Now I'm not!" announced Lord Salvador of wisdom with a note of pride in his voice. "Right, I'm listening. What do you want?"

Jurka coughed to clear his throat but was unable to utter a word. The change of scene had been so unexpected that he still wasn't sure if he should speak or if it wasn't better to keep quiet. What if the lord was making fun of him again?

"Well?" said Lord Salvador and the gleeful company's eyes were all fixed on Jurka and his friends. "Are you going to tell me or shall I carry on having a good time?"

Johara, calm and determined as always, spoke first.

"Lord Salvador of wisdom, we've come here to ask you to clear up something..."

"I know, I know," Lord Salvador interrupted. "That's why I'm wise. I know everything!" he boasted and started to laugh once more. At this, everyone else in his cheerful company burst into laughter.

Johara gave the other two a dubious glance. If he knew, why didn't he tell them? Or was he just fooling?

Milo, anticipating Jurka's anger, proposed that they put an end to all the joking around and cut to the chase. "You have to tell us what's happened, Lord Salvador of wisdom..."

"Is that so, big boy? You want me to tell you what's happened? To the lovely Nefeli, I presume..."

"Yes, yes, go on, tell us," all three answered as one, while Milo grew impatient. "Go on then, tell us Lord Salvador. You're driving us crazy. I'm all ears. I'm listening," he added.

"Are you sure?" Lord Salvador of wisdom replied at once, and Milo wondered what he meant.

"That you're all ears," the lord said to him and the big-bodied pupil instinctively felt his ears. Fortunately they were both still in place...

"Ha! I got you, big boy! I got you there, young man," Lord Salvador guffawed triumphantly and did another somersault. The rest of the party rocked with laughter once again.

Jurka could stand no more. "Oh come on, that's enough! Stop joking around, Lord Salvador. Since you know everything, being all-knowing and wise, just tell us where Nefeli is. How is she? How can we find her?"

"No need to be in a hurry, young man! Everything in its own good time...in its own good time," replied Lord Salvador. "Can't you see that we're having a party?"

Johara was about to ask what kind of party it was and on what occasion it was being held when, suddenly, the lights went out and from the depths of the hall the well-known song "Happy Birthday to You" was heard. A group of dwarfs, holding up their tiny arms, carried an enormous cake whose countless candles lit up Lord Salvador and friends' dark palace of fun. Everyone started to sing "Happy Birthday" to the celebrating lord who appeared to be enjoying himself again since he'd already opened a bottle of champagne and was spilling its froth everywhere. The dwarfs drew near and placed the huge cake at his feet. It was time for him to blow out the candles.

Lord Salvador imposed total silence, ostentatiously sucked in the air and then gave a gentle 'puff' as he exhaled. The candles flickered out while the dwarfs were propelled to the opposite wall like seeds, causing more delirious outpourings of enthusiasm and celebration in the now brightly-lit hall.

"Well, aren't you going to wish me a happy birthday, o triad of the Nectar Brotherhood?" asked the lord as he swigged champagne from the bottle.

"Many happy returns, o Lord Salvador of wisdom, and may you live to be a hundred," answered the three friends as one.

Lord Salvador made a 'glug, glug' sound and appeared to be close to choking.

"Not a hundred, you guys, not a hundred," he replied angrily, and the three friends looked at him, bewildered. What was wrong with what they'd wished him?

Lord Salvador gave a crafty laugh. "Hmm, tell me, how old do you think I've turned tonight?" he asked them. "How old am I, eh?" he repeated.

Milo hurried to correct their mistake: "Fifty!" he shouted, and his lively entourage fell about laughing.

"Fifty? No Big Milo, you're way off, a long way off. How about you, Jurka, how old do you make me?" the lord asked.

"Hmm, I'd say..." Jurka hesitated. "Sixty?"

More bursts of laughter and cackling echoed through the hall.

"Nooooooo... no way!" said Lord Salvador and turned to Johara. "Well, little girl? What do you say? I'm listening..."

"A thousand!" said the annoyed Johara.

A long-drawn out "nooooooo...."was heard in the hall and Johara blushed a deep red with anger.

"Well, tell us then, Lord Salvador of wisdom. Stop playing games with our nerves..." shouted the small, short-haired young woman and she fixed her big black eyes on the moon's screen. Everyone was waiting for the celebrating lord's reply.

"We'll tell you!"

A harmonious chorus of voices was heard and, from the back of the hall, half a dozen women came forward in a line. Behind them followed a crowd of children, boys and girls, white, black and yellow, of various ages and sizes.

"Tonight, dear young friends, Lord Salvador of wisdom turns 821 years old!" chanted the women and children as one.

More pandemonium broke out as everyone rushed to kiss Lord Salvador who sat back in his armchair and delightedly received their birthday wishes.

"I can't believe it!" said Jurka. "The lord's having us on again," he remarked and Milo agreed: "Did you hear that? 821 years old. As if..."

Johara disagreed.

"Perhaps you'd like to tell me why not? He works miracles doesn't he? He can do anything he wants, and he can be as old as he likes. I was right to wish him to make it to a thousand..."

"Well done that girl, bravo Johara! By Hahanoff, the prime minister of the gods, you're a clever little thing. Well done!" Lord Salvador was addressing Johara delightedly. "Of course I turned 821 tonight, my friends. Here are my witnesses," he added, pointing to the six women and countless children. "Please meet my family," Lord Salvador of wisdom said proudly.

The women bowed politely to the three friends and greeted them in unison. Jurka, Johara and Milo instinctively replied "pleased to meet you" and the party started up again. Only this time Lord Salvador wasn't taking part – he was scoffing large mouthfuls of the cake he'd been brought.

"Guys, enough is enough. Lord Salvador is just fooling with us," said Johara who was wishing that she had never come to Bald Hill.

"Let's wait and see what's going to happen. It'll be fun," replied Milo who always enjoyed a party. "In any case, he knows why we're here, and he must have the answers too," added the swarthy giant.

"We've come this far. There's no going back," Jurka agreed. "We just need to be patient, that's all..."

"Hey, Lord Salvador, aren't you going to give us some of your cake?" called out Milo who reckoned that soon there would be none left for anyone else.

"Cake? What cake?" replied Lord Salvador. The cake had disappeared.

"Oooooooh!" screamed the entourage with disapproval, while the dwarfs began to chant "shame, shame..."

Lord Salvador gave a crafty smile. With a gesture he again imposed silence, the lights dimmed and the music began to play a lively polka.

"Here, my dear subjects," the stylish lord declared majestically, "here is my birthday treat for you!"

Lord Salvador pressed a button, took up a pose, closed his eyes and, as if by magic, a door opened in the rear. The lights went out and only the bright, tight beam of a spotlight played on the open door. An old cart, pulled by an ancient white horse, appeared...

"Aaaaah..." echoed the room as the cart slowly made its way towards lord Salvador, loaded with straw and hay.

Jurka, Johara and Milo burst out laughing, while long-drawn-out jeers filled the room.

"Eat and drink as much as you like!" commanded Lord Salvador, who had not yet opened his eyes.

"Eat it yourself!" responded his guests with one voice.

Lord Salvador opened his eyes and saw the old horse with the cart loaded with straw and hay in front of him.

"Oops, pardon, made a mistake!" he apologized and performed a somersault.

"That's what happens nowadays when you put your trust in technology," he announced in a very official tone. "Let's see what we can do to fix it... I think we have to take things into our own hands," he added with a cunning grin.

The showy lord stood up on the armchair and stretched out his hands towards the cart. There was total silence as everyone watched Lord Salvador perform his magic.

"Right, dear friends. In the beginning was the loaf..."

Lord Salvador wiggled his little finger and on the cart there appeared delicious loaves of bread. "Perhaps you'd like a little venison?" he asked the astonished crowd as, with another movement of his fingers, he turned the straw into wonderfully smelling freshly-cooked meat.

"Oh, ah, oh, wow!" came the sounds from his friends as the appetizing smell reached their nostrils.

Soon the cart had been transformed into a sumptuous buffet with every kind of dish imaginable.

"Enjoy the food and the sweet wine," Lord Salvador ordered his fun-loving company. "I have some work to do, please excuse me," he added and, with one bound, he was again right at the front of the screen, staring straight at the three friends of the Nectar Brotherhood.

"Now, what were we saying?" he asked, bells ringing.

Jurka reminded him that they had come to request his advice concerning the matter of Nefeli's abduction.

"If it really was an abduction..." Johara remarked pointedly.

"Ah, yes, that's what you came for. I'd forgotten for a moment," the lord replied.

"So let's see where your Nefeli is and what she's up to. Ready, set, go!"

The three friends sat down and once again formed a triangle, holding hands and silently watching Lord Salvador. He did a somersault and positioned his thin body upside down, supported by this slim arms.

"I see better this way up," he explained.

From his eyes came a beam of blue light.

"Ah! There she is, there's your friend," he shouted. The gaze of the three friends focused on the other end of the wall, where the beams of light ended, forming a small screen. Nefeli could be seen clearly, dressed in a white gown, looking ethereal, as if flying among high golden ears of corn. Her blonde tresses waved, as always, like winged beams, while her eyes gazed into infinity. Her steps were heavy and tired, as if they were seeing her in slow motion, and her divine face looked pale, like the moon. In her hand she held a small mirror and every so often she would stop, look into it and sigh: "Aaaaaah!..."

Jurka could not restrain himself. "There! See what I told you? You see how unhappy she is?" he shouted and no-one was in any mood to get into an argument by disagreeing. "Where is she now, Lord Salvador of wisdom? Where's Nefeli?" Jurka asked anxiously.

The lord performed another somersault and found himself back on is feet.

"Behind here," he replied simply, pointing over his shoulder.

"Behind where?" asked Johara.

"Behind the moon, where else, silly girl?" replied Lord Salvador.

There followed an embarrassed silence since none of them had understood precisely where Nefeli was. Behind the moon were millions of heavenly bodies. On which of them should they go looking for her?

"Lord Salvador of wisdom," said Milo, "couldn't you be a bit clearer?"

"I'm not getting any clearer! You've seen it all, I showed you everything, didn't you see? It's not my fault if you're blind," Lord Salvador answered, shaking his head. The bells tinkled again. "Which is a pity, because I had you down as clever kids," he concluded.

Jurka asked for time out so as to consult with his friends.

"The corn is the key, guys," said Slavik, but Johara disagreed. "There are lots of planets where they sow cereals Jurka. How can that be the key?"

"Yes, but how many of them could Nefeli be taken to in, what, six or seven hours?"

"That's right," said Milo who suggested that they work it out using a process of elimination, starting with the closest ones to the region in space behind the moon.

"Ha!" said Johara. "Don't count the hours in earth time," the black-eyed girl commented. "And, if you'll pardon me, behind the moon but in which direction? The moon's in orbit…" she pointed out.

"Where it is now" insisted Milo. "We're talking about right now, not in a general, vague way. Lord Salvador was clear: 'Behind the moon,' isn't that what he told us? Of course he meant right now…"

The lord's chin jangled. He nodded and Milo was encouraged, since it was evident that he was right about where they should be looking.

"Fine, that helps tremendously," said Jurka. "So let's begin. How many planets with crops growing are there in this region?"

"Ah, for those kinds of calculations we need the astronomical maps, man," said Milo and he was right about that. How could they work out the moon's orbit?

An impasse was looking all the more certain, Lord Salvador was whistling indifferently and Jurka Slavik proposed that they return to base so as to examine the maps at once.

"Hold on a minute," Johara blurted out suddenly. "I think we're making a very big mistake here. The corn was a clue but not the only clue," she elaborated.

"What do you mean?" asked Jurka, confused. "Explain yourself, kiddo. Where are we going wrong?"

"Try and remember," Johara insisted. "How did Nefeli and Tao Li's gang of Tigers leave?"

"How did they kidnap her, you mean, Johara," Jurka corrected her straight away but the slim-built girl paid no attention.

"Remember how she left!" she persisted, and Lord Salvador's chin jangled in approval at her thinking.

"It was in a black cloud, wasn't it?" said Milo.

"Precisely!" replied Johara triumphantly. "Well, clever boy Jurka, where's Nefeli then?" the dark-haired girl challenged her friend.

"Lord Salvador of wisdom! On planet Black Cloud, where else?" Jurka declared triumphantly, quite sure of himself.

"Bravo! Bravo!" chanted Lord Salvador ironically. "What took you so long?" he reprimanded them, at which the three friends of the Nectar Brotherhood protested.

"You misled us with the picture you showed us, Lord Salvador," said Jurka Slavik, "but that's another matter. The main thing is that we now know where to find Nefeli," he concluded.

"The main thing, my friends, is that you have to set off on your journey right away. You're off to Black Cloud, that's the most important thing," Lord Salvador told them as Johara wondered aloud: "Really? And how are we going to get there?"

"Not on foot, that's for sure, my girl? Not on foot," answered Lord Salvador.

"So how?" Johara insisted.

"That's how. Look behind you!" the wise lord ordered the three friends.

An odd-looking jalopy that looked a bit like a car appeared before them.

"You'll be going in that," Lord Salvador explained in all seriousness as the three friends looked at one another, bewildered. "Go on, try it out," he told them.

Milo rushed to sit at the wheel and tried to start the car. First a loud 'boom!' was heard and then the old wreck started to rattle, like a machine gun. The engine revved up with a deafening 'vrooooom!,' the whole thing lurched half a metre forward and suddenly disintegrated into dozens of spare parts. Milo found himself sprawling on the ground, the steering wheel still in his hands. Lord Salvador rolled around on the ground, his arms and legs kicking the air like a mule, dying of laughter. His whole crazy entourage followed his lead, laughing until it hurt.

"By Hahanoff, prime minister of the gods, this is fun. I got you again kids! And you, big boy Milo, how did you end up on the ground?"

Lord Salvador was enjoying himself. "Only teasing..." the wise lord managed to say when he had pulled himself together.

Milo blushed with shame and his large black lips were trembling from his anger. Johara tried in vain to restrain herself but she, too, burst into laughter, holding her belly. Jurka didn't know how to react. On the one hand he wanted to laugh at the lord's fun and games but, on the other, he was fretting because time was passing and every second counted on the mission to save Nefeli. Who was in the mood for joking at such a crucial moment?

"Phew, you're going to make me die laughing here," said Lord Salvador when his energy had finally dissipated. "Time for work," he added and turned once more towards the members of the Nectar Brotherhood. "Now don't give me that miserable look, I can't stand it," he told them. "I had a bit of fun That's it, over and done with. Let's get serious now," he concluded, but the three friends were still looking at him with mistrust. "What else has the joker lord of wisdom got up his sleeve?" they were thinking.

"C'est fini mon ami, c'est fini," Lord Salvador insisted, in French this time. "Look behind you. Now!" he ordered.

Jurka, Johara and Milo turned and focused on the distant horizon. Before them stretched the trees of the forest, while further down in the distance they could make out the roofs of their orphanage and, higher up, in the sad, evening sky, the infiniteness of space, sown with countless stars. But apart from this, they could see nothing special and their mood naturally turned to one of mistrust again. Was their protector and mentor Lord Salvador of wisdom going to give them yet another shock?

Suddenly, Milo's trembling voice pierced the silence of the night.

"Look!"

His shout was stifled by his unexpected emotion at the sight he was the first to see. They all turned their eyes to the direction in which Milo was pointing his raised hand. From the distance, above the roofs of the houses in sleeping Heliopolis, amid the reflections of its lamps which gilded the pitch black horizon, a small, completely white cloud appeared, spreading a beautiful, pale silver light all around. The white cloud travelled slowly but steadily towards Bald Hill, moving in waves like a snake and, as it drew closer, it grew in size and the light surrounding it shone brighter.

The white cloud hung over Bald Hill and over the heads of the three friends who remained motionless like statues, watching the unexpected and uniquely beautiful sight. Lord Salvador, now enthroned in his favourite armchair, was enjoying his champagne. He smiled with evident pleasure, constantly shaking his head and causing repeated rhythmical janglings of satisfaction. All around him were seated the members of his family, while the circle was completed by the dwarfs and the rest of his lively entourage. For the Nectar Brotherhood it was now time for action.

"Wow!" shouted Milo enthusiastically, slapping the other two on the back with his huge hands. "Now we're talking. Now we're getting somewhere...," he said, turning to his friends. The famous White Cloud, about which Lord Salvador had spoken to them so many times, was there, alive and shining in front of them. All three looked at the wise lord in anticipation of his next move.

"Ah! Leave me out of it now. I want to spend some private moments with my family," he said. "See you!"

Lord Salvador made a movement of his hand, his fingers quivered together and, the next moment, the screen disappeared as if by magic. All that remained was the full disc of the moon looking down with its eternally pale sad face upon the three friends.

"So now what do we do?" asked Milo and Johara replied that there was nothing they could do but wait, as they watched the magical white cloud above their heads.

Jurka nudged the other two. "Look, something's happening," he said, pointing at the white cloud. Indeed, all around the cloud, which was hovering and undulating, there suddenly appeared a ring of light, like a halo. Thousands of tiny multicoloured lights flickered on and off, sparkling in the sky while seeming to dance as they changed position and followed one after another in a feast of colours and shapes.

"Gosh, this is something else!" said an admiring Milo, who was the first to come out of the protracted bout of gazing.

"My God, that's beautiful," whispered Jurka. "Guys, the time has come. It's time for the big journey. Let's make the sign of the Brotherhood," he added in a voice trembling with enthusiasm and emotion.

Jurka gestured to Johara and Milo to follow him as he led them to the very centre of Bald Hill.

"Now let's join hands," he said. They each joined hands in a clenched fist. "Index fingers aloft!" Jurka ordered. "And now, point both index fingers at the white cloud and close your eyes," Jurka continued the orders. "Now we press the ends of our index fingers hard," he added.

The other two made the sign of the Brotherhood perfectly, exactly as Jurka had told them to. The next moment felt like an eternity. Of course, they could not see how the multicoloured ring around the dazzling white cloud formed a bright beam which gradually approached, like a colourful ribbon, the point that the three friends were forming with their fingers. And when it gently touched them, a sudden flash, like silent lightning, went on and off, absorbing the beams of light – together with the bodies of the three friends.

ᔕ

A moment later, when they opened their eyes, they saw something they had never seen before. Jurka Slavik was standing on the bridge of a spaceship, wearing a tight-fitting, blue uniform that appeared to have been stuck on him. Johara stood beside him, dressed in the same outfit but deep green in colour, while Milo resembled a weightlifter in his yellow clothes. On the front of their uniforms was a big white letter "N".

"Good Lord," Milo cried out. "Is this what I think it is or am I dreaming?" he asked in his deep voice and Jurka nodded. "Look around, Milo. Look and see for yourself..."

All around was a smooth, soft white surface that seemed neverending. On the bridge were white seats made of some unknown material that looked more like plasticine than anything solid and sturdy. In front of these, at the front of the ship, was a curved recess, in the middle of which appeared a circle in a golden tone which, like a dying wave, caressed the surface. And right in the middle, a small, curious object that looked like a psychedelic disc with tiny lights and lamps flickering on and off, pulsating continuously like a heart.

The unending white surface of the spaceship resembled the inside of an enormous pipe. Its monotonous monochrome was broken by lots of tiny multicoloured rectangular shapes, like windows, placed symmetrically with wonderful precision one next to the other. Inside the hull of the ship they could see a transparent whitish-grey screen waving like a veil, persistent and tiringly so, to the same repeated rhythm.

Milo remained speechless, while Johara could not take her black eyes off the ship and the three friends' uniforms. They each looked as if they were seeing the others' ghosts. Their protector and mentor, the wise Salvador, had given them many surprises in the past but this was definitely the most impressive. It was Jurka who brought them back to reality, by telling the other two that, yes, they were on the spaceship for the great journey in search of Nefeli. "And this," he added, "is all thanks to our protector, Lord Salvador of wisdom."

Johara was about to say something when an invisible, metallic voice was heard instead.

"Welcome, Nectar Brotherhood space travellers. This is the captain of the White Cloud, awaiting your orders."

The metallic voice was so clear that Johara immediately turned to look at the small disc which was pulsating like a heart. She had noticed how, when the invisible metallic voice of the captain was heard, the tiny lights and lamps had been blinking on and off.

"What? Now what?" wondered Milo and Johara replied by pointing to the pulsating disc. "That's the captain of our ship. Please meet Nec-Tar 1," she declared pompously.

"Nec-Tar 1 awaiting your orders!" answered the metallic voice straight away.

Johara was speechless. She had never expected that the joke she had played on Milo would end this way. She looked bewilderedly at Jurka who, in the meantime, had settled into the first seat that he had come across.

"I'd very much like to know where we go from here," she said.

Jurka replied that their destination had been and still was planet Black Cloud and their mission was to save Nefeli. He had not finished speaking when the metallic voice confirmed: "Destination planet Black Cloud, space location Galaxy of the Two Suns. Estimated duration of voyage: Seven sunrises and seven suns." The invisible Nec-Tar 1 concluded his report.

"Yippee!" shouted Milo enthusiastically and the unseen voice asked at once: "What does voyager Yippee require?"

Jurka and Johara burst into laughter as Milo hurried to clarify that his name was not Yippee. "Jurka, why don't you introduce us to Nec-Tar 1?" he said complainingly.

"Nec-Tar 1 is listening!" the metallic voice of the invisible captain echoed once again and the light-haired inmate of the orphanage rushed to comply with his friend's suggestion.

"All right, Captain Nec-Tar 1. I am Jurka Slavik and this big friend of mine is Milo..."

"Why Milo other colour?" asked the voice.

"Hey, you can see too, Captain Nec-Tar 1?" asked Johara but received no answer. Jurka whistled spontaneously.

"Wow!" he shouted "That's amazing,,, Er... This is Johara... er... she's a girl," Jurka hurried to explain so as to pre-empt, for better or worse, any comments from Captain Nec-Tar 1. "We are the Nectar Brotherhood, faithful comrades and followers of our mentor and protector, Lord Salvador of wisdom."

"Lord Salvador of wisdom, father... Give order!" clarified the invisible voice.

"That's great, Nec-Tar 1. And now that we've all got to know one another, how about starting up for the journey?" proposed Milo and the voice replied at once:

"Take up your positions!"

Johara and Milo sat down in the spacecraft's two other seats. As soon as they were all in the strange white seats made of unknown material, a muffled humming sound came from the depths of the spaceship. At the same time, their armchairs reclined and a curious, transparent veil covered them, enclosing the three young space travellers inside a peculiar, soft shell.

The next second their eyes had closed and in their sudden deep sleep they began to experience strange visions and illusions. There was a shining planet, illuminated by two suns. This curious planet was made up of four different sections, one for each earthly season. Its inhabitants spoke an unknown language which was broken up by continuous short syllables, composed of sounds that came from their round mouths which did not open or close. Their round, watermelon-like heads were identical but of different sizes according to their origins and the social or professional rank to which they belonged. Like decorations, they had two big ears sticking out at the sides like perfect crescents while on their noseless faces were two eyes – sunken, empty and black, unfocused. Their bodies were slim and tall while their long arms and legs ended in four fingers and toes respectively, joined by a membrane at the extremities. Around their necks they wore a narrow choker, on the wrist of each hand two more bracelets and on each ankle three more. They dressed in monochrome gowns which differed only in colour, according to their particular section of the population. Around the middle of their identical bodies was a strange belt, which resembled a computer screen, pulled tightly around their gowns. In the centre of their foreheads, right in the middle above their deep-set, expressionless eyes, was a small metal triangle which stuck out like a small horn on their brows.

Their cities were divided into neighbourhoods, each of which had a distinct purpose – work, recreation, entertainment, learning, residence and administration. All the neighbourhoods were linked by terrestrial and aerial corridors where, according to the district, pedestrians walked or flyers moved around, either in their own vehicles or as passengers. The four sections of the planet were linked in a similar fashion, except that here, aerial communications dominated, with air taxis, small and large private ships and even flying animals available according to choice. The two suns illuminated the planet without interruption. The large sun covered the largest part while the small sun caressed the Winter Section, maintaining an eternally chilly season, with snow, rain and cold. Night did not exist on the shining planet, except deep in its bowels, from where Cre-matum, the planet's most precious asset, was mined. Slaves and convicts, exiles and outcasts lived and worked there. They laboured day and night for a plate of food, under the supervision of the terrible Cig-ants and other guards or mercenaries, usually settlers from neighbouring poor and infertile planets. At the very centre of the planet's sky hung a single, huge black cloud, shining like a chandelier...

The strange, shared dream of the three friends was suddenly interrupted when the White Cloud shuddered so intensely that Nec-Tar 1 was obliged to place them on alert.

"Awaken!" The order was heard and the three travellers immediately found themselves standing. They looked at one another, with no concerns or questions, as if nothing had happened, as if they had always been on the spaceship from the very first moment and the long voyage lasting seven sunrises and seven suns had not taken place.

"What's going on, Nec-Tar 1?" asked Jurka and the voice replied that they were being attacked by Locusts. "Nothing serious," he added. "Sit back and watch the battle. Screen, now!..." Nec-Tar 1 ordered and the walls of the spaceship around the three friends were transformed into a panoramic screen. Wherever they turned their heads, they saw infinite space, the majestic landscape of the Galaxy of the Two Suns. It was a phantasmagorical sight and the three friends, open-mouthed, could not get enough of it. Colours everywhere made up the surrealistic painting of the unknown galaxy. Colours that changed with every new location, colours that formed shapes and pictures of infinite beauty, amid stars and comets, moons and rainbows, planets large and small, near and far.

All around the White Cloud spacecraft it was easy to spot the spaceships of the pirates of the galaxy. They did indeed resemble enormous dark-coloured locusts, from which small red shells were being fired, one after the other in waves against the spaceship. These missiles swooped down en masse from all sides like birds of prey and when they were within firing range of the spacecraft they exploded loudly, with the aim of making a hole in its hull, shifting it off course and, once it was immobilised, boarding it as triumphant victors for the spoils. Such a perfect craft as the White Cloud would definitely make them a tidy profit on the planetary black market.

"Nectaroids, battle stations!" ordered the invisible captain of the spaceship and suddenly, from among the small, window-like rectangular shapes emerged a line of tiny robots. Their yellow and black colouring made them look more like huge bees leaving their hives together as they flew off, humming throughout the craft, ready to take up their positions. Soon, the voice of Nec-Tar 1 rang out again as he ordered:

"Arm the torpedoes! Circular aim! Fire!"

The spaceship's screens clearly showed round, rotating torpedoes, like balls, leaving the barrels of the White Cloud's defence weapons system at high speed. The arms of the pirates were immediately ranged against them and began hitting them with continuous fire. The shells struck the rounded surface of the torpedoes and ricocheted without doing them any damage. The Locusts then turned their ships against the flying torpedoes in an attempt to trap them in crossfire from bigger guns resembling cannons.

Suddenly the torpedoes stopped moving and hung there in space. They were a perfect target for the enemy's lightning strike and that would mean their destruction.

"Why?" wondered the three friends...

The voice of Nec-Tar 1 gave the answer. "Forward Explosion" he ordered and the three hanging torpedoes that were covering the forward part of the spacecraft exploded with a loud bang. A yellow gas spread out through space, melting as it did so, any pirate craft that was flying in the vicinity.

"Stern Explosion!" the invisible voice commanded and the Nectaroids activated the mechanism that controlled the torpedoes covering the stern of the spaceship. The three friends turned their eyes towards the tail of the craft and saw the same thing happen there.

Nec-Tar 1 did not need to give another order. The attacking ships of the Locusts had disappeared, retreating in disarray into the depths of the far galactic horizon.

"At ease!" the invisible metallic voice ordered and the guns fell silent.

"Nectaroids, take up your positions!" he commanded once more and the tiny black and yellow robots disappeared into the strange rectangular windows from which they had sprung earlier.

"Screen forward!" ordered Captain Nec-Tar 1 and all the screens disappeared apart from the one at the front. "Magnification now!" he continued and the picture became clearer. Before them stretched a brightly-lit strip, illuminated by two suns and, in the background, was the shining destination of their voyage.

"That's planet Black Cloud!" shouted the three friends in unison and Nec-Tar 1 confirmed it: "Planet Black Cloud. Distance two million kilometres. Approach within orbit from the side of the Summer Sector Portal..."

Jurka could not restrain himself and he sprang up: "But I know this planet," he said enthusiastically. "I saw it in my sleep..."

"What? You too, Jurka?" asked Johara in astonishment, and the two of them turned in curiosity to Milo. He nodded. "What a stupid name, Black Cloud. It's shining like a spotlight," the black giant remarked, pointing at the planet.

"It's a euphemism, Milo... It's the first time you've seen something like it?" said Jurka.

"Yes, but look at that pitch black cloud hanging over it, like Death," said Johara as, from the depths of their visual field, the impressive shape of the Black Cloud gradually came into view.

"Pitch black cloud – Aerial Fortress," clarified Nec-Tar 1 at once.

As the White Cloud approached ever closer to the planet, Nec-Tar 1 ordered the three friends to take up the safety position in their seats. At the same time, he readied the Nectaroids. The spacecraft was now entering the upper atmosphere of planet Black Cloud. The captain gave the command for a circular journey around the planet, evidently wanting to take a closer look so as to choose the most suitable and accessible landing site. He finally decided to attempt a descent from the side of the Portal of the Summer Sector, exactly as he had planned, and gave the relevant technical orders to the ship's navigation instruments.

ᔕ

Inside the luxurious apartments of the Aerial Fortress, there was a great deal of movement at this hour. The Council of Elders was meeting in order to determine export prices for the next quota of Cre-matum which the wholesale merchants from the neighbouring planet Short Time would be receiving to sell on to other planets in the galaxy. The guards in their black uniforms ostentatiously marched up and down in twos, overseeing the smooth functioning of the headquarters' security, while in the private apartments of the Observatory, the highest point of the Aerial Fortress, their leader, the famous Three Star Commander, Master Zar-ko, was continuously receiving reports, giving orders and waving his staff – from which he was never separated – up and down.

On the screens of the Observatory, the four sectors of the planet were being monitored in great detail. Another screen showed the situation in the mines, while a circular rotating antenna constantly monitored the space traffic around the planet. Always next to the Commander, ready to carry out his every wish, was the Head Guard, Taka-mura.

"Bring in the traveller Tao Li," ordered Master Zar-ko and Taka-mura passed the order further down the line.

"Take him to my private apartments," added the Three Star Commander and headed for the side reception room, waiting for the traveller from the distant planet Earth. Tao Li entered the comfortable apartment accompanied by the Head Guard. The Commander gestured to Taka-mura to leave them alone.

"My respects, Three Star Commander, Master Zar-ko," said Tao Li and his host returned the greeting. "Welcome to planet Black Cloud, Tao Li. May the Two Suns illuminate your path."

Tao Li sat down where Zar-ko had indicated.

"Will you have a cocktail with me?" the Commander proposed and Tao Li replied that, having travelled from so far away, it was worth trying anything. Zar-ko clapped his hands and from nowhere appeared a hologram of a shapely woman. From her dress and appearance, Tao Li concluded that the hologram was of someone who was not local. "Well, well, the Commander's got good taste..." he thought.

"Bring us two special cocktails," his host ordered. "With plenty of ice. Isn't that how you drink them in your homeland, Tao Li?" he asked and his earthly visitor nodded in agreement.

The shapely beauty returned as suddenly and quietly as she had appeared the first time and soon she had placed before them two huge, square, silver utensils that looked more like games than glasses.

"Let's try some of this wonderful drink," said Zar-ko and Tao Li was curious to know what he was going to be drinking. "Drink up and you'll see," answered the Commander, downing his glass in one. Tao Li hesitated for a while but decided that his mission demanded sacrifices. He would drink the unknown cocktail and God help him…

The taste wasn't so bad, he thought. But its smell was not like any with which the earthly visitor was familiar.

"Well, young man, did you like our cocktail?" asked Zar-ko and Tao Li replied that its smell was difficult to pin down.

"Well, that's perfectly natural," explained Zar-ko, "since in your homeland you don't have the Eternal Tree. That's what this special juice is made from… from its leaves, to be precise," the Commander explained.

"So may we be eternally remembered, then…" murmured Tao Li. "Anyway, I didn't travel for so many suns to drink juice," added the arrogant young earth visitor.

Zar-ko waved his staff in the air. "I agree," he said. "So, I'm listening. What bright sun has brought you so far?"

"I'll get straight to the point, respected Commander," replied Tao Li. "The Tigers, whom I represent, would like to propose taking up the representation and distribution of Cre-matum on Earth. Our planet is in a state of underdevelopment and the controlled introduction of Cre-matum into the market will create a new situation, with unknown and unimaginable possibilities for the perceptions of the inhabitants of Earth. Cre-matum will conquer the Earth," boasted Tao Li, "precisely because it will provide the inhabitants with more opportunities to use and exploit it than they could ever imagine in their wildest dreams. Not in a million suns… New horizons will be opened up and your wonderful system will be imposed on Earth too, I suppose you realise that, Commander?"

"We do know that, young man," replied Zar-ko," and we've tried it with many other planets. The Cre-matum market, by Doctor Soc-rat, is booming. But as far as new exports and expansion are concerned, the decision rests with the Council of Elders. They alone determine the quantities that are exported, where to and at what price. They don't want to ruin the market by thoughtless trade in our planet's most precious resource. They don't want to drop the price and they always definitely weigh up the benefits involved, you do realise that, Tao Li?"

"Allow me to comment that all that is just old-fashioned, Commander. We are taking about the same thing but you're putting it back to front. I say yes to exports, but in controlled amounts and, as a consequence, at a controlled and beneficial price. Increased demand through a new market will create upward pressure on the price but is it possible that the Elders can't see that? Anyway, we're talking about a completely new intergalactic market, one to which you've only carried out familiarisation visits so far…" concluded Tao Li.

Master Zar-ko remained pensive for a while. The young visitor from Earth had made some persuasive arguments. It seemed that he had been well coached. On the other hand, the Commander knew very well that obtaining a final, positive decision would be no easy matter. Many wheels would have to be oiled and that, in turn, would push up costs. As if he had foreseen these thoughts, Tao Li spoke again,

"Would you let me finish telling you what I've been thinking, Commander? I'd like to stress another significant advantage. What's that? Well, of course, the dependence that will be imposed on my compatriots' way of life. And also, the opening up of the labour market and migration which will naturally follow this commercial activity. Your mines, not to mention services in the other Sectors of Black Cloud, are in urgent need of labourers, isn't that right Commander? And when you're importing settlers from planets like Foxtail and Mousehole, I don't think I need to say anything more... Earthlings are much better and, more importantly, cheaper. It's one thing to travel for seven sunrises and seven suns and another to be waiting two whole winters for your workers to arrive…"

Again, Zar-ko didn't reply at once. As he brandished his staff up and down, he was already thinking that this business could bring him benefits. And he knew which ones…

"Let's have another drink. It might give us some fresh ideas," the host proposed, clapping his four-fingered hands to call his servant. "So, what will it be, dear Tao Li?" he asked. Tao Li smiled inwardly. That 'dear' was a sign that everything was going as he had wished.

"Zi-van, is there any zi-van? May I try your famous drink?" the young man asked, looking at the shapely hologram who was awaiting orders, expressionless and silent.

"You're a silly boy, Tao Li. Can you imagine us not having any zi-van, our national drink? In Doctor Soc-rat's name, what kind of a question is that? Of course we've got zi-van. The very best, naturally..." the Commander clarified and he nodded to the servant to fetch his guest's order.

Soon the young woman re-entered the room and left in front of Tao Li a transparent cup containing a steaming, thick, black tar-like liquid. Tao Li jumped up, his eyes bulging.

"What... what's that?" he shouted. "Don't tell me I'm supposed to drink this... this... what should I call it, this nasty black soup!"

Zar-ko burst out laughing. "How naïve and backwards you earthlings are compared to us," he remarked. "So naïve that you still judge everything by appearances and nothing more," he added. "What you see here, my dear Tao Li, is the most precious, the most refreshing, the most delicious drink in the entire universe. And you're disgusted by what it looks like?" The Three Star Commander paused and tasted the zi-van. Then he looked at his earth visitor and smiled. "Do we look a bit more attractive to you, young man? Nicer than this liquid?" Master Zar-ko waved his staff in Tao Li's face. "Or rather, let me put it the other way round: Do you know how horrible and unpleasant you look to us Black Cloudians, dear Tao Li? With that hairy head, yuccchhh!" The Commander grimaced in disgust. "And those living holes that you have in the place of eyes? Yeccchh!" he uttered again, "they remind us of prehistoric animals. And what are we to say about the drill sticking out of your face... a nose, isn't that what you call it? It makes you look like a grated rock...to say nothing of your bent body, with curves front and back that remind us of our old trees... Go on, taste it, it'll make you feel good..."

Tao Li was speechless at the description of the imperfections of the Earth's human race, not knowing whether to laugh or cry. In the end he decided that a glass of black liquid, however disgusting it looked, was not going to prevent the successful accomplishment of his mission. Armed with all that remained of his will, he sipped the contents of the glass and cursed the moment he had asked for zi-van. In the entertainment dens in the various Sectors of Black

Cloud, they at least had imported drinks from their intergalactic trade. But here?

Zar-ko scratched his bald head which was perspiring from his laughter and he fixed his soulless, round black eyes on his visitor. It was the time for some decisive moves on the chess board of negotiation. Had the hairy, ugly young earth boy got the message?

"All right, let's get back to business. Where were we?" asked the host and Tao Li reminded him that he had been listing the many advantages that trading Cre-matum on earth would bring.

Tao Li had been around and it was no coincidence that he was the leader of the infamous Tigers gang. He was a crafty one and he now needed to prove it to the Commander. For a start, he had drunk the black liquid without showing any sign of disgust.

"I was talking, honourable Commander, about the benefits that will arise for all of us if you begin trade with my home world. And I had enumerated only a few of the... what shall I call them... additional advantages of such business: a cheap, good quality labour force, the settlement of your planet by Earthlings and many others. They'll definitely be profitable for you..." Tao Li concluded his brief monologue.

"Hmm, hmm... profitable, yes. I can see that. But for whom?" asked the old fox.

"For everyone, Commander, there will be something for everyone!" replied Tao Li who felt that the time had come for him to play his ace. "For example, honourable Commander, you could be our Agent here on Black Cloud. All the imports of labour, all the immigrants in all categories, would have to go through you, crediting you, of course, with a great deal of Value Units – isn't that how the system works here?" explained Tao Li, quite sure of himself. And then came his trump card. "What's more, since you will be the one to steer the decision through the Council of Elders and obtain the export and commerce license, it's only natural that the Cre-matum will soon bring you that much-desired fourth star on your lapel. As for us, we'll be the general commercial agents for Cre-matum and immigration, all right dear Commander?"

Tao Li was on a roll and nothing could stop him. The zi-van had indeed made him feel good and he was talking non-stop.

Master Zar-ko was no newcomer to such matters. How many times during his long career had he taken care of cases such as this? Countless times. He was well versed in negotiation tactics, especially when his counterpart was playing with what was essentially a marked deck. He decided to prolong the time that he would keep the young visitor from Earth on tenterhooks.

"Your views are interesting, dear earthly visitor. Now that I am familiar with them, I need to talk to my people and see how to handle the various issues. This is not a game, we're talking about matters of planetary policy. So, I'll have to see how we can take things further..."

Tao Li realised that the fish had bitten. From here on it was only a matter of time. And time, thank God, was something he had plenty of. And pleasant time too, since he had taken care that they brought, like booty, the gorgeous Nefeli for company. He wouldn't find anyone better, not only on Black Cloud but anywhere in the infinite galaxy of the Two Suns.

"It's a deal..." Tao Li began when, without warning, Taka-mura rushed into Master Zar-ko's private apartments. The Commander uttered a screeching sound.

"What are you doing in my apartment uninvited, Head Guard? What's up now? Go on!", Zar-ko ordered and Taka-mura stood before him like a stone statue.

"Sir, a craft of unknown origin has been spotted in the space triangle of the Summer Sector. Give your orders!"

"Have you checked the craft's identification? Looked up its license?" asked the Commander.

"Yes, Master Zar-ko," replied the Head Guard.

"And...?"

"It's an intruder, Commander. Consequently it should be declared hostile. Give your order!"

"What in Vasi-Vuzuk's name!" swore the upset Zar-ko. This incident had come at the most inconvenient time, just as he was about to conclude what would definitely be his most interesting conversation with the visitor from Earth.

"Handle it in accordance with the code. Readiness at Guard level," ordered the Commander.

"The guard has already dealt with the matter, Master Zar-ko," shot back Taka-mura.

Before the Three Star Commander could say anything, a warning whistle was heard and a screen came to life. The familiar figure of one of the Elders of the Council filled the screen.

"Master Zar-ko..." he began in a soft, weak voice and the Commander was suddenly standing to attention.

"At your command, Elder!" he screamed and the Councillor clapped his hands over his enormous crescent-shaped ears.

"Quiet, Master Zar-ko, quiet or you'll deafen us..." complained the Elder. "The Council wishes to speak with you on a matter of high planetary security. At once," the aged Councillor added as the other five members of the Council of Elders appeared on the screen.

"Ready. Elders... At your command," replied Zar-ko who suddenly remembered that a foreign being was still present in his chambers. "Allow me to accompany the honourable Tao Li, my visitor from planet Earth, as he leaves," he added but the aged Councillor told him at once not to do such a thing.

"Let him hear. His presence may prove to be useful," ordered the Elder and Tao Li, who had been awkwardly following their conversation, grew bolder. "At your service, Elders. Your wish is a pleasant command to me," he said in a servile tone.

"Good. Now listen. The uninvited craft is extremely dangerous and must be dealt with at the highest level of readiness for the sake of intergalactic security. Reverse analysis has shown that it has come from quite some distance and must have been travelling for at least five or six suns, if not more. Our agents inform us that the Locusts suffered heavy losses when they attacked it. The unidentified craft is unaffected by their fire and armed with new generation weapons of the third century since the disappearance of the Third Sun..."

"Oooohhh! By Vasi-vuzuk, that's incredible..." stammered Zar-ko, while the perplexed Tao Li looked on, feeling dizzy. He could not understand their conversation and it seemed to him that he was out of place and, even more, out of time. What era of a lost Third Sun were they talking about?

The aged Councillor nodded his head and the other Elders did the same, confirming the information. Their wisdom was unique and beyond the comprehension and knowledge of their ordinary subjects. Consequently, their verdict was final.

"The planet's intelligence services have also informed us that, as they learned from the Locusts, the craft is peculiar insofar as it moves like a wave, like the snakes we have in the Museum of extinct species..."

"Aaaahh!" uttered Zar-ko and Taka-mura imitated him. Tao Li pricked up his ears. What he was hearing was very interesting. And it reminded him of something...

"As for the passengers and crew, zero," the Elder went on.

"Our spectral rays failed to penetrate the craft, the same for the antisonic measurements..."

The aged Councillor paused. The other Elders again nodded their heads affirmatively, as if to prove their wisdom.

"One final thing... and the worst of all," concluded the Elder, pausing for effect. "It is all white in colour!"

"Oooohhhl" echoed everywhere at the Councillor's extraordinary revelation. "White! But... but... how can that be?" said Zar-ko and Taka-mura as one.

The Elders of the Council again nodded their huge round, bald heads meaningfully.

"Hold on a minute! I've got it!"

The voice of Tao Li was heard, like a terribly jarring note. They all turned their attention to the repulsive face of the visitor from Earth. "I think I know the unknown visitors that you're looking for," said the leader of the Tigers gang triumphantly.

"You know them?" answered the Black Cloudians in unison.

"Yes, I do!" replied Tao Li with certainty. He had remembered the conversations and arguments that he'd had with the Nectar Brotherhood and he recalled vividly how they had boasted about the fantastic, invincible spacecraft of their protector and mentor, Lord Salvador of wisdom, which was called White Cloud. Yes, by all the indications and reports, it must be that one...

Tao Li was like a cockerel now, inflated with his own self-importance at having shown how useful, how indispensable he was to them. "And naturally, all this comes with a price, doesn't it?" thought the leader of the Tigers with satisfaction.

Tao Li struck a pose as he set out in great detail his theory about the provenance of the terrifying white ship and its passengers. He took care to elaborate his story with cosmetic improvements to make it more important and, mainly, to bestow terrific, amazing abilities on to his detested rivals of the Nectar Brotherhood. When he reached the part of his description that concerned the Brotherhood's mentor and protector, Lord Salvador of wisdom, a worrying buzzing sound drowned out his words. Tao Li wondered what he had done wrong...

"Lord Salvador of wisdom?" echoed the Elders with a single voice. "The same Lord Salvador with whom we had so much bother and trouble at the time of the lost Third Sun? The one it took three winters to remove from our galaxy...?"

Tao Li could only look on in embarrassment, now at the screen with the Elders, now at Zar-ko. He did not understand what they were talking about, nor did he have any idea bout wars and exiles. He had only heard about Lord Salvador, never even having seen him. "Yes, I presume that we are talking about the same person," stammered the leader of the Tigers.

The Council of Elders disappeared from the screen and the Commander explained to his earthly visitor that they would discuss the matter in private. "The wise Elders now have to come to a decision, my dear Tao Li," said Zar-ko simply. "We can do no more than wait for their decision and their instructions. Another drink?"

"No, no, nothing to drink or to eat," Tao Li was quick to answer.

After a while, the characteristic whistle was heard once again and the Elders of the Council appeared on the big screen.

"We have decided, for the sake of maximum security and defence, to activate the planet's plasticanopy. Master Zar-ko, you will have the honour of overseeing the implementation of our decision, together with the men of the Guard," announced the same Elder who had first appeared on the screen, on behalf of the members of the Council.

"Oh, by Doctor Soc-rat, this is a great honour, Elders," responded the awestruck Three Star Commander, lifting his staff into the air in a gesture of respect and acknowledgment. Deployment of the plasticanopy had not take place for a great many suns, not since the time of the great Five Star Commander.

"Ah, now that you mention it, Commander," continued the aged Councillor, "we have sent an intergalactic signal to Doctor Soc-rat, requesting his return to the planet as soon as possible. His presence and his valuable experience are indispensable to us if we are to deal with the invaders' craft and, above all, our eternal enemy, Lord Salvador of wisdom. We wish you good luck!" he said, and the screen went blank.

Zar-ko wasted no time, ordering Taka-mura to gather his men together. He needed to give them the correct orders and, at the same time, they had to make sure that the Council of Elders' commands were carried out. The plasticanopy, the unique object of pride of intergalactic technology that protected the planet, had to be activated at once. And what an honour it was that this task had been given to Commander Zar-ko! That Fourth Star would undoubtedly be his great and well-deserved reward. All he had to do was succeed in the new mission with which the Council of Elders had entrusted him. And who could say what would follow...

Master Zar-ko stood motionless and emotional as he touched Tao Li with his four-fingered hand. Then he gave the order: "Om-niscient, take us to Military Headquarters!" and they suddenly found themselves in a circular room in which, all around and even on its dark dome, was nothing but screens and countless tiny lights. Right in the middle was the only object in the quiet room that Zar-ko referred to as his Military Headquarters. It was an egg-shaped protruberance on the floor with translucent grey pipe-like fluting, in which there appeared to be a continuous and steady flow of pink liquid. It was the Om-niscient. Tao Li trembled at the thought that, if you touched it, it might be holed and bleed.

"Activate visuals!" ordered Zar-ko, wasting no time. All around and on the dome there formed a panoramic screen, illuminated by the planet's suns and bringing life to the quiet room that was Military Headquarters. The view was sensational but the Commander had not come here for the view. His next order drastically altered the appearance and the atmosphere of the room.

"Sweep the Summer Sector to a depth of one Sun!" ordered Zar-ko and Tao Li at once felt himself travelling at dizzying speed into the depths of vast space, among stars and nebulae, comets and spacecraft.

"Circular sweep!" continued Zar-ko and everything seemed to be spinning round unstoppably. Tao Li felt lost, as giddiness struck his head without mercy and he suddenly lost consciousness but the Commander paid him no heed.

"Identify craft on the frontier!" said Master Zar-ko and the rotating, alternating pictures froze. On the screens, one by one, appeared all the spaceships that were travelling in the area according to their position. The Commander's experienced eye could not detect any craft that corresponded to the specifications provided by their informers.

"Luckily they haven't made it inside the inner fence," he murmured and lifted up Tao Li. "You mustn't miss this," he told the Earthling once he had come round. "It's unique," the Commander added, talking more to himself. "Because even I have never seen it before..." he added before giving his next and most important order.

"Om-niscient, activate the Plasticanopy... Execution now!" commanded Master Zar-ko in his steady, monotonous voice.

Within the Headquarters came something resembling a distant hum and it felt as if the place was shaking slightly. The hum went on for several minutes, as did the trembling of the room, and Tao

Li turned his head in curiosity, looking for the plasticanopy, but he could see nothing at all.

"So, you see that, earth visitor?" asked Master Zar-ko but Tao Li replied that he could not make out anything special.

"Ah, yes, of course my dear Tao Li. How can you see since your earthly eyes are blind and weak before the perfection of this, our technology?" replied the Commander and gave further orders to the Om-niscient.

"Place optic filters on the visitor!" he commanded and Tao Li felt his eyes close like the lens of a camera. When he opened them his vision was different. He saw everything with a tint of mauve and he quickly realised that his eyes focused in a different way, according to the distance of an object and their viewpoint which expanded dramatically.

"Wow!" he shouted enthusiastically, "I can see to the sides too!... Oh, what's that then?" he asked as, with his new eyes, he could now clearly see what Master Zar-ko and the Elders called the plasticanopy.

A cover, invisible to earthly eyes, as if it were made of something immaterial, began to inflate over the whole of planet Black Cloud. Like a huge bubble, it expanded outwards across the surface of the planet, moving away while forming an invisible protective cover. When it had reached the desired height and distance, it stopped spreading and, at the very top, right over Military Headquarters, a valve opened. From the bubble's opening stretched a long, transparent ribbon which terminated in the room at headquarters and was connected to the egg-shape protruberance that was the Om-niscient.

Commander Zar-ko's order had been carried out impeccably and fast. The planet was now protected by the plasticanopy and no presumptuous enemy would be able to break through it and enter the territory of Black Cloud like some undesirable parasite.

The Commander immediately reported to the Elders that the plasticanopy had been activated and he set the coordinates of the invisible entrances and exits of Black Cloud. The Om-niscient registered and encrypted them while Taka-mura charged his men with overseeing and coordinating intergalactic traffic from then on. No spacecraft, whether from the planet or foreign, would be able to move without first obtaining permission from Headquarters.

Zar-ko gave a sigh of relief. Everything had gone as hoped for and he would now be able to complete his negotiations with Tao Li. Everything was going fantastically well for the Three Star

Commander and that longed-for Fourth Star was already looking like a tangible reality.

ᔕ

"Crew, attention!" came the order from Nec-Tar 1 as the spacecraft completed its reconnaissance of the ground around planet Black Cloud. "Seats for landing..." it added and Jurka, Johara and Milo settled into their seats.

"On course for the Summer Sector, maximum approach speed, activate now!" the unseen Nec-Tar 1 continued and the spaceship, after turning slightly so as to be heading in the right direction, set off like a speeding bullet towards planet Black Cloud to make a landing on the planned site. The three friends felt their blood flow faster through their veins. Their heartbeats grew louder from the tension which was now reaching its peak as the end of the journey approached. White Cloud was taking them to their destination where they would have to carry out their successful mission.

Suddenly a prolonged noise, like a grating sound, came from the front of the spacecraft. The noise grew louder and immediately afterwards the whole ship began to shudder. It then became clear that its speed had started to decrease drastically and was gradually reduced to zero.

"What's happening, Nec-Tar 1?" asked Jurka but, before he could hear the answer, something unexpected happened. The spacecraft was flung backwards, as if from some gigantic catapult, and it sped through space out of control, spiralling like a crazy shell that had ricocheted off its target.

"Activate stabilisers!" came the clear order from the steady, expressionless, metallic voice of Nec-Tar 1 and the spacecraft gradually stopped revolving, disorderly and unprogrammed, like a spinning top.

"Boosters, maximum reverse thrust," the voice ordered and within a minute the crazy backwards course had been halted.

"Stable position now!" commanded Nec-Tar 1 and White Cloud hung motionless and steady in the vastness of space.

"Nectaroids, damage inspection. Report!" came the invisible voice and the tiny black and yellow robots poured out in every direction to carry out the order.

The three friends got out of their seats, bewildered. They were still in a state of shock.

"What can have happened?" stammered an embarrassed Jurka.

"We seem to have had some kind of accident..." replied Johara, while Milo was still trying to recover from the unexpected incident.

The eyes of all three focused on the small disc pulsating like a heart.

"Nec-Tar 1 is processing chronoscopic data. Analysis incomplete," said the voice.

Several minutes of silence and anticipation passed.

"Screen now. Give us visual contact, Nec-Tar 1," ordered Jurka who considered that a picture would perhaps explain better at this stage what had happened to their spacecraft.

The front screen was activated and the three friends stared at it. Before them unfolded an incomprehensible sight. They could see nothing that reminded them of planet Black Cloud or even the presence of the Locusts, the space pirates in the vicinity of the galaxy of the Two Suns.

"Where are we? Does anyone know where we are?" wondered Jurka but he received no answer from his friends, and not even from Nec-Tar 1.

"We must have hit something," said Milo.

"Yes, but couldn't our good friend here have predicted that? I consider an accident highly unlikely," remarked Johara and Jurka agreed with her at once.

"Whatever it was couldn't have been predicted," he said. "It must have been something unexpected... something unknown," the light-haired youth concluded.

"Like what, man?" Milo wondered aloud.

"Hmm, something like an ambush, for example..." replied Jurka, hesitatingly.

"An ambush? You must be joking. Who would want to ambush us?" persisted Milo, but no-one could give him an explanation.

"I don't know, man, I don't know," murmured Jurka. "What I do know is that it's not only friends that we've got in these parts of the galaxy. We're not welcome visitors to everyone, are we? Remember the Locusts..."

Johara remarked that the way it had all happened was completely unorthodox. "Whatever it was that stopped us in our tracks, we need to think about it," she said. "It didn't seem to hit us with a weapon or even rays..." she concluded.

"Let's hope that our friend here will give us some answers, and the right ones," said Jurka, pointing to Nec-Tar 1. "Hey Nec-Tar 1, buddy, what's happening?" he asked.

"Nec-Tar 1 analysing information," came the metallic voice.

"Great! So, let's wait and see. What else is there for us to do?" said Jurka and the three friends returned to their places in the middle of the spaceship's bridge. The Nectaroids were still scuttling continuously from one side to the other and disappearing into the bowels of the ship where none of the three members of the Nectar Brotherhood had yet attempted to go.

"I wonder what's going on in there..." whispered Milo.

"Where do you mean?" asked Johara and the her big dark-skinned friend nodded towards the back of the ship. "Over there. Behind the dark grey screen," he explained.

"Do you think it's wise to go and see? Uninvited?" Johara asked.

"I'm not sure. What do you say, Jurka?" replied Milo.

"Why don't we ask our all-knowing friend here?" suggested Slavik, pointing once more at the throbbing heart.

"Leave it, Jurka. It's better if he tells us first what's happened. Don't let's be bothering him every so often with unimportant things. He might get blocked in the end," Johara commented.

Milo hastened to say that he hadn't meant that they should go to the back of the ship at that very moment. That could wait.

The waiting got on their nerves. When there is nothing to do except sit and wait, it feels as if all your energy, that precious commodity, has been imprisoned. On the other hand, what else could they do? Did they have any choice?

The voice of Nec-Tar 1 suddenly made them jump as he broke the painful silence.

"Analysis complete," came the Captain's simple announcement. "Spaceship halted by impenetrable plasticanopy over planet Black Cloud. Immediate reduction of speed to zero. Irregular unprogrammed reverse propulsion to distance of three suns. Damage slight. Reverting to correct course, now..."

Upon completion of this last directive, the familiar hum was heard once more from the bowels of the ship. The White Cloud was again on course for planet Black Cloud.

"Screen now," ordered Nec-Tar 1 and the front of the spaceship was once again lit up. The three friends stared into the infinity that stretched out before them. Again they saw familiar sights which, like multicoloured paintings, appeared one after another in a unique heavenly spectacle. The light played hide and seek with the darkness as the spaceship headed at untold speed past successive suns, covering distances of many sunrises before reaching its destination. When it arrived in the upper atmosphere of Black Cloud, Nec-Tar 1 gave the order to stop.

"Magnification!" he ordered and the planet filled the screen. Nothing looked any different from how it was on the previous occasion, nor could they observe anything odd. No movement, no alarm, no guards.

"So where's the plasticanopy?" asked Milo.

"Hmm, it has to be out there somewhere," replied Jurka. "If we could see it, we'd have avoided it the first time," noted the light-haired young man and the slightly-built Johara added a simple "that's right."

"Captain Nec-Tar 1, dear friend Nec-Tar 1, can you show us the plasticanopy?" asked Milo as a joke, addressing the throbbing heart and the voice answered at once that the ultraspectral ray system was being activated.

"Process complete," announced Nec-Tar 1. "Activate now!" he added and on the large front screen of the spaceship a miracle began to take shape. Suddenly, as if from nowhere, a wave of light poured out of the ship and spread out gradually to the surrounding areas, making visible anything that was previously invisible. The plasticanopy took shape with all its magnificence and detail before their eyes, encircling the whole of planet Black Cloud on all sides like a transparent skin, protecting it with incredible strength from any invader.

"Plasticanopy in sight" announced Nec-Tar 1, as the ultraspectral process was completed.

"Wow!" shouted Milo. "That's what we hit, guys. It grabbed us like a spider, stopped us in our tracks and then slung us back like some tiny, insignificant thing from an enormous catapult," he reasoned. Jurka agreed with his friend. "Yes, that must be exactly what happened. That's why we were flying backwards and out of control," he said.

"The question is: what do we do now, everyone?" interrupted Johara who had a practical mind. "Honestly, how are we going to reach the planet? How are we going walk on its surface?"

Johara's question could not be answered by Jurka or Milo. The only one with the answers was the throbbing heart of Nec-Tar 1.

The three friends turned to the invisible captain, awaiting his answers. Nothing. No reaction. Nec-Tar 1 was not responding because he appeared to be occupied, as evidenced by the multicoloured lights on the throbbing heart that were continuously blinking on and off.

Jurka took a decision.

"We need to speak to Lord Salvador," he proposed. "He's the only one who can tell us what to do," he added, as Johara and Milo continued in vain to call Captain Nec-Tar 1 into action. The throbbing heart of the spacecraft was still not responding.

The three space travellers joined hands and formed the familiar triangle. Jurka Slavik was about to begin the Hymn of the Brotherhood when, from the bowels of the ship, there came a familiar voice.

"Ahoy there friends!"

"Lord Salvador!" shouted the three in unison, turning to where Lord Salvador's greeting had come from.

No-one appeared.

"Hmm, let's see how you're going to get out of this mess," came Lord Salvador's voice. "Let's see..."

"How? Tell us, Lord of wisdom," begged Jurka, impatient as always.

"Well, since you've had something of a shipwreck, there's only one thing to do now my friends," the lord's voice was heard once again. "You'll just have to swim for it!"

The three friends looked at one another in surprise and mistrust. Their concern was well-founded. Swim? Where to and how?

"Come one, come on, don't be like that. I'll lose my temper," Lord Salvador reprimanded them. "What I've told you is so simple and so obvious that it really annoys me that you're even thinking about it, like children. In any case, I have nothing more to add. Ask your Captain for the rest. All I've given him are the basics," Lord Salvador added and his voice went silent as quickly as it had been heard earlier.

Their attention now focused exclusively on the throbbing heart. At last, Nec-Tar 1 spoke,

"Change to action plan," he announced.

The captain of the White Cloud explained to them that since it was impossible for the spacecraft to penetrate the plasticanopy, they would have to take matters into their own hands. They would leave the spaceship and attempt to reach planet Black Cloud through the safety valve that connected the plasticanopy to Military Headquarters. The Nectaroids would provide them with the famous

AETP (Automatic Energy Transformation Package) space suits and all the right equipment. This was the latest miracle in futurist technology and there was nothing like it in any of the known galaxies of the universe. Nec-Tar 1 himself would programme their course and would be in a constant state of alert so as to bring them back to the ship if anything happened or when they had achieved their mission, or whenever they wished. All they had to do at this point was lie back in their seats…

The three friends followed Nec-Tar 1's orders to the letter. Once again, they all had the same dream. In it they were dressed in the famed AETP suits and they miraculously knew all its multiple uses and capabilities. The helmets, so light and close-fitting that you would have thought they were a natural extension of their heads, comprised, like a brain, the centre for all the senses. The wave-like vests consisted of countless voice-activated fibres which carried out every order and function simply by hearing the wearer's voice, while their sleeves and self-adhesive gloves doubled as deadly, multi-purpose weapons. The belt around the waist served not only as an extremely valuable tracking and locating device but also as a tool for repelling all foreign bodies and unwanted matter. The close-fitting trousers resembled, more than anything, a collage of different, small, coloured sections while their boots, which you would have thought no different from normal, actually concealed microchips of enormous capacity and with a huge number of applications. Down their backs, attached to the reverse of the vest as if in pipes, were built-in navigation and propulsion systems while at the very centre of their helmets, as tiny as a stamp, were the control mechanisms of the complex space suits.

When they awoke, they did indeed feel as if they were swimming in the vastness of space. The automatic course control mechanisms had been activated and the three friends, like astronauts in their protective masks and uniforms, were travelling in the bright sky towards the heart of Black Cloud. They would shortly reach their destination and from then on, they would have to fend for themselves.

Entering by the central valve of the plasticanopy into the Military Headquarters area was not especially difficult. The problems began when they were already inside the circular quiet room. The Omniscient sounded the alarm. Now they had to act lightning fast before Taka-mura and his guards arrived.

Jurka took a quick look around the Headquarters. There were two possible escape routes, One was through the door that most likely led to the interior of the Aerial Fortress and with certainty into the hands of the guards. The other was through the walls in which there must be windows that were not visible. Jurka activated the spectroscope and made a sweep of the whole room.

"There it is! That's the escape window," shouted Jurka Slavik to his comrades and, wasting no time, gave the order:

"Beam out now!" he said and he other two repeated the same command. The moment their dematerialised bodies crossed the room and passed through the window, the door opened and Taka-mura and his guards rushed into the Headquarters. All they managed to see was a triple flash that, like a comet, illuminated for some fractions of a second the part of the inner wall where the window lay before it disappeared.

"Damn them by Me-gaera," cursed Taka-mura on realising that they had arrived too late. "Guards, call Master Zar-ko, over," he said and at once came the reply, "Tell me!"

Taka-mura gave his brief report and this time it was Zar-ko's turn to swear. "Damn you! What happened then? Where are the invaders right now?" he asked in a voice that rang like steel.

"Obviously, they've landed on the planet, Commander," replied Taka-mura in a steady voice. "Give the order!"

"What order do you want me to give? You're the Head Guard, don't you know your job? I want you to take them alive for interrogation. At least one of them. You said there are three of them, Taka-mura?"

"Yes, Master Zar-ko. I managed to catch three flashes..."

"So what are you waiting for? Sweep the Summer Sector. Locate them and arrest them. Whatever it takes! And keep me informed. The Council of Elders is already extremely concerned, got it Taka-mura?"

"Yes, Master Zar-ko!"

"Go on then, action stations!"

Taka-mura ordered his men to follow him and they all went to the operations room of the Aerial Fortress. Tao Li was waiting there, tense and worried.

"Head Guard Taka-mura, it is the Commander's wish that I should come with you," he explained and the leader of the Guard gestured to the earthly visitor to follow him.

"Put this on!" he ordered and Tao Li at once donned the uniform he was shown.

"You'll go with me, Tao Li," added Taka-mura, as he mounted the two-man craft that resembled a covered scooter. The guards did the same and they all took off without delay for the planet's Summer Sector. That was where the three invaders must have landed.

ꙮ

The landing on planet Black Cloud had been a perfectly smooth one for the three friends from distant Earth. The golden corn all around reminded Jurka of the picture of Nefeli and he sighed.

"At last, we've reached our destination," he said. "We need to look for Nefeli somewhere around here, and right now. Something tells me that she's not far away..." he added, but Milo stopped his train of thought.

"What are you talking about, Jurka? We saw her before we set off, remember. How long has it been since then, eh?"

"Oh dear, have you remembered Nefeli again? We've hardly landed and you're on about her already," remarked Johara. "Well, Milo's right," she added and reminded Jurka that they'd been travelling for seven suns.

It was hot and they ordered the AETP to regulate the temperature to a comfortable level. Milo looked around. They needed to start somewhere but the big question was: which way should they go? And how? On foot? Through the air? At what altitude? And what speed?

"Reconnaissance antenna, activate!" said Johara and at once an aerial rose from her helmet. "Observation, now," the young girl ordered and the aerial began to rotate slowly in every direction. When it stopped, they knew that it had identified the location of the city. The three friends activated the optical fibres in their tunics and, on their arms, like illuminated windows, arose small screens.

They had just started to study the images as they appeared one after the other when Milo's voice interrupted the procedure.

"We've got company," was all he said and pointed towards a clearing. Through the corn they could make out three figures.

"We're lucky they're not guards," said Jurka confidently and Johara added, "My friends, it time to get to know the Black Cloudians properly..."

The three figures were identical except in height. The tallest of them approached the Earthlings with light, almost ethereal steps. It stood right in front of Jurka and the deep-set, black holes in the place of eyes, focused on the youth's forehead. It then went back to the other two figures and the three of them began to rock about in a funny way, as if they were wound-up like clockwork.

"What's happening, man?" Milo asked Jurka but it was Johara who answered at once.

"They're laughing at us, that's what," the young girl explained.

"What for?" Milo insisted, only to receive his answer from Jurka this time.

"Because we're different, Milo. And obviously, to them we're funny too," he added, at which his dark-skinned friend laughed out loud. "We're funny? What does that make them, then?" Milo managed to utter between guffaws.

The tallest of the three figures eventually returned to where Jurka was standing. In a single movement, it stretched out its right hand, opened its four-fingered palm and turned it upside down, offering it to the light-haired youth.

"Take a look at this! What does it want now? Is it asking you for pocket money, Jurka?" asked Milo in a loud voice.

"Well, it couldn't possibly be a handshake, could it?" answered Johara. "It's making the introductions," explained the petite girl, who remembered better than Milo the details of the dream they'd all had.

"Johara's right," said Jurka. "So let's get to know each other..." he said, stretching out is right hand, palm upwards.

The Black Cloudian bent over and looked at it for a while. Then it lifted its round bald head and uttered:

"Jur-ka!"

The other two figures followed like an echo: "Jur-ka..."

"Yes, Jurka. Jurka Slavik," the young man confirmed rather comically.

"Let's see who you are..." he said, gazing at the Black Cloudian's open palm. In his ears the answer rang out from the nano-data processor.

"Ti-hon..." he said and at once the three figures echoed, "Ti-hon!"

Soon, all the introductions had been made. Ti-hon was the head of the family, Ma-ru his partner and Lu-gi their child. The classification of labour by the Council of Elders had placed them in the farming category until they had completed their fixed duties and achieved the aims of the plan that they had been given. If they were lucky enough to collect a few Value Units, they might be transferred to another, better category, who knows, suppliers or, even better, superintendents.

"What Jur-ka and friends want on planet Black Cloud?" asked Ti-hon, when the introductions and explanations were over.

"We're looking for Nefeli," Jurka replied mechanically. "She was abducted from Earth by Tao Li's Tigers and they brought her here," he explained.

"Ah! Nefeli... Tao Li." Ti-hon repeated the names and gestured to their child: Lu-gi find," he said simply, touching the little one's narrow, small shoulder with one hand. Ma-ru did the same with the child's other shoulder. All three stood motionless, as if in prayer. The small triangle on Lu-gi's forehead started to flash as the three earthly friends watched the never-experienced ritual with obvious curiosity but tension too.

Suddenly a strange sound resembling that of a bell was heard from Lu-gi's wide open mouth and the other two looked concerned.

"Lu-gi feel danger. Lu-gi feel guards... Tao Li city," said Ti-hon as Ma-ru and the little one rushed to disappear like the wind into the corn.

They received no answer about Nefeli. At that moment, an alarm sounded in the ears of the three friends. Their sensors had been activated and there followed a warning from the nano-computer which was clear:

"Hostile guards on the border fence. Take protective action!"

Jurka, Johara and Milo activated their self-defence system and their jetpacks without delay. They had to get away from their pursuers. They absolutely had to get into Summer City and look for Nefeli before the Black Cloud guards caught wind of them.

The jetpacks worked perfectly and the three friends were soon flying at speed towards Summer City They flew low, caressing the golden corn as they passed, having left behind them the guards who had arrived on the scene seconds earlier, led by Taka-mura. They had not been fast enough to catch the Earthly invaders and the Head Guard cursed again, as he usually did in such instances.

"Damn Vasi-vuzuk! The ugly devils have got away... But where are they going to go? I'm going to get them, I'll get them," he said to himself angrily, as he prepared to report back to Master Zar-ko.

CHAPTER 2

The sirens in Summer City sounded three times, signalling that another working day was over. And, as if by some miracle, the roads and air corridors were suddenly full of people. Black Cloudians, wearing their recreation outfits, foreign visitors and tourists, as well as all sorts of settlers from near and distant planets, hurried about like machines so as to take advantage of the time they had before the sirens sounded again, signalling that it was time to go to their homes, shelters and hostels to relax, regain their strength and get a little sleep.

All roads led to the centre of Summer City and the three young travellers from Earth, wearing simple long capes over their uniforms, decided to follow the crowds who appeared to be heading for one and the same building complex: the 'Bax-e' Universal Arcade that dominated the structure of the city like a jarring note. Firstly, it stood out because of its bulk: as tall as it stretched upwards, it had the same again in depth. Then, there was its pitch black colour.

The extent that it covered was enormous in comparison with the surrounding settlements, but that was perfectly natural since it was the only Universal Arcade in the city. It was here that the foreign settlers rushed to drown their sorrows and troubles in drink; it was where the locals hurried to do their shopping; it was the only place of entertainment for young and old; it was a place of fun for the Mace-bearers, those Black Cloudians who belonged to the higher class of clerks. The "Bax-e' Arcade was paradise to them, even if only for the brief relaxation period.

Jurka entered the front gate by himself and glanced around. Brightly-lit signs informed visitors about everything they needed to know while the screens showed a constant stream of commercials, short films too, all about the planet's famed product. A voice like that of someone narrating a fairy tale spoke the permanent advertising slogan: "Cre-matum – total pleasure..."

In front of the central screen which dominated the enormous ante-room, beings and creatures from every corner of the galaxy jostled, while the touts loudly proclaimed the services on offer, mainly in the 'Ba-xe' Arcade's Pleasure Department. Inspectors walked nonchalantly among the crowd in twos, taking care to make their presence known for better or worse. No-one seemed to be paying attention to the small-built visitor from Earth and Jurka Slavik decided that it was safe to call his friends in.

"Hey, this is really cool this... this... thing," said Milo on seeing the inside of the building complex.

"It seems fine to me," remarked Johara, who was quick to note that the mass of people and the noise, the overwhelming mix of movement, sound and images, suited them unbelievably well.

"I agree," Jurka said, adding, "OK, we're in the Arcade. Now we have to work out our plan of action. Where do we go? Where do we look for information? And who will we get it from?"

A tout appeared in front of the three youngsters from Earth who, he thought, appeared to be idling away their time. His long snout and his sparse, trembling whiskers revealed his origins.

"Young Earthly friends, allow me to offer you my services," began the settler from planet Mousehole with wonderful professionalism. "What are you interested in today? Shopping? Games? Entertainment? Whatever interests you, I'm at your complete and exclusive service..."

Jurka thought that they should not trust a touting vole from Mousehole but Milo had a different opinion.

"We're interested in finding others from our country," said the dark-skinned giant. "To socialise," he added.

"A-ha! There's no better place than Entertainment Square 12 in Section B. That's where your Earthly friends go, my young friends," he said and paused. "Of course, they go to other places too but you can't go to them," the Mouseholian clarified, winking craftily. "You're underage..."

"What places?" asked Milo, full of curiosity, and the vole whispered in his ear, "The Pleasure Baths. Not allowed," as he opened up a path through the crowds to lead the three young friends to their destination.

"Just a minute. Hold on one moment, Mister," said Jurka and the tout stopped, wondering what the problem was. The sparse whiskers at the end of his snout were playing, as if he was trying to smell out their decision, while his shining eyes sparkled as they opened and closed impatiently. If he managed to take the three youngsters to Square 12 of Section B, he would immediately be credited with three times five equals fifteen Value Units. "A good haul for one or two minutes' work," he was thinking.

The three friends gathered some distance away.

"What's up, Jurka? Why the hesitation?" asked Johara.

"I think we need to cover our backs first. I can't trust a vole who's a tout..."

"So what do we do? What exactly are you thinking? Go on..." said Milo.

"Well, I'm saying we should be careful. Not put all our eggs in one basket, that's what I'm thinking," Jurka explained.

"Hmm... You may be right, my man," remarked Milo. "What do you say, Johara?"

"I'm not sure. If we split up, there's always a risk of getting lost and we're not so strong apart. On the other hand, we're more likely to run into Tao Li and his Tigers, not to mention finding Nefeli in here. I can't imagine what she's doing in this... this, what shall I call it, this enormous stable," said the girl with the short black hair.

"Well, Jurka, what's it to be?" asked the impatient Milo who always wanted to be in the thick of things.

"OK, big man, let's do it. We'll all go and we'll see," Jurka decided and nodded to the vole to take them to where they wanted to go.

Square 12 of Section B was nothing more than a smaller version of the entrance. There was a noisy square full of people and creatures while all around you could see the various shops and haunts offering their wares. The upper floors of the section were similarly arranged while in the aerial corridors flew winged stewards, scooters for one and two riders, flying servant-beings out on errands for the Mace-bearers and other members of the privileged elite. In the intervening space, between the floors, huge screens put out a constant stream of sound and sensory pollution.

The Mouseholian led them to a haunt where they could only move with difficulty due to the mass of people there.

"Here we are my friends," announced the vole-tout as, pushing and cursing, he managed to find them seats among some of his settler compatriots. "Here, in the corner, it's very convenient... It's something like an observatory, since there's a wonderful view. And the service is first-rate, ask my fellow villagers over here..." the tout finished. "And whenever you need me, you know where to find me," he added as he headed for the bar from which the place was run by a fat settler from a planet in the constellation of the Little Bear. The tout would settle up with her.

"What would the Earthlings like? To eat? A drink? A soft drink?"

The voice of the waitress demanded the attention of the three friends of the Nectar Brotherhood. Milo was quick to ask whether they served ice cream and the hologram of the waitress nodded: "Of course," she said and noted his order. Jurka ordered a lemon-flavoured drink and Johara asked for plain water. The waitress hologram disappeared.

The nearby customers from Mousehole had already had plenty to drink and were quietly singing the blues in sorrowful tunes from their homeland, pushing one another.

Life is a but a dream
Yes a dream, just a dream
Moments are more precious
More precious than they seem
But I'm going home
Home, yes home…

The waitress warned them that it was time for them to sober up as they risked violating Regulation 323 of the Good Behaviour Code.

"No more zi-van. You're over the limit," announced the waitress in her expressionless voice. "Your drink now is so-ki," she continued, undaunted, despite the protests and bawling of the voles, who were demanding one more alcoholic drink. Order was, of course, imposed on the voles since once they'd drunk the so-ki, they magically became sober. Only then did they notice that they had company.

"Hello to the young friends from Earth," they said as one and the three returned the greeting.

Jurka raised his glass of lemon-flavoured liquid.

"Cheers!" he said and the voles bowed. "Your health," they said.

"What good sun brings you here to planet Black Cloud?" the oldest Mouseholian asked Jurka.

"We're searching for a friend of ours," the light-haired young man replied as simply and naturally as he could. "Nefeli," he added, hoping that the name might ring a bell with them. No reaction. The settlers from Mousehole made an indifferent "a,a,a..." sound and that was the end of the subject.

"And Tao Li, leader of the Tigers," added Johara.

The company of voles livened up.

"Tao Li? But who in here doesn't know the famous leader of the Tigers...?" they said as one.

"Bingo!" shouted Milo enthusiastically, making the rest of them wonder what was up.

"Bingo? No, we don't know anyone called Bingo," said the oldest one who appeared to speak on behalf of the whole vole group.

"No, no, we're not looking for anyone called Bingo," Jurka was quick to explain. "It's Tao Li we're after. Would you know where we can find him?"

"No, but they should know," replied the oldest Mouseholian, pointing with his snout to somewhere high up, on the first level.

The three friends had no trouble recognising several members of the Tigers who were eating and drinking and generally living it up with some shapely female holograms.

It seemed that the restrictions on drinking that were imposed on those lower down did not apply to customers on the upper level.

"Bingo!" shouted an enthusiastic Milo once again. "This discovery calls for another ice cream," he added.

Johara leaned over to Jurka's ear and suggested that they activate their image magnifiers.

"We need to look at who they're with from close-up," said the young girl and Jurka added that it was essential not to lose sight of them now. The Tigers would lead the three friends to Tao Li and, through him, they would definitely find Nefeli.

They examined the members of the Tigers in the magnifiers. Tao Li was nowhere to be seen, nor was there any other Earthling near them apart from the holograms. They were clearly having a terrific time, indifferent to everyone else around and unconcerned by the occasional presence of the patrolling inspectors. They evidently enjoyed special privileges and treatment, Jurka thought, and he was not wrong.

"Let's go, guys," said Johara. "Time to go," she added, as it appeared that the Tigers had received orders to get up.

At that precise moment, up on the top level, Tao Li came into view with Taka-mura and two guards. They quickly opened a path through the crowd, approaching the Tigers who had taken care to get rid of the holograms and were now standing to attention, waiting for their leader. It was clear that Tao Li was bringing news.

"Sit down a minute, kiddo," whispered Jurka to Johara.

"Let's see what's going on," he added.

"Attention! Attention!" came a voice over the main loudspeaker.

"This is a special announcement," it continued, and Master Zarko's ugly features appeared on all the screens.

"The Council of Elders has announced that three dangerous Earthlings are wanted for violating the Interplanetary Cooperation Code and illegal entry to the planet. All remain in your places for checking. Any information leading to their arrest will be rewarded with one Cre-matum and, for Black Cloudians, with promotion to Mace-bearer. End of message..."

Portraits of the three members of the Nectar Brotherhood appeared on the screens.

The announcement continued to be transmitted via the screens in the Universal Arcade as a long-drawn-out commotion filled Square 12 of Section B. A Cre-matum and becoming a Mace-bearer was not something to be sniffed at.

"We've got problems, guys," said Johara, and the three friends were forced to lower their hooded heads. Soon every Earthling in the area would be checked.

"Time to beat it, big man," said Milo, with which Jurka agreed. "Yes, but how are we going to get away unnoticed?" he asked. Johara came up with the answer: "In disguise, that's how!"

It was not to be. The elderly Mouseholian stuck his face in among the faces of the three friends. His tiny eyes fixed on them, one after the other, as if he was counting them. His whiskers played craftily as he smelled them and his horrible voice was heard:

"That's them! They're here!"

Suddenly all hell broke loose! Everyone focused their attention on the corner where the three young friends were sitting and, scared and upset, they all pointed at the wanted trio. The voles tried to surround and trap the youngsters but they had neither the strength nor the means to do so. In any case, the voice of Tao Li put everyone back in their places.

"Stand back, everyone! They're mine!" he shouted and ordered the Tigers to arrest them.

"Hit them with stun rays!" he ordered. "They want them alive. Take them prisoner now!" he added and rushed down to the ground-level Square 12 of Section B. He was followed by Taka-mura and his two men, screaming at people to make way and open up a corridor for them to pass through.

Then came utter chaos!

Tao Li fired the first shots and the bright pink stun rays from his machine gun randomly hit the unfortunate customers who found themselves in the line of fire in Square 12 of Section B, knocking them down as if they were wilting plants. The Tigers copied their leader while Taka-mura and his two guards fired pellets containing knockout gas in the direction of the Earthly enemies.

From one moment to the next, the place turned into a battlefield. First to fall were, of course, the voles since the shots were aimed first and foremost in their direction.

The three friends of the Nectar Brotherhood immediately threw off their capes and prepared to take emergency action. The only good to come from the instinctive behaviour of the stupid, arrogant Tao Li was the fact that all those near his three earthly targets had been neutralised. Jurka managed to order the activation of the anti-gas protection device and pointed to the bar where the fat woman from the constellation of the Little Bear still seemed to be conscious.

"Let's go to the bar for cover!" shouted Jurka as Milo returned fire, throwing out smoke bombs which immediately covered the area with a thick curtain that prevented visual contact.

"Keep firing, men!" came Tao Li's voice as he leapt from counter to counter, descending to the ground-floor level. Taka-mura, more experienced and cool-headed than the arrogant youth from Earth, at once ordered his men to fire gas to clear the smoke. He knew very well that if he did not locate them fast he would lose them again. And then who would save him from the anger of Master Zar-ko?

The three friends hid behind the counter of the fat woman's bar but as soon as she saw them she began screaming uncontrollably. A dose of knockout gas from Johara made her fall silent. Now they had to find a way to repel their enemies before reinforcements arrived. They needed to get away right now...

Tao Li and his group arrived on the ground floor and took up positions opposite the bar.

"Stupid little Slavik, can you hear me?" he called and signalled to his men to stop firing. Taka-mura made certain that all the exits of the Universal Arcade had been secured. The wanted Earthlings were trapped.

"I hear you, Tao Li. What do you want?" replied Jurka.

"I want you to surrender right now. There's no point in resisting. You're surrounded and trapped in the building..."

"Surrender? What for? What have we done that we need to explain ourselves?"

"You're illegal invaders, that's what..."

"A-ha! And you and your gang are legal, are you? After kidnapping Nefeli and bringing her here against her will..."

Tao Li responded with a loud, sarcastic laugh.

"Kidnapping her? That's a good one! What nonsense are you going to come up with next, young and stupid Slavik? Anyway, what's it to you? What are you to the girl? Her guardian?"

Jurka did not answer the question. Johara signalled to him that it was time to prepare for the fight, while Milo had already armed his multispectral gun.

"I'm going to tell you one more time: Surrender, you've got no choice..." insisted the leader of the Tigers and collaborator with the Black Cloudians.

"Why don't you bring her out here in front of us and let her speak for herself so that we know the truth, eh? What are you afraid of, Tao Li?" Jurka persisted.

"I don't need to explain anything to anyone! And I'm not afraid of anyone..." replied Tao Li, furious. "Especially a baby like you. Anyway, that's enough talk. Surrender, yes or no?"

The quiet hum of two-man vehicles arriving at Square 12 of Section B interrupted the dialogue. Master Zar-ko jumped down from the first one, startled.

"What's going on here? Any longer and we'll be sending them kisses, eh Taka-mura?"

"No, Master Zar-ko! The Earthlings just started talking to one another..." the Head of the guard said in his defence but the Three Star Commander was having none of it.

"Silence!" he thundered. "Get out, Taka-mura, go on, outside. You and I will talk later," ordered Zar-ko and the Head of the Guard left, tail between his legs. "As for you, Tao Li, let me remind you that without me you are nothing. So cut out those Earth habits and don't overdo playing the clever devil," Master Zar-ko chastised him. He then turned towards the bar and gave his men their order.

"Hit them from the air!" he ordered and at once several two two-man vehicles lifted off and reached a considerable height. When they had manoeuvred into the best position for taking aim, they fired a succession of knockout gas pellets down towards the bar. At the same time, Zar-ko ordered the rest of his men to attack the bar head-on and arrest the three young fugitives.

"All fire!" came the Commander's order and all hell broke loose. Milo returned fire and his multispectral gun proved to be a treasure since it forced the guards' two-man craft to crash-land. Johara set off a series of smoke bombs and Jurka Slavik, using his repulsion pressure pump, successfully dealt with the attacking guards and Tao Li's Tigers, drenching them with sticky liquid.

"Damn Vasi-vuzuk!" cursed Master Zar-ko upon realising that his orders were not bringing about a positive result. The three young fugitives were repelling their attacks with ease.

"Hold your fire!" ordered the Commander and the weapons fell silent.

The ground floor of Square 12 of Section B looked as if it had been hit by a hurricane. Variously shaped bodies of customers, creatures and beings from the ends of the galaxy lay untidily on the ground, unconscious and immobilised. Liquid and solid remains of drinks and food soiled the surrounding areas, while many of the screens had stopped working, fatally struck in the crossfire.

Master Zar-ko gathered his men together and gave new orders.

"Forget the knockout gas," he said. "The two-man craft will capture the area around the bar with the Intangible Net," he added. "And you, Tao Li, will rush them with your Tigers when I give the order and you'll capture them," said the Commander.

"Yes, Master Zar-ko," responded the guards and the Tigers with one voice. "At your command!"

Master Zar-ko felt satisfied. "Why didn't I think of it from the start? If I'd done that we'd have finished in no time without any upset, without any fuss, all nice and clean," the Three Star Commander said to himself.

Jurka, Johara and Milo looked up. Nothing. No moves at all from the other side.

"They're up to something," said Johara and Milo was forced to agree with her. "Look, those two-man craft are taking off again..." he remarked.

"Hmm, hmm, yes, that's interesting. Why aren't they attacking us?" wondered Jurka. "Why are they hovering there with their engines on?"

"Let's ask our macro-analyst," said Johara while Milo suggested hitting them right away as they were perfect targets.

"We've not got time for analyses, kiddo," said Jurka.

"Whatever it is, is going to happen now," he added.

"So let's hit the bums. Right now!" repeated Milo, brandishing his pride and joy, the multispectral gun

They didn't have a chance to do any of what they were planning or thinking. An invisible force began to press down on them like a nightmare, pushing them slowly but surely to the ground. Jurka at once activated the repulsion pump but without success. The invisible pressure did not stop and their Earthly eyes could not see the huge Net which, like a spider, had suddenly trapped them. Milo fired two or three hopeless shots but, again, without being able to stop the strange pressure which had forced them to the ground and restricted their movements, trapping them like wild animals in an invisible, unassailable cage.

The triumphant voice of Master Zar-ko was now heard: "Now you see the result of my genius. The Intangible Net has done its job, by Doctor Soc-rat! Look and learn, you useless guards. Dear Tao Li, prepare to arrest the fugitives once you've neutralised the source of their energy. Meanwhile I shall inform the Council of Elders," the Commander ended, filled with pride.

"As you wish, Three Star Commander!" replied the leader of the Tigers who would now have the great pleasure of destroying their AETP system.

Behind the bar, the situation looked hopeless. However great their efforts, whatever they tried, the three friends could not do anything. They were like mice, caught in the invisible trap that Master Zar-ko had set for them.

Suddenly, a creaking sound came from the floor of the bar and the three trapped and immobilised friends were startled to see a hidden trapdoor open up like a ship's porthole. Gradually the round head of Lu-gi appeared.

"Lu-gi help... Lu-gi friend..."

These sounds from the wide open mouth of their unexpected little visitor rang like bells of salvation in the ears of the members of the Nectar Brotherhood, trapped and incapable of reacting. Their escape to safety would come through Lu-gi and the underground tunnels of the Black Cloudian city.

"Quick!" came the sound of Lu-gi's voice once again and Milo nodded at Jurka to crawl away first.

"No, you go first Johara. Now!" the light-haired youth whispered and the tomboy with the short black hair managed to slip nimbly into the tunnel. Milo signalled to Jurka to follow while he kept guard, shooting blindly to delay the guards and Tao Li's Tigers, who had started moving towards them, for as long as possible. When Jurka was safely inside the tunnel, Milo dragged his body towards the little trapdoor entrance, only to discover, to his horror, that he couldn't get into it!

"This can't be happening, damn it," cursed the big black boy. "Help, guys, I'm stuck!" he shouted to his friends and Jurka grabbed him by the shoulders, pulling his friend with all his strength. Nothing. Johara joined him to help but still they couldn't get him through. Milo was trapped in the door's entrance and nothing looked like freeing him.

"Well, that's just great," shouted Milo upon realising that he'd lost the game. "You two get away, get away now!" he screamed at his friends and Lu-gi echoed him: "Get away, quick, get away..."

Jurka gestured to Johara to pull one more time. Still no result.

"Get away, for Lord Salvador of wisdom's sake, get away!" Milo begged them as the moment of reckoning approached.

Lu-gi grabbed Jurka and Johara by the hand and pulled them towards the underground tunnel.

"Get away! Now..." cried the little Black Cloudian and the two friends, with heavy hearts, let go of Milo.

"We'll be back for you, big man!" shouted Jurka, as Lu-gi led them to an old carriage, ready to take them out of danger through the labyrinthine corridors of underground railway lines in the now abandoned and haunted Old City.

"See you soon, man! Keep strong, kiddo!" rang out Milo's voice as he bade them goodbye.

Darkness prevailed in the Old City. The small, ancient carriage creaked as Lu-gi guided it from the driver's seat with extraordinary skill past ruins and platforms and down tunnels. Jurka and Johara collapsed, exhausted, into the dusty seats, looking at each other with sorrow written all over their faces. They had not yet grasped the fact that Milo had been left behind and would now be a prisoner in the hands of the hated Tao Li and Master Zar-ko's guards.

"We shouldn't have left..." the light-haired youth kept repeating to himself. Johara pointed out: "We had no choice, Jurka. It's just that…" the girl hesitated for a moment, "well, it's a bit odd. This bit, Jurka, it wasn't in my dream."

"You're right, I didn't have it either," the young man agreed. Then he looked around. "Where can we be going?" Jurka wondered.

They both looked totally lost…

Lu-gi said nothing. The ancient little carriage continued on its way until Lu-gi brought them back to reality:

"Nearly there," he said and the two youngsters from Earth realised that life hadn't come to an end with Milo's arrest.

"We're nearly where, Lu-gi?" asked Jurka.

"'Cen-tro' station, entrance to Spe-ranto headquarters…" replied the little Black Cloudian train driver with precision.

'Cen-tro' station must once have been the jewel of the city's underground railway. Its architecture was imposing, though old-fashioned, and, of course, it bore no similarity to the majestic buildings of the modern Summer City which stretched over the ground above them. Total darkness and a deathly silence prevailed on the platform, which underlined the ghostly nature of the Old City.

The ancient carriage creaked as its steel wheels braked in front of the dusty platform. The beams of light from the Earth visitors' built-in searchlights penetrated the darkness and shone on the two figures who were standing on the broad platform steps. Jurka and Johara followed Lu-gi whose deep-set eyes had no vision problems, and they approached the waiting Black Cloudians.

It was Ti-hon and Ma-ru.

"Lu-gi, bravo!" The youngster's parents patted the child's round head, praising him for successfully carrying out his mission.

"Jur-ka, Jo-hara, follow us," they said in unison and, fleet of foot, they ascended a set of steps which took them to a huge hall. On its walls all around were faded posters that were a reminder of how once, many suns ago, there had been life in this haunted place. Then they headed for a side door and soon emerged on the station's upper level. There, in a large room with a very high ceiling, a group of Black Cloudians was waiting for them.

"Ben-azir, Spe-ranto leader," announced Ti-hon, pointing to the figure sitting in the middle of a raised platform. The mysterious figure looked at them in curiosity while a green shawl bearing the emblem of the Third Star waved in the air. The other Black Cloudians stretched out their hands, palms upwards, ready for the introductions. Jurka and Johara stood before them and, as one, introduced themselves, offering their hands at the same time.

"Good work Captain Lu-gi," the figure called Ben-azir praised the youngster. It was clear that he was the leader of these people who called themselves Spe-ranto.

"We want to thank Lu-gi, Captain Lu-gi, for saving us," said Jurka politely. "We're most grateful to you, Mr Ben-azir..." the young man added politely, only to be corrected at once by the leader: "Ben-azir woman," she clarified.

"Oh, sorry," Jurka apologised at once.

Johara decided that they had no time to waste and needed to find out more about the Spe-ranto but – most importantly – about Milo's fate.

"Madam Leader," she said, "may we learn who you are? Why have you saved us? And what has happened to our other friend, Milo?" The young girl was straight to the point. Jurka nodded his head in agreement. "Yes, tell us... please..." he added.

Ben-azir descended slowly and majestically from the raised platform, followed by her entourage. When she was near the two Earthlings, she told them to close their eyes. Jurka and Johara did exactly as they were told. Ben-azir first rested the shawl with the emblem of the Third Star on Jurka's head and then touched the girl's short black hair. Each of the other Black Cloudians placed their hands on the narrow shoulder of the other, forming a living chain. Then they all started to utter the same sound from their unmoving mouths. In the ears of Jurka Slavik and Johara, there sounded, like a chanted psalm, a strange, entreating hymn:

"O shield of memory,
O armour of silence,
O, vision of Grace
Receive this prayer
And allow them
To enter through the eternal portals
Where everything was born.

"O shield of memory,
O armour of silence,
O, vision of Grace
Receive this prayer
And place them
At the right time and place
Where everything is known."

When they opened their eyes, the two youngsters from Earth felt as if they had always been members of the Spe-ranto guerrilla organisation. They knew everything and, more to the point, they were ready for anything.

"Madam Leader, Ben-azir, we are in urgent need of an action plan," Jurka said, wasting no time. "First and foremost we have to rescue Milo. Then we have to look for Nefeli..."

"Just a moment, Jurka, you and your Nefeli," Johara interrupted. "We're stuck and you still can't get Nefeli out of your mind..." the girl with the short black hair said bitterly. "I think," she went on, "that first of all we should be thinking about Milo. Then we have to plan the decisive battle with Master Zar-ko's guards. At the same time, we've got to demand the rights of the Black Cloudians. What kind of Spe-ranto members are we?"

"That's what I'm saying, kiddo. I said, Milo first...," Jurka insisted. "Without him we can't do anything. He's our friend and our firepower, let's not forget that," he remarked.

Johara looked at Ben-azir, who had silently followed the conversation. "What do you think, Madam Leader?" she asked.

"Ben-azir think both right," she replied and explained: "Mi-lo freeing first, then Spe-ranto battle with Council. Same target," the Black Cloud guerrilla leader clarified laconically.

"That's fine, then. How do we proceed?" asked Jurka.

"Captain Lu-gi, what do you feel?" Ben-azir addressed the miraculous powers of the young warrior.

Little Lu-gi remained motionless as Ti-hon and Ma-ru pressed down on his shoulders. The small triangle on his forehead blinked on and off several times before the familiar sound emerged from his open mouth like that of a bell.

"Mi-lo torture," Captain Lu-gi announced plainly. "Mi-lo hold firm," he added. "Mi-lo tired," the little Black Cloudian said, concluding his brief report.

"Torture? Who's torturing him, Lu-gi? Where? How?"

Jurka and Johara began bombarding Lu-gi with questions but received no reply. By contrast, Ben-azir the leader requested their attention and put things in their place.

"Mi-lo torture, Pleasure Baths," Ben-azir clarified.

The two young friends remained open-mouthed.: "What! Torture at the Pleasure Baths?"

"My young friends, prepare for action. Young Earth allies with Spe-ranto, assault liberation Mi-lo," ordered the calm voice of the leader Ben-azir.

"Hurray!" came the shouts of the Black Cloudian guerrillas as their leader gave the green light to carry out the mission to free Milo.

"Let's go!" ordered the leader.

Captain Lu-gi led the group to the lower level of 'Cen-tro' station where from one of the platforms they all climbed aboard a carriage and the little captain set off.

They must have travelled for twice the amount of time it had taken to reach 'Cen-tro' station from the Universal Arcade. Jurka calculated that their final destination must be some distance from the centre of Summer City, somewhere on the outskirts. When little captain Lu-gi applied the brakes and they got out of the carriage, they realised that they had indeed travelled to the City limits. On the dusty signs on the half-ruined walls of the underground station they could just about make out the faded letters of the name "Acro-pol".

"We've arrived, Madam Leader Ben-azir."

Captain Lu-gi gave his report and the leader ordered the guerrillas to line up in twos with herself and Captain Lu-gi at the front of the parade and, right behind them, the two friends from Earth. Then followed Ti-hon and Ma-ru and the other warriors. Jurka and Johara carefully checked their AETP uniforms. Everything was working perfectly.

The procession made its silent way through the darkness. They went up a floor and then another before little Lu-gi activated his sensor once again. Everything was OK since he could sense neither traps nor guards. They continued on their way, ascending another floor. The leader Ben-azir gestured to them to stop. The steps led them straight into walls.

"Dead end," Jurka thought but Johara nudged him: "Look, Jurka," she said, pointing to an area high up on the ceiling. "Isn't that light up there, coming through the crack?" she asked.

Ben-azir confirmed Johara's observation, since she had already given orders to Lu-gi to investigate the source of the light. The little captain flew up to the ceiling and scrutinized the crack. Then he came down, reporting that, yes, that must be the opening of the old trapdoor which ought to lead straight to the Pleasure Baths.

"One moment, we can check that quickly and surely," said Jurka and he gestured to Johara to follow him. The two friends from Earth flew up to the place where the light shone through the crack.

"Reconnaissance antenna!" Jurka ordered the AETP and Johara did the same.

The miracle of futurist technology responded impeccably and two miniature aerials squeezed through the tiny crack and, without difficulty, maintained their path towards the surface.

"Activate visuals!" said Jurka and on the ceiling there appeared, as in an old panoramic cinema, a screen. It was, indeed, the striking hall of the Pleasure Baths in all its majesty.

The two youngsters landed back on the floor where, with the guerrillas of the Spe-ranto organisation, they watched the circular transmission of images from inside the famed torture chambers of the Pleasure Baths.

Amid the rose-scented steam and the mountains of fragrant shrubs and flowers, seated in a circle in raised booths were various notables and officials from the whole of the planetary system of the galaxy of the Two Suns. Among them it was not difficult to distinguish Tao Li and his Tigers who were enjoying themselves with holograms of Earth women. There were Black Cloudian Mace-bearers too, with their followers, various other notable subjects, chosen members of the community, as well as spies from the service of the Council of Elders, accompanied by their holograms.

They were sucking liquid into their wide open mouths while their holograms and other servants rubbed their backs with a thick powder resembling sand. An enchanting melody filled the air while, as in an ancient Roman arena, the prisoners jostled in the pit below. They had been stuck to the floor, unable to move, and waves of half-naked beauties of all types and races were let loose, teasing them with unheard-of sensual tricks. They were kept there, hungry and thirsty, while all their senses and weaknesses were challenged, as those around bet convertible Value Units on their reactions and endurance.

The wonderful smells of the galactic titbits literally pierced the senses of the hungry and thirsty captives who regularly fell down, senseless and even dead from physical and, mainly, mental exhaustion. Which races from the galaxy could withstand this constant trial? And for how long?

"Good Lord! These aren't Pleasure Baths. They're… they're an Inferno," Johara shouted angrily.

"Torture of the spirit and the senses, that's what it is, Johara. The worst, most inhuman torture of all!" murmured Jurka angrily.

"So you know that there are different types of torture?" wondered Ben-azir aloud, but she received no answer from her Earthly friends.

After the first, strong shock, Jurka and Johara focused their eyes on the screen. "Where can Milo be?"

The dark-skinned giant was nowhere to be seen. However, in the middle of the torture pit, a strange creature that resembled an Earthling, danced and swayed, all the while changing its appearance. One moment it had the head of a stylish young male dancer, as handsome as Adonis. The next moment, this head had disappeared and in its place that of a beautiful woman magically appeared. Then the two heads merged, like Siamese twins, in a sensual embrace, rhythmically shaking their single, shared body.

"Two heads on the same body! Lord Salvador of wisdom, I've never seen that before!" said Johara.

"I don't believe it," added the astonished Jurka. "Where is that creature from? Or is it a hologram?" he asked Ben-azir.

"Ah, that's the Viv-andré," the guerrilla leader said simply. "Dangerous agent of Doctor Soc-rat. Control everything."

"Doctor who?" asked the two friends in unison.

"Doctor Soc-rat. President of Elders," Ben-azir replied coldly.

The strange hermaphrodite creature that Ben-azir called the Viv-andré, slid like an eel among the ill-fated captives, provocatively caressing their tormented bodies. It stood in front of them, rocking while its two heads ostentatiously sucked up water or food, both laughing hysterically.

When they reached one corner of the room, a shout from captain Lu-gi rang out like a joyful bell.

"There, friend Mi-lo!" he shouted, pointing to where, surrounded by earthly beauties, sumptuous dishes and drinks, Milo lay, exhausted but calm.

The dark-skinned youth was still wearing his AETP uniform which, however, had obviously been neutralised by the organs of Taka-mura and Tao Li's Tigers.

"Get away from me, you disgusting creatures!" Milo screamed and shouted as the Viv-andré moved closer, trying to attract him with its various tricks.

"Milo, would you like some water?" asked the male head while the female one echoed in song, "water... water..."

Milo turned his head away and spat in disgust.

"Get away from me, tormenter," he cursed but however much as he tried to repel it, the more the two-headed creature took advantage of him and his pain. And each time it played with his senses, attacking his nerves with various instruments of torture, the gallery of guests burst into enthusiastic shouting. Bets were being made all the time while Tao Li's Tigers constantly cheered the creature on: "Get him, Viv-andré! Give him smells to make his mouth water!"

Jurka grew ever more angry at seeing his faithful friend being tormented by the Viv-andré and mocked by the Tigers and the collection of high-ranking galactic officers. Johara, no longer able to bear the awful sight, lowered her head, too upset to see any more...

"Johara, get the penetration bombs ready. It's time to get even with those idiots. You're going to pay a high price, you scum! Yes, you're scum!" screamed Jurka, raising his fist threateningly. The girl replied at once that everything was ready. Jurka turned to Ben-azir.

"Madam Leader, we need to surprise them, to catch them unawares. We launch a lightning attack, like commandos, and we free our friend Milo and as many more of those poor captives as we can," he proposed. "What do you think?"

"Ben-azir say yes. Only, before plan, wait," she replied.

She then called two fighters to her side and once they had embraced, they turned their heads around in a circle, carefully examining the ceiling.

"What are they doing?" asked Jurka and Johara guessed that they must be studying the layout of the ceiling in relation to the space of the Pleasure Baths.

"Good move," Jurka commented. "You need to know where you're going to enter and what part of the room you're going to hit," he added.

Ben-azir and her men completed their study and she turned to her two Earthly allies.

"Plan ready," she announced. "Spe-ranto attack there," she clarified, pointing to the other side of the enormous ceiling. "There, other passage. First, distraction. You help penetration bombs. You hit here," she explained, pointing to the crack above their heads.

"A-ha, the plan seems OK. We need the diversion," Jurka agreed. He turned at once to Johara, giving her orders. "You get ready to hit there first, where the leader showed us..."

"Mi-lo opposite," Ben-azir explained, pointing in the direction where they had found the captive member of the Nectar Brotherhood. Then he addressed her guerrillas: "Ready?"

"Hurray!" shouted the Black Cloudian guerrillas.

The leader of the Spe-ranto raised her hands high. "By the vision of Grace," she declared.

"By the vision of Grace," repeated the chorus of guerrillas, hands held high.

"Battle stations!"

In a single movement they all armed whatever weapon they were holding while flying upwards towards the location of the attack and taking up their positions.

Jurka took one last look at the screen. Nothing had changed in the Pleasure Baths. The lively torture party was still going on, just as when they had first seen it.

"Johara, fire!" the light-haired youth ordered in a voice full of anger and the girl stretched out her hand in the direction of the target.

"By Lord Salvador of wisdom, I'm going to rub their face in it," she shouted in her high-pitched voice. Then she pressed a button on her arm and the penetration bomb slowly fluttered towards the point of contact. When it arrived there, it stopped and Johara pressed another button. The penetration bomb attached itself to the ceiling like a mine.

"And now, get a load of this!" said the young girl through her teeth as she pressed the third button on her arm.

A prolonged rumble was heard as the bomb was detonated. The sound grew louder, like an alarm and when it reached its highest point the bomb exploded with a deafening bang, hurling into the air everything that lay above it. A large cavity opened up, through which furniture and utensils, drinks and food started to fall like rain and smash onto the unwelcoming floor of the Old City's underground.

In the Pleasure Baths themselves, chaos reigned. The guards and the Tigers began firing blindly, cursing amid the panic, while the holograms disappeared. The captives, regaining courage and mobilising the very last drops of their strength, shouted for help.

Ben-azir shouted out the battle-cry: "Brave Spe-ranto, attack!"

The Black Cloudian guerrillas flew, quick as lightning, towards the open passage and fluttered, like angels of salvation, into the hall of the Pleasure Baths. The battle flared up at once, with Tao Li and his Tigers starting to fire on the invaders. The guerrillas whirled around with amazing speed and precision, avoiding the enemy fire. At the same time, by carrying out these dangerous aerial manoeuvres, they attracted the attention of their foes in the area of the Pleasure Baths, exactly as planned.

Jurka and Johara watched the battle anxiously and when they judged that the diversion had succeeded, they decided that it was their turn to act. The girl activated another penetration bomb and guided it to the crack above their heads.

"Picture end!" she ordered and the screen went black. Immediately she pressed the button for the controlled explosion. A new hole was created in the ceiling and the two young fighters made their kamikaze-like entry into the other side of the Pleasure Baths where only the Viv-andré, some servants and unarmed officers had run for cover and protection.

"Johara, take care of them!" Jurka shouted, pointing in the direction of the Viv-andré. "I'm going to get Milo," he added.

"My pleasure, Jurka, my pleasure..." the young girl replied, already aiming her repulsion gun at the two-headed monster.

"Eat this! Nice cakes..."grunted Johara.

The repulsion shell found its target, precisely where the girl had aimed. It touched the creature's body at speed... and went straight through it without leaving so much as a scratch. Johara could not move. She'd never seen anything like that...

The hermaphrodite being waved on, untouched. It turned in curiosity towards Johara and extended its two heads, both of which were grinning sarcastically. Then, two tongues popped out of its mouths and, after moving around and licking up saliva, it stuck them out like two sharp red blades. The two-headed creature made a sound of "Ummm...ftoogh" and shot two fiery strips of flame at Johara.

The small-bodied girl jumped nimbly into the air and evaded the flames which burst with a bang at the end of the room, immediately starting a fire there. The Viv-andré coiled itself up once more and from its two mouths came the curse: "Damn you, by Me-gaera!" It then took up a new position and aimed once more at the flying girl who was still spinning through the air, trying to hit her with its red-hot shots.

In vain. Johara got away again. Now it was her time to attack. She stretched out her hands, aiming at the two-headed creature with the Stink gas. When she pulled the trigger, a line of small yellow pellets left the gun, spinning like tops towards their target. The Viv-andré curled this way and that, it attempted to fly up high, then to dive through the air and, finally, to hide behind the officers' boxes. But the little yellow balls followed it, like a nightmare trapping it wherever it tried to hide.

Johara ordered "Fire!" and a series of successive explosions shook the place. For the Viv-andré, the only way of escape from the Stink gas was to break out. Otherwise it would pay a high price since, once hit, it would be transformed into an aged, abominable creature. Without paying a great deal of fuss it conceded defeat and scurried away from the Pleasure Baths. Flying, screaming among the flames and smoke it disappeared.

"Hurray!" shouted Johara, in imitation of Ben-azir's guerrillas.

"Come to think of it, what are they up to? What's happening with Jurka and Milo?" the girl wondered aloud and tried to see all around.

In the area where the diversion had been created, the fighters of the Spe-ranto organisation were doing fine. They fought bravely against the guards who had now been reinforced with more men and two-man vehicles. On the side of the captives, Johara was unable to make out a great deal, since the smoke from the exchange of fire and the fire bombs had seriously restricted any vision. She decided to fly in Milo's direction when, in the opposite corner, amid the smoke, she spotted the figure of Tao Li crawling cautiously towards the area where the captives were. He was armed with knockout gas grenades which he carried on his back while, in his hands, he was clutching the famed multispectral gun that belonged to Milo.

"Lord Salvador save me!" Johara shouted in terror as she thought about what Tao Li could do to them with the multispectral gun.

Jurka had neutralised whatever resistance he came across with comparative ease and was fighting to free Milo from his imprisonment. It would be easier for the two of them to then free the other captives and to get away as fast as possible. At the very moment that he was lifting up his dark-skinned friend, Tao Li appeared before them like Satan himself.

"Where are you rushing off to, guys?" he laughed scornfully. "Have you got permission from this little devil?" he said, ostentatiously waving Milo's multispectral gun around. He gave another loud laugh and pushed the two friends to the ground.

"Two birds with one stone," boasted Master Zar-ko's arrogant collaborator. "I wonder how much your arrest is going to cost the Commander?" Tao Li wondered complacently. Two or three of the

Tigers who were following him jumped for joy. They'd be taking their share too...

"Not so fast, hard man!"

Johara's voice interrupted the fantasies of the Nectar Brotherhood's Earthly enemy.

The young girl, leaping like a wildcat, suddenly found herself hooked behind him, breathing heavily on his neck. In one move, she inserted the anaesthetic in his neck and with the other hand grabbed the multispectral gun from him. Before he knew what was happening, she had disarmed him and completely neutralised any reaction. Milo rushed to regain possession of his fabulous gun, caressing it like a baby.

"Come to uncle, baby, come to Uncle Milo..." the dark-skinned giant said over and over. Then he turned to Tao Li who was standing there looking lost, his expressionless eyes staring at them.

"As for you, you filthy devil, sweet dreams!"

Milo clenched his fist with as much strength as he had left after his sufferings in the Pleasure Baths and landed it in Tao Li's face. "I owe you that for cheating on Sports Day," he shouted. "And this one for what I've been through in here," he added as a second fist hit Tao Li on the forehead.

The usually bold Tao Li collapsed with a thud to the ground, while his Tigers had already run away.

"Bravo, Johara, well done girl!" Jurka called out enthusiastically while Milo placed a kiss on the girl's cheek.

"Thanks Johara, you're very brave," he said with emotion.

"All right, all right, that's enough. Now what do we do?" the girl asked.

"Our objective has succeeded completely. It's mission accomplished," replied Jurka. "We have to activate Milo's AETP as soon as we've got out of here before it's too late. Meanwhile, let's free the other captives," said the light-haired young man and the three of them set to work.

"Be careful!" shouted Milo as, from the direction of the roof, reinforcements appeared led by Master Zar-ko himself. The Commander scrutinized the scene, unable to believe his eyes. How could the hated guerrillas have struck inside his lair, the unassailable Pleasure Baths? How could they have turned the most sacred place of torture on the whole planet upside-down? How had they managed to catch the guards unawares?

"Vasi-vuzuk take me!" Zar-ko swore as he searched for his men among the ruins and the chaos in an effort to work out what had happened and to launch a counter-attack.

Too late! The guerrillas had already completed their task, Milo was free and Ben-azir had given the order to retreat to the underground of the Old City, where no Black Cloudian guard dared to set foot.

"Lu-gi, accompany friends," she requested the little captain and Lu-gi sped like a bullet into the torture chamber.

"Lu-gi lead friends out," he announced. "Go this way," he added and opened the way, flying towards the ceiling. Jurka and Johara grabbed the enormous Milo by the shoulders and, carrying him like a flying sack, followed Lu-gi.

"By Vasi-vuzuk, they're getting away!" Zar-ko was heard shouting angrily as the four figures whistled past him and his two-seater like bullets.

"All fire!" ordered the Three Star Commander.

The salvos from the stun guns exploded in the void, colouring the air, but the birds had already flown to freedom. The three friends of the Nectar Brotherhood, together with Captain Lu-gi, had escaped, flying safely to where the little guerrilla was taking them.

ᔓ

When the mountain top with its green trees appeared on the far horizon, illuminated by the rays of the great sun, Lu-gi swooped down towards the ground. The three friends followed.

"Stop here," explained Lu-gi laconically. "Here Forest Zone, Autumn City. Here Elves," he concluded, pointing towards the mountain top. The three friends looked at the mountains that stretched out along the horizon.

"Forest Zone? Elves?" wondered Jurka aloud. "What's that you're saying, captain Lu-gi? Explain..."

They knew about Autumn City since they had seen it in their dream. But they had neither heard about nor seen any Elves...

Lu-gi repeated what he had said, unable to enlighten them any further. No Black Cloudian from Summer City had ever been to this region. Here lived different types of inhabitants, he explained. Whatever he knew he had learned from space travellers and settlers.

"All right, captain Lu-gi. Johara will examine the situation but first let's activate Milo's AETP," Jurka proposed.

"How are you, big man?" asked Johara. "What happened in there? What did those bastards do to you?"

"Hmm, it was a bad experience, guys. I'm OK but I almost lost it in that cage. My belly suffered a bit, but luckily you arrived before I died of hunger... So I say we have a bite to eat before we do anything else...Eh? What do you say?"

Jurka burst out laughing. Johara insisted on first activating Milo's equipment to be on the safe side.

"All right, do it now. Let's get it over with," agreed Milo impatiently. "Anyway, how can I eat if the AETP isn't activated?" he added.

"OK, and in the meantime you can tell us what happened," said Jurka and the three friends got on with relaxing and snacking while listening to the details of Milo's adventure. Fortunately the AETP menu was a rich one...

"Reconnaissance antenna. Activate!"

It was Johara who gave the order as all three brought their screens into operation. Lu-gi watched the now familiar observation process that his friends from Earth were implementing.

Onto the small, high-resolution screens, picture after picture appeared. A seemingly endless wooded area spread out in the sector of Autumn City, passing through mountains and ravines, rivers and torrents. Right in the middle of the green forest, as in a dream, lay the Lake of Youth, resting in the palm of the surrounding mountains. It was a serene, deep green lake, wreathed by countless flowers of rare beauty. All around, planted on its magical shores, like multicoloured toy boxes, were the beautiful country houses of Autumn City, home to the privileged.

"Lake of Youth!"

Little Lu-gi, who seemed to know everything, explained that, according to what he had heard, anyone bathing in the lake's waters would be given eternal youth. This was why not just anyone could set foot in Autumn City. And any mad fool trying to do so was signing his own death warrant. The Elves, those vigilant guardians of the cities, were on the look-out...

"Hmm, interesting," said Jurka Slavik to no-one in particular. "By Lord Salvador of wisdom, Nefeli must be here," he shouted.

Johara gave a grimace of disapproval but said nothing.

"If she's there, we'll find her, man, don't worry. These things don't make mistakes – or do they?" wondered Milo who had suddenly realised that neither Nefeli nor any Elves were anywhere to be seen on their screens. "And what about the Elves? Where are the Elves? How come we haven't seen them?" asked the dark-skinned giant.

"Hmm, yes, where are the Elves, captain Lu-gi?" asked Johara but the youngster shrugged his shoulders. How was he to know?

They completed their reconnaissance of the land and the mountainsides in the forest region without finding anything to worry about. The three friends decided that it was time for action. They had to travel towards Autumn City and accomplish their mission. But first they needed to get some things straight with captain Lu-gi. Was he prepared to go with them? Did he want to?

The little Black Cloudian didn't hesitate. "Leader Ben-azir, order with you," he said and that was the end of the matter.

The flight of the four took place at some altitude. They considered that, since they were entering an unknown and probably dangerous area, it would be better to fly high so as to see better what was happening around them.

Nothing. As they flew over the fallow ground, everything looked fine. But when they reached the first treetops on the edges of the mountainsides, they decided that it would be better to travel at a lower level, under cover of the trees.

They had not gone very far when, suddenly, Lu-gi checked himself and stood behind a branch. The other three were forced to imitate him.

"What's up, captain Lu-gi?" Milo asked. The multispectral gun was already in his hands in a state of readiness.

"Lu-gi feel strange," replied the little creature, as the triangle on his brow blinked on and off.

The little captain immediately activated his belt and some lights flashed on. Then he pressed a button with one hand and raised the other into the air.

"Vision of Grace, captain Lu-gi feel danger but no see!" His voice came bland and calm from the depths of his open mouth, while his deep-set, empty eyes focused without expression on the trees around.

Jurka, Johara and Milo were all in a state of alert. Since Lu-gi sensed danger but couldn't see it, things might be worse than they'd calculated. And yet, they too saw nothing around them; nothing could be heard, nothing moved. Where was the danger coming from? Who was it?

The big question was answered by little Lu-gi when, suddenly, with one bound, he found himself hiding behind Milo's huge back.

"There!... And there!...And there!" shouted Lu-gi, pointing at the trees all around them.

It took several moments, which seemed endless, for the three friends of the Nectar Brotherhood to realise exactly what Lu-gi was showing them.

What they saw left them rooted to the spot!

All around, the trees at first seemed to come alive. Then, gradually, they began to take on the shape and form of green monsters, transforming their trunks into bodies and their branches into arms and legs. Once formed they looked like gigantic beings...

"The Elves! By Master Hahanoff, it's the Elves!" screamed Johara and Milo felt Lu-gi trembling behind him. A long-drawn out sound left his wide open mouth.

"Ooooom... Ooooom..."

Lu-gi was quaking with fear and he clung like a leech to Milo's back, preventing him from manoeuvring with his jetpack.

"Jurka, what do we do now?" the dark-skinned giant called out to his friend who was still frozen by the unexpected sight.

"Jurka, snap out of it!" It was the voice of young Johara, who at once ordered: "Defence mechanism – circular cover!"

The other two copied her at once, since they were all on the ground surrounded by the tree-like Elves. Luckily they were in time because at the very next moment, the strange beings, one after another, appeared to puff out their cheeks and to blow in the direction of the group of intruders in the forest area.

First to blow was the pine Elf that stood opposite them. A hail of sharp needles was repelled with a bang by their shields. The other tree-like Elves followed one after the other and soon the four friends had come under a pitiless bombardment of strange, very strong missiles of nuts, leaves and branches. Their endurance was quickly being tested since they could not help bending under the continuous, merciless, intense bombardment.

When the first wave of the firestorm eased and the Elves fell quiet, the three friends and Lu-gi counted their losses. Milo's multispectral gun had done them some damage since it had sliced through some of the Elves as if they were cucumbers but it could not provide total cover from all sides. Their uniforms had been damaged by the violent, repeated hits from the strange missiles and the risk of destruction of their precious AETP mechanism was now very real, as their nano-computer had been warning them constantly.

"What are they up to now?" Milo asked aloud. No-one was in any position to give a logical answer. Johara nudged Jurka.

"I say we try the herbicide," she suggested but the young man hesitated. "It's a shame," he said. "So many trees will be destroyed..."

"Jurka, wake up, they're not trees! They're... illusions of trees," the young girl replied but still Jurka was not sure about using the herbicide.

"So, what are we going to do?" interrupted Milo, while trying to place little Lu-gi more comfortably on his back. "Make your mind up fast, yes or no? These things aren't joking," he added, pointing in the direction of the Elves which had again begun to move.

"For Lord Salvador's sake, Jurka, take a decision..." Johara cried out.

"No!" answered Jurka in a firm voice. "We're not going to bring about ecological destruction," he added.

"So what do we do, then?" asked Milo.

"Wait and see what they do first..."

The Elves regrouped and it looked at first as if they were retreating.

Wrong!

The tree-like monsters were not retreating but carrying out tactical manoeuvres. Slowly they moved to the sides and soon they had opened up a corridor, like a clearing, in the depths of which the three friends and Lu-gi could make out a small, black moving mark. The mark grew and grew until it was clearly visible.

"Good Lord, what's that?" Milo wondered aloud.

'That' was a flock of bird-like creatures which, seemingly jet-propelled and in battle formation, were flying towards the four trespassers in the forest. When they were within firing range, they split up into groups, surrounding their target. Everything was ready for a new attack.

The situation was looking hopeless and Jurka Slavik reactivated the defence mechanism.

"Hmm, I think they're going to attack us, that's for sure. But I'm not sure that that they're going to hit us," conclude the light-haired youth.

"For better or worse," Milo proposed, "let's defend ourselves by attacking the birdlike things with pesticide," but Johara had a different idea.

"I'm afraid we won't get very far like that. If I'm right, this army of bird-like creatures must be inexhaustible. We're not going to get rid of them with pesticide. We need to use a different tactic!"

"Such as?" asked the other two in unison.

Johara said nothing. She merely placed her hands on her helmet and gave the order: "Triple image multiplier. Projection now!"

Next to Johara there suddenly appeared from nowhere... three more Joharas! And another three!

Lu-gi uttered a cry: "Vision of Grace..."

Jurka and Milo could only stare open-mouthed at the images of Johara.

"Go on, what are you waiting for? Do the same, right now!" the girl ordered them.

The next moment the place had filled with identical copies of the three members of the Nectar Brotherhood. Only Captain Lu-gi remained untouched, watching the earthlings and their miraculous creations.

"Hide him, Milo, hide him!" Johara shouted since Lu-gi could unwittingly betray the presence of the real bodies of the three friends.

Milo opened up his waistcoat, grabbed the little Black Cloudian and tucked him into the dark safety of his uniform. They were now ready to take on the bird-like troops of the Elves.

The enemy must have been taken by surprise at the unexpected spectacle when, suddenly, the place filled up with copies of the three Earthlings. Johara gave the order to rotate and a small cyclone of people and images mixed everything up. When the cyclone petered out, copies of the three Earthly intruders could be seen everywhere. The bird-like creatures waited patiently for the order to attack but, when it came, it was too late. The enemy targets had multiplied and were flying around from tree to tree, others ran left and right and others jumped about provocatively on the ground. Which of all these should the bird-like monsters hit?

When the order came, the flocks of flying monsters dived, whistling, onto their targets. They were shooting to kill but their guided missiles merely passed through the images and were lost in the air.

Jurka gave the order and their identical copies moved around in the middle of the battlefield and lined up at about the same height. This manoeuvre proved to be their saviour and the destruction of the bird-like creatures was immediate and spectacular. Their missiles were turned into crossfire and, as a result, they were soon annihilating one another and, at the same time, hitting the Elves too.

The untidy retreat that followed gave the intruders a chance to confer about their next steps. Johara's trick had succeeded perfectly and they could now breathe more easily. The bird-like creatures had disappeared and the Elves had taken cover in the thick foliage of the trees, unable to stop the group that had invaded their zone. The road to Autumn City and the Lake of Youth was open.

∽

In the observatory, Zar-ko, the Three Star Commander, Taka-mura and his guards were counting their losses and drawing up new plans. The Council of Elders chastised those responsible for security and maintaining law and order and warned them meaningfully that Doctor Soc-rat would be there at any moment.

The once bold Tao Li now resembled a plucked bird as he wandered about with his head bandaged and sporting two black eyes, provoking sarcastic comments from Master Zar-ko and the guards.

"Where are they going to go? Won't they fall into my hands again? I'll show them who Tao Li is. I'll beat those punks to pulp," he said to himself, trying to persuade himself more than the others.

The Three Star Commander stood bending over the computers and data transmitters, studying the situation as shown to him by the Om-niscient. All around sat the members of the war council. It was not difficult to identify the precise location of the three enemies from Earth, nor to monitor their movements at any given moment. Of course, the latest news was not good at all. The invaders had succeeded in getting past the Elves and neutralising the attack of the bird-like creatures. Things were growing difficult and Master Zar-ko knew better than anyone that he had to do something. And he had to do it both quickly and successfully. Who could say what might happen if the three earthlings and that accursed guerrilla reached Autumn City and the Lake of Youth?

The war council had reached an impasse and Taka-mura proposed to his boss that they try the Intangible Net again.

"Yes, I've thought of that," Zar-ko replied, "but I doubt that they'll be taken unawares this time. They'll have learnt their lesson. And if we're unlucky enough to fail, Taka-mura, we're really going to be in trouble..."

The Captain of the Guard did not respond. What could he say, anyway?

"No, we need to think of something else, something more effective. A surprise," concluded the Commander, challenging the guards to put forward their suggestions.

In the observatory the familiar whistle was heard and the Elders appeared on the main screen.

"Well, Master Zar-ko, what have you decided?"

The Three Star Commander was scared.

"We're studying the situation, Elders. Give us a little more time and shortly we'll announce the headquarters' action plan," was all Zar-ko managed to say.

"The only thing that we don't have, Commander, is precisely that: time," said the most senior of the Councillors pointedly and the others agreed at once, ostentatiously nodding their heads as usual.

"Yes, Elder, yes, we know. That's why we'll soon be in a position to tell you exactly how we're going to proceed..."

Master Zar-ko was saying the first thing that came into his mind. All he wanted was for them to leave him alone to think of something, to plan something, to report something, anything. The Elders disappeared from the screen and Master Zar-ko vented his anger on the members of the war council.

"Say something for heaven's sake. Give me an idea, help us get somewhere..."

An emboldened Taka-mura proposed using knockout gas. "We lie in wait for them in the valley of the marshes between the mountainsides and then we bombard them from the air with knockout gas. It could work, Master Zar-ko, you never know."

"Hmm I've thought of that, Taka-mura, but I'm afraid it won't work. They seem to have all the answers, those..." replied a pensive Zar-ko. "What if we try to hit them with soundwaves? We stun them first and then we can use either the Net or the gas. Maybe the two together, by Vasi-vuzuk!" thundered the desperate Zar-ko.

"Just a minute!"

Tao Li interrupted the discussion of the Black Cloudian military chiefs and, in so doing, caused great annoyance among them. Why was the Earthling getting involved?

Master Zar-ko, however, had grown wiser. "Let him speak," he ordered and the murmuring subsided.

The malicious Tao Li may not have known much about the strategy and tactics of conventional planetary warfare but he knew something that the Black Cloudians did not. He knew that Jurka Slavik was crazy about Nefeli…

"I have a plan," and he forced them to be silent, whether they wanted to or not. All their attention now focused on him.

Tao Li explained to the members of the war council that there was one way, and only one, to achieve their objective: through deceit and ensnarement!

As he explained to them, this method had been tried and tested on Earth and always worked, especially when you had suitable bait at your disposal. And there could be no better bait than Nefeli. The earthly beauty would be taken at once to Autumn City and the Lake of Beauty – indeed, what girl wouldn't want to swim in its waters? – and Jurka Slavik, like a fool, would fall into the expertly set trap and lead his group towards her. Right into the arms of Master Zar-ko and his guards. Tao Li explained that on Earth people had the bad habit of falling in love and becoming blinded by their passion, leading themselves to destruction…

The trap was perfect and the operation, with the unwitting contribution of Nefeli, would be crowned with total success. No risk, no Net, no kinds of gas. The Om-niscient would take care that Nefeli would become its instrument and through her it would hypnotise Jurka and his band of friends. The rest would be a simple, routine matter. As soon as their protective suits had been neutralised, they would be transformed into harmless sheep and probably sent to mine Cre-matum in the bowels of the planet. As for Nefeli, she would be his reward, along with two or three Cre-matum…

Master Zar-ko remained thoughtful for a while. His deep eyes stared blankly into the void, irritating Tao Li a great deal.

What would the small blinking triangle on his forehead advise?

What would the Three Star Commander decide?

Master Zar-ko let forth a shout from his wide open mouth: "Perfect!"

Taka-mura and the other guards, members of the war council, repeated in chorus: "Perfect!"

The die was cast. The decision had been taken unanimously. Now Master Zar-ko had something to say to the Elders…

CHAPTER 3

The flight of the four friends to Autumn City was, rather surprisingly, not interrupted by any more unpleasant incidents. When they landed in the glade in front of the first houses, they decided to carry out a new reconnaissance mission on the land around. It would be much more useful since they were now in the garden of the city.

Johara's antenna brought magical images to their screens: the beautiful, serene Lake of Youth, the flowers and the blooms caressing its shores, and young girls bathing in its miraculous waters. Nearby, privileged young men, musicians and courtiers enjoyed the sweet sounds of a harp while, with their melodic voices, singers accompanied the laughter and exclamations of blissfully happy couples.

Suddenly Nefeli appeared on the small screen, like a fairy among a company of little princesses. She was bathing her half-naked body in the waters of the lake like a swan enjoying the pleasure of universal admiration in its proud solitude.

"Stop! Stay here kiddo," ordered Jurka, as the vision of Nefeli, so near and yet so far, had upset him.

"See, we've found her, chief," said Milo, while Johara feigned indifference.

"Yes, we've found her," repeated Jurka. "Now we have to get nearer to her. And I'm not sure how we're going to manage that. Any ideas?"

Lu-gi reminded them that they should not do anything foolish or hurried. "Lu-gi no know Lake," the little captain explained apologetically.

"Well, what does your sensor say, captain Lu-gi?" asked Jurka.

"Nothing. Zero..." came the reply.

"So what are we worried about? We haven't seen anything to concern us, captain Lu-gi hasn't sensed anything, what are we waiting for? Since there's no visible danger, I say we make our way to the lake. Being prepared, of course, for all eventualities," Jurka was quick to add.

Johara was not persuaded.

"And who can guarantee that we won't go through the same as we did in the forest, Jurka? Eh? Or am I wrong in thinking that from the first moment we set foot on the planet – what am I saying? – from the moment we entered the vicinity of Black Cloud, we've had nothing but problems? If we're going to proceed – and I say we should so as to get this business over with – we have to do it carefully, taking every possible precaution, ready for anything," the young girl said.

"Well, this baby is definitely ready," added Milo at once, stroking his multispectral gun.

The dark-skinned giant turned to Jurka but his friend looked abstracted. His eyes were fixed on Nefeli and he appeared unable to get enough of the goddess he was admiring so ecstatically.

Milo nudged Johara. "Come on kiddo, bring him back to earth," he whispered. Johara deactivated the reconnaissance antenna and the images from the Lake of Youth disappeared.

Only then did Jurka come back to reality.

"Sorry guys, I got carried away," admitted the lovestruck, light-haired youth with admirable frankness. "Right, what do we do?" he repeated his question.

'What do you say?" Milo asked him.

"I say we proceed with the original plan. We very carefully get close to her and we ask her to come with us. Isn't that what she wants? And then we get out of here and go home..."

"Are you so sure about that Jurka?" wondered Johara.

"Absolutely! Nefeli is here under duress, against her will," insisted the young man.

"Well, it doesn't look like it," said the young girl ironically, pointing to the screen which was on again. Nefeli was clearly enjoying every moment.

"All right, what do you say we should do? How do we go about this?" asked Jurka.

"I think we should aim some hallucinatory spray at her and grab her. As soon as she's in our hands, we call for the White Cloud and off we sail..." proposed Johara.

"Don't even think about it, kiddo, not for one second!"

Jurka reacted immediately and with determination. "Spray her! With hallucinatory spray, at that... Are you all right, Johara?" added the young man.

"Completely!" replied the black-haired girl in a steady voice. Her big black eyes were giving off sparks... "What can we do that's easier and more certain than that? All she'll do is lose her senses for a while. So what?" insisted Johara.

"What are you saying, kiddo? Why should we treat her worse than we would our most dangerous enemy? We're not thinking straight, by Lord Salvador of wisdom, not thinking straight at all..."objected the young man.

"Well then, why don't we ask the wise lord to tell us what to do?" proposed Milo in an attempt to find a third alternative to resolve the dispute between his friends which looked like growing worse.

Milo's idea stopped the other two from arguing further. They realised that they had gone too far and that such behaviour was to the detriment of their mission.

"Hmm... there's a fresh idea," said Jurka. "I'm sure that Lord Salvador will agree with me..."

Johara added that, if they had no other mutually acceptable choice, she would agree with Milo's suggestion.

"Right then, what are we waiting for? Let's call on him, here and now!" enthused the dark-skinned giant. And, no sooner said than done, without waiting for a reply he began singing the Hymn of the Brotherhood. The other two, whether they wanted to or not, followed his lead.

Little Captain Lu-gi observed the ritual with his expressionless, deep-set eyes, without saying a word.

"Ahoy there, Lord Salvador of wisdom!" Slavik gave the traditional greeting.

The reply was immediate: "Ahoy there to you too, Jurka Slavik!"

Lord Salvador of wisdom appeared on their screens, making them burst out laughing. He was in a chaotic kitchen, wearing an enormous white chef's hat. An apron was tied around his neck and he was covered in flour, as he attempted to cook pancakes. His gestures were clumsy and, as a result, he would let slip the bottle of oil or forget the quantities for the ingredients, or even drop his cooking utensils on the floor.

The three friends were dying of laughter, and even captain Lu-gi was having problems, rocking his little body.

"What are you doing, Lord Salvador of wisdom?" asked Jurka.

"Making pancakes, idiot!" replied the wise lord. "I'm having guests tonight and I'm getting ready. Why do you ask, Jurka Slavik?"

"Well, I... er, we got the impression that cooking was something you're not too good at, Lord Salvador," the light-haired youth explained.

"Who, me? I, the great lord of wisdom, the one and only, the inimitable, am not too good at it? What nonsense are you spouting now, young man?"

Lord Salvador raised one hand high, holding the frying pan, and covered his yes with the other.

"May a pancake be created!" he ordered.

The frying pan gave off steam and a delicious smelling sweet appeared on the table. "Now, what were we saying, dear friends?" asked the lord teasingly.

The three friends of the Nectar Brotherhood were obliged to make a grovelling apology for doubting the culinary skills of their mentor and protector. They should have known better about his miraculous powers...

Jurka explained that there was disagreement among them about the way and the method by which they should free Nefeli. They wanted to consult him and benefit from his wisdom.

"Hmm, these are difficult questions you're setting me, very difficult..." murmured Lord Salvador, scratching his chin. "And since, my dear young friends, you know my saying about "what you sow, so shall you reap", don't you? Well, think a bit. Put your minds to work. I can't do everything for you..."

And before they had a chance to say anything, Lord Salvador of wisdom had disappeared from their screens.

The three friends were back to square one.

"Great! That's really fantastic! Our good lord has left us in it yet again..." Jurka shouted. "Left us in the lurch and disappeared," the young man added, but Johara didn't agree.

"What do you mean, Jurka? He gave us the key to decide. What do you say, Milo?"

"Mmm, I say... er, I say we think about it" said the dark-skinned giant hesitantly.

"Think about what?" insisted Jurka, who would naturally have liked to receive clearer guidance from the wise lord.

"Think about what that 'what you sow, so shall you reap' business means, that's what," said Johara with certainty. "I must say that I'm worried..." added the black-haired girl.

"Oh? And what would you be worried about then, kiddo?" asked Jurka.

"Well, about... look, if I understood rightly, if we give what I had suggested - and it was the only concrete suggestion we had, the one about the hallucinatory spray – then we'll get the same thing back, that's what I understood... What does it mean, do you think?" Johara asked pensively.

"A-ha! Now you're talking! Didn't I say so? You see why we mustn't go to extremes with the hallucinatory spray?" stressed Jurka triumphantly.

"That doesn't solve the problem. We're still at a dead end," the girl remarked.

"Back to the beginning again, in other words..." murmured Milo.

The three friends remained pensive and unspeaking. Suddenly captain Lu-gi broke the silence.

"Lu-gi idea," he said in his bland tone.

"You've got some ideas, captain Lu-gi?" asked the three.

"Lu-gi find solution!" replied the little one calmly.

"What? You've got a solution?" shouted Milo and Jurka rushed to add: "Come on then, captain Lu-gi, tell us what it is!"

Johara said nothing but looked at the little Black Cloudian with mistrust. "What solution is he going to come up with when everyone else has failed?" she thought.

"Solution simple: Jurka carry out his plan. Johara her plan..." replied Lu-gi.

"What do you mean? Explain, captain Lu-gi..." said the bewildered Jurka.

"Simple. Jurka go to Nefeli. Johara and Milo ready cover, hallucination spray," explained the little Black Cloudian.

The three friends looked at one another. Could little Lu-gi be right?

"Hmm... it's both simple and good," appraised Jurka and Milo agreed with him. "Simple definitely has its good points," he remarked.

Johara was still adding up the pros and cons. On the one hand, they would be risking everything by placing all their eggs in the one basket that was Jurka's plan. On the other hand, there was always a greater risk if Jurka went to Nefeli by himself. It would be a major problem if they were to come under attack. But then again, Milo with his multispectral gun and she with the hallucinatory spray would be on permanent alert and able to cover for him against any danger of attack. And in any case, little Lu-gi would be able to give them good warning of any danger. Hmm, the plan might work, why not? Anyway, did they have anything better? No, they didn't...

"OK, I agree with Lu-gi," said Johara and Jurka hurried to praise her.

"That's it kiddo, bravo!" he enthused and gave her a kiss on the cheek. Johara blushed but remained silent.

"Great, we're all agreed at last... Thank you captain Lu-gi," said Milo and gave the signal to start preparing the operation.

The three friends turned their attention to the monitors once more and began observing the Lake of Youth again. Nothing appeared to have changed. The same scene, same people, no guards, no Elves, nothing.

The earthly beauty was bathing, carefree and enjoying every moment with her friends... The sweet melody of a song dedicated to Nefeli reached their ears like a caress, as the girls and the boys accompanying them sang of the beauty of the visitor from Earth.

"Like the sun you shine at dawn
Like a lily in the day
At evening time you are a rose
Lovely priestess, here you'll stay..."

Jurka Slavik flew among the bushes until he reached the clearing in front of the first house. He passed like the wind among the plants and garden decorations to find himself in the front yard which led straight down to the lake shore. There he weighed up the situation and reported back to his friends.

"All clear. Everything's open. Proceeding towards the lake..."

The AETP changed to amphibian uniform mode and Jurka headed undisturbed for the water. No obstacles. He entered the calm waters of the lake and swam towards Nefeli and her entourage. When he was at a safe distance, he called out her name.

"Nefeli!"

The beautiful young girl turned in the direction of the voice. For a moment she stared at the young man who appeared to have called her by name and then she gave a broad smile. Her pretty eyes sparkled as she answered in a melodic voice: "Jurka, is that you? Oh Jurka Slavik, what a nice surprise!"

Jurka felt the familiar sweet paralysis take over. He stayed there, speechless and motionless, staring like a fool at the blonde goddess who was now moving towards him with her usual coquettish air.

"Jurka, Jurka…" murmured Nefeli. "Oh Jurka, I've missed you so much…"

Jurka wanted to say something but he could not utter a word. He wanted to move but his legs would not do what his brain was telling them to. He wanted to reach out his arms and embrace her but, again, nothing. He was like a shadow turned to stone, seeing but feeling nothing at all.

"Was this the height of happiness? Was this the paralysing glory of love?" Jurka Slavik's unsteady mind wondered.

He received no answer. He simply felt Nefeli touch him, pull him gently by the hand and lead him to the shore. There, amid the intoxicating fragrances of lemon and jasmine blossom, Jurka was suddenly in paradise with his beloved Nefeli. He surrendered totally and unconditionally to her charming beauty and felt incapable of reacting, of saying or doing anything. It was as if he had been taken over by the pleasure of an incredible dream which was leading him to previously unknown and inaccessible places.

But where were they going? By Lord Salvador of wisdom, why was the Lake of Youth disappearing from before them? What was this cold and unwelcoming place? How on earth had they ended up among glaciers and snow-covered mountains? And this terrifying gate, how did that get there? Where would it lead them? Why was it suddenly so dark? What on earth were those noises like drumbeats that were coming closer?

Jurka Slavik suddenly felt himself alive. An icy current pierced his body, causing him to shiver.

He turned to Nefeli but there, facing him, was the hated figure of Master Zar-ko. Next to him stood Taka-mura and Tao Li.

"Welcome to the underworld of Winter City, young man," came the voice of the Three Star Commander.

Jurka Slavik suddenly awoke from his lethargy. He looked around. Darkness and emptiness dominated the place from where linking tunnels could be seen leading in various directions down into the bowels of the Black Cloudian soil. It was from somewhere down there that the rhythmic drumming noises were coming.

"Young and foolish Earthling, you're going to spend many suns here," continued Zar-ko's voice. "And that's thanks to Nefeli, may Doctor Soc-rat keep her well," he added.

Taka-mura moved towards Jurka and the young man tried to react by giving orders to the AETP: "Defence protection – now!" he said, but the other three burst into laughter.

"Defence protection – kaput!" said Tao Li sarcastically. "My boy, you can forget all you knew. Down here you're on your own and helpless. One more labourer in the Cre-matum mines... What am I saying? You won't be on your own for long. You'll have your pals for company. Where are they going to go? You think we won't arrest them too?" said the leader of the Tigers.

"I don't get it... I was with Nefeli..." stammered Jurka, now feeling totally lost.

"Really? Let me explain it then, clever boy. Yes, you were with Nefeli, but not exactly. You thought you were, because her vision did a good job for us. It hypnotised you, and here's the result. You're here in the mine, alone and helpless. And the main thing, you're as weak as a reed on the plain without the AETP. So that's what happened... you thought you were travelling to Paradise but your destination was hell..."

The nightmare took control of Jurka Slavik as soon as he realised what had happened. He'd been caught like a mouse in a trap and now he would have to pay the heavy price for it. As for Nefeli, fortunately she was acting unwittingly. But Johara had been right all along. They should have been more careful.

Johara... Milo... Yes, what had happened to his friends? What had happened to Lu-gi? "Phew, at least they had got away," Jurka thought as Taka-mura implanted the miner's code in his neck before handing him over to the duty inspector.

ᔓ

Johara was inconsolable while Milo resembled a wounded animal. Only captain Lu-gi stood firm, not showing any emotion. His Black Cloudian upbringing did not allow him to reveal his grief.

"How could this happen? How did we fall into their trap, like inexperienced cadets?" the desperate Milo kept repeating over and over. "What are we going to do now, Johara?" he anxiously asked the young girl.

Everything had happened so quickly and unexpectedly that they had not been able to react at all. They had been completely fooled and neutralised since Milo could not risk using his multispectral gun nor Johara the knockout gas.

Jurka had been abducted by Nefeli and the enemy and heaven only knows where he had been taken.

"There's only one solution," said Johara pensively. "We call on Lord Salvador of wisdom one more time an ask for his advice. What do you say, Milo?"

"I think you're right, kiddo. I don't see what else we can do," replied the swarthy giant. "Unless captain Lu-gi here has a better idea," he added.

"Lu-gi think," the little Black Cloudian answered at once.

"OK, think and let us know," said Milo, expecting Johara to express her opinion. The girl didn't respond. She was studying the recording of what had taken place and was trying to understand it. Where had they taken Jurka?

"Lu-gi ready," the young captain said and approached his two friends from Earth. Without saying another word he placed one hand on Milo's shoulder and the other on Johara's.

"Close eyes!" he ordered them and from his wide open mouth a strange sound began, something like a lullaby: "Mmmmm.... Mmmmm...."

When the murmur intensified, Milo and Johara's closed eyes suddenly came alive. Before them appeared scenes from a cold, dark place. Its surface was covered with snow and glaciers, while deep underground many creatures appeared to be working with identical rhythmical movements, to the sound of drums and under the supervision of enormous, snorting creatures that spewed out hot flames from their nostrils...

Lu-gi removed his hands and the two friends from Earth opened their eyes.

"Winter City, Cre-matum mines. Cig-ants," Lu-gi announced, straight to the point.

The Cre-matum mines lay deep beneath Winter City and those guarding them were none other than the terrible Cig-ants, the planet's fire-breathing dragons. It was there, among the miserable convicts and exiles, the outcasts from society and the oppressed, that Jurka Slavik must be.

"Lord Salvador of wisdom, I can't stand it," sobbed Johara and Milo tried to raise her spirits. "Come on, kiddo, don't be like that. Things are going to be all right, you'll see..." he consoled her. "We'll do something, we've got to, we're not going to stay like this with our hands tied, are we now?"

Johara took a couple of deep breaths and replied that she was ready for anything.

"Let's go then, what are we waiting for?" said Milo and started up his jetpack. "Lu-gi, show us the way," he ordered the little captain and the three of them set off in the direction of Winter City.

"Lord Salvador of wisdom, help us!" wished Johara.

The cold was unbearable. The glaciers had transformed the landscape into an infinite white carpet out of which, like mushrooms, arose icebergs and white, snow-capped mountain peaks. There was not a soul to be seen, only infinite desert.

The three travellers appeared to have no problems with the bitter cold. The rings around their necks and on their hands and feet worked continuously to keep their body temperature stable.

"Now we have to find the gate that leads to the mines," said Johara, rubbing her hands together.

"We'll find the gate, Johara. The question is, what do we do after that," Milo remarked pensively.

"It's clear that we'll need reinforcements. How are we going to deal with the Cig-ants? By ourselves?" asked Johara. "Could the Spe-ranto guerrillas help?" she asked captain Lu-gi, only to receive a simple 'no'.

"That's what I thought. They can't come here, isn't that right captain Lu-gi?" she asked again and once more the young captain responded with a single word: "Yes."

"I wonder what Lord Salvador of wisdom has to say?" Milo got straight to the point. "He's the only one who can get us out of this impasse. And now that we're where we are, what else can we do except call him up again?" he added.

"You're right, Milo," said Johara. "Yes, that's what we've got to do. Right now!"

The two members of the Nectar Brotherhood wasted no time starting the ritual.

"Ahoy there, my friends!" came the familiar voice of Lord Salvador.

"Having a good time?"

The wise lord appeared at the opening of a cave. He was dressed in only shorts, an underwater mask and flippers. In one hand he was holding a harpoon and in the other a fish was quivering.

"By Hahanoff, prime minister of the gods, what's going on that you should be bothering me when I'm busy with my favourite pastime?"

he asked the two friends who gazed at him, wide-eyed. The sight of the half-naked fisherman made them shiver.

"Well, are you going to talk to me or shall I get out of here? I have other things to do, I'm not a time-waster..."

Johara was the first to come round and she spoke: "Lord Salvador of wisdom, Jurka has been taken prisoner and is in the Winter City mines. There are two of us – three with Lu-gi. How are we going to manage to fight the army of the Cig-ants? We need urgent reinforcements," the young girl concluded.

"Well, I haven't got time, let's make that clear," Lord Salvador interrupted her.

"All right, OK, you're busy fishing. But what about us? What do we do?" said Milo.

"You go and bang your heads on the ice, over there..." replied the wise lord, pointing to the snow-covered wall of the cave.

"Come on Lord Salvador, stop joking!" said Johara angrily but their wise mentor and protector insisted.

"Listen to what I'm saying, you guys. Go on, Milo, bang your head on the wall..." he told the dark-skinned giant.

Milo shook his head. "Ah, no Lord Salvador, you're not going to trick me again," he said stubbornly.

"How about you, Johara? Do you want to bang your little head on it, eh?"

Johara was similarly in no mood for practical jokes.

"Lu-gi bang head!"

The little captain put an end to their quarrelling.

"Lu-gi bang head!" repeated the little Black Cloudian and without a second thought he had head-butted the icy wall.

The layer of ice appeared to crack and Lu-gi banged his head on the same spot once again.

That was when the unexpected happened. The layer of ice crumbled away and, from the crack that had formed, dozens of tiny black and yellow robots started to emerge, filling the place like a swarm of bees.

"The Nectaroids! By Hahanoff, prime minister of the gods, it's the Nectaroids!" shouted Milo as Johara jumped for joy. Little Lu-gi withdrew, startled and frightened, but his friends calmed him down, explaining that these little flying things were their reinforcements.

"Oh thank you, Lord Salvador of wisdom!" declared Milo but there was no-one to be seen at the entrance to the cave. Lord Salvador had disappeared. He had let go the fish he had been holding and it had dived into a small pond and swum away.

The swarm of Nectaroids, having made a few circles of the cave, lined up in a formation that resembled a honeycomb, awaiting orders.

"Forward for the Nectar Brotherhood!" screamed the two friends as they led their army out of the cave.

Finding the entrance to the Cre-matum mines was not difficult for the Nectaroids' scouts. Nor did they have any trouble breaking through the gate and opening up an entrance to the bowels of the planet.

Milo gave the order and the Nectaroids sent their scouts on ahead to monitor the entry of the others to the workshop where the valuable commodity was mined and processed. The tracking instruments were infallible and the rhythmic sounds of the drums that were heard shortly afterwards proved that they were on the right course.

How far away were the Cig-ants?

There was no need for an answer to the question. Two pairs of flaming eyes fixed on the scouts and a roar followed. The advance guard of the Cig-ants had located the Nectaroids and was preparing to welcome them. The huge nostrils of the two Cig-ants gathered all the force they could and, exhaling, hit the Nectaroids with their burning flames. The fire quickly spread to the walls and a river of lava began to flow everywhere, forcing the invaders to remain in constant flight.

From the depths of the tunnel came the sounds of clattering feet and snorting. It was obvious that reinforcements were arriving. The drums could now be heard more loudly. They must be near the mine itself.

Milo armed his multispectral gun and Johara decided to activate her knockout gas launch mechanism. The defence mechanism of both earthlings was operational, while captain Lu-gi followed close by ready to sense any danger.

The Nectaroids took up battle positions. One group formed a shield while the others filled out the sides. The scouts were the first to come into contact with the Cig-ants. And then, battle commenced!

The fire-breathing dragons rose up in the passage to form an impassable wall and started to shower the scouts with flames. The Nectaroids swooped down at speed on the monsters and burst with a bang on their huge bodies, causing injuries and wounds. But the two Cig-ants resisted strongly, despite the non-stop, merciless bombardment by the Nectaroids. Milo gestured to Lu-gi to go in front and the youngster flew ahead, avoiding the flames and the lava that flowed everywhere from the surrounding walls.

"Milo, try out the multispectral gun!" shouted Johara when they were within firing range of the Cig-ants.

"With great pleasure!" replied Milo and he fired off his first round.

The shells pierced through the flaming scene and burst with a bang on the huge bodies of the Cig-ants. Traces of smoke rose from the points of contact but nothing much had been accomplished. The ammunition had been wasted. Milo was speechless. "Lord Salvador of wisdom, these are invulnerable, even to the multispectral gun!" exclaimed the dark-skinned giant.

"Hmm, it seems that the weapon isn't so effective beneath the surface of the planet. Unless these monsters are immortal..." concluded Johara. "Try again with more power, Milo," she said.

Milo turned the weapon to the maximum, took aim again and pulled the trigger. Nothing again...

"Zero to the umpteenth, kiddo," whispered the young man desperately. Johara launched her knockout gas but to no avail.

Meanwhile, the two Cig-ants had been joined by other monsters and were making life difficult for the Nectaroids. They were repelling the waves of attacks from the tiny black and yellow robots with relative ease, preventing all access to the mine. The battle appeared to be lost...

Then Captain Lu-gi exclaimed: "Look!" and pointed to the lava which was flowing down towards the mine.

"Look!" he shouted again.

The two Cig-ants of the advance guard had opened their legs, allowing the red-hot stream of lava to flow between them.

"A-ha. It seems that they're not very fond of lava," said Milo and Johara added that it might be their weak point. "Let's see how much they like the flame throwers," added the small-built girl.

"Lord Salvador, 'what you sow, so shall you reap', wasn't that what our wise protector told us?" enthused Milo.

The multispectral gun was suitably configured and Milo responded to the fire with flaming pellets. Johara and captain Lu-gi looked on anxiously.

And then the unexpected happened: The two Cig-ants opened their huge mouths wide and swallowed the fiery pellets as if they were sweets! And as if that was not enough, they snorted them out of their nostrils, returning the fire at double strength…

Failure… Impasse… Crisis… The size of their failure began to weigh extremely heavily on the minds of the friends, still under attack. What else could they do?

"We've got to find a way of fooling them… There's no other way," shouted Johara.

Captain Lu-gi grabbed the girl by the hand: "Lu-gi find solution," he said in the nonchalant way that typified the little Black Cloudian's way of speaking.

"Solution? What solution? Be quick, captain Lu-gi, come on, we've no time…" Johara begged and Milo pricked up his ears. "Go on!" he called out.

Lu-gi pointed with his small, delicate hands towards where the lava was flowing. "We pass through Cig-ant legs," he explained.

Johara and Milo were speechless. How come they hadn't thought of that? How had they failed to perceive the only visible weakness in the Cig-ants' camp?

"Captain Lu-gi is right," declared Johara. "That's the only way we can fool them and make our way into the mine. What do you say, Milo?" she asked.

"I agree. I don't think there's any other way," said the swarthy giant.

"So, what are we waiting for?" asked Johara, but little Lu-gi interrupted her. "One moment. One moment. First, let loose Nectaroids on Cig-ants," he proposed.

The little Black Cloudian was proving to be an expert at tactical manoeuvres.

"Yes, of course, we should send out the Nectaroids on a diversionary attack. Bravo, Lu-gi," said Johara. "And then we speed like bullets between the dragons' legs. How will they stop us?" said the young girl.

"That's really cool, I agree. This is going to be good!" said Milo, full of enthusiasm. "Captain Lu-gi, that bald head of yours has a very good brain inside it!" he added.

Johara gave orders to the AETP and the two earthlings returned to launch mode. Lu-gi was already fully prepared for the low flight between the Cig-ants' legs that would take him to the Cre-matum mines and to Jurka Slavik.

"Nectaroids, target the enemies' heads. Strike in waves!" ordered Johara and the tiny robots lined up at once in the right formation.

"Fire as you go – now!"

On receiving Johara's order, the yellow and black robots set off in threes, only aiming high, straight into the source of the enemy's fire, the repulsive heads of the Cig-ants. It was definitely a suicide mission but the Nectaroids undertook it without a trace of hesitation. After all, this was their destiny, as expendable items…

Milo flew in front, opening a path through the flames, the pitch black smoke and the fiery pellets. In the middle, holding onto his legs, flew Lu-gi while Johara followed as the rearguard, with the aerials of her tracking system fully activated all the time. With unique skill and at remarkable speed, the AETP led them through the legs of the dragons which didn't even see the trail of smoke behind them.

Soon the three invaders were inside the mine. What they saw there would remain forever etched in their memories. A golden glow was given off by the walls of the mine, dimly illuminating the place. In every corner were dozens of creatures from every planet in the galaxy jostling along in groups, one leaning on the other in an effort to protect themselves against stray missiles and to avoid the Cig-ants' wrath. All around were iron gates, guarded by the dragons, while in the middle, a pool for cleaning the precious ore gave off steam and scolding hot bubbles. Next to the small artificial lake were the automatic Cre-matum processing machines, waiting to be carried to the outside world through a tunnel.

"Jurka! Jurka Slavik, where are you?" Milo called with all the strength he had left.

Nothing. No answer. Milo called again, this time with Johara, but their voices merely echoed in the void. Jurka did not reply.

The third time they called his name, something unexpected happened. The other convicts, who had in the meantime grown bolder, stretched out their hands and pointed in the direction of the tunnel: "In there!" resounded the voices as one.

Lu-gi whistled a warning: "Cig-ants coming," he said and leapt onto Milo's back.

"Let's go then, what are we waiting for?" Johara called to the others as the glow of the Cig-ants' fiery snorting appeared in the surrounding galleries.

The three winged invaders now flew into the only tunnel and into the unknown. When they emerged into a clearing, they saw a platform in what was evidently a transit station used for checking the Cre-matum. The employees sitting behind the registration counters were Black Cloudian bureaucrats who did not present any particular risk. They immobilised them easily with knockout gas and captain Lu-gi undertook to interrogate the one who appeared to be in charge of the group.

The Black Cloudian clerk played it tough with the little guerrilla, but when Lu-gi stretched out his hand and pressed the triangle on his brow, he changed his tune.

Yes, they had seen the prisoner from Earth. Yes, he had been taken to the mine but when the attack started, they carried out the orders they had been given. Meaning? Meaning that he was in solitary confinement, under constant guard. Who was guarding him? Who else but the Cig-ants at the gate and Taka-mura's men in the detention cell...

Lu-gi had an idea. He took his Earthly friends to one side and explained what he had in mind. Milo was enthusiastic and Johara was forced to stifle her misapprehensions.

Captain Lu-gi's plan was simple and clever and, in the circumstances, it might be the only feasible one, and perhaps their salvation. The three friends would disguise themselves as Black Cloudian clerks and, after fooling the Cig-ants, would enter the isolation cell – supposedly to carry out an inspection – and fight Taka-mura's guards to free Jurka.

Lu-gi copied the codes of the civil servants' compatriots and soon the three of them were continuing their underground journey towards the prison area, disguised as Black Cloudians, towards the place shown on the maps that they had seized from the clerks.

They didn't have to go very far. At first they came up against the checkpoints on the inner perimeter fence, where they presented their fake identity cards to the Cig-ants and passed further inside unhindered, since the only thing that interested the dragons was news of the battle in the mine. When they reached the prison gate, a guard appeared, asking them to pass through triangle control. Captain Lu-gi went first into the monitoring station and when he emerged, he simply said to the other two: "Let's go!"

The automatic inner gate opened wide and the three, passing under the noses of the guards, entered the prison forecourt. Straight away they came across the isolation cells. They were set in a row in the actual rock of the surrounding walls and, through the iron bars at the front, the discarded bodies of prisoners could be distinguished in the semi-darkness.

"Where is Jurka Slavik?" they asked the guard on duty. He pointed at once to the furthest cell. They had just brought him there, he explained, and the prisoner was still suffering from the effects of the exhausting interrogation at the hands of Taka-mura himself. He must be especially dangerous, he told them, since Master Zar-ko had been present throughout the proceedings.

But what did the three civil servants want with him, the duty officer wanted to know.

"We're taking him away from here for security reasons," Milo explained. The battle in the Cre-matum mine was still raging and there was always a danger that the enemy might enter the isolation cells, he explained.

The Black Cloudian guard asked them to give him a moment to check with headquarters.

"It's routine. Regulations..." he said and activated the communications system with headquarters and Taka-mura.

Milo gestured to Johara that they needed to act at once and lightning fast. There was no time to waste or to come up with a new plan of action and escape. They had to free Jurka first and then they would work out how to get away. Johara acted with characteristic speed, injecting a good dose of knockout fluid into the guard's neck. The way was now open to Jurka's cell or, at least, that was what they thought. But the moment they touched the iron bars, the automatic alarm was set off. A piercing, repeated sound was heard and at once red lights began flashing on and off. The communication channel with Headquarters was immediately activated while the escape routes were sealed off one after another.

Taka-mura's voice echoed through the semi-darkness of the prison.

"What's happening, guard?" he asked but received no answer. "Speak, for Vasi-vuzuk's sake, what's going on?" the Captain of the guard asked once more.

Silence again.

"Attention, attention! This is an urgent to call for immediate action! All prison guards in the highest state of readiness. Cover the exits and arrest the intruders!" Taka-mura's orders, explicit and immediate, rang out clearly.

Johara shot an anxious glance into the cell. There, in a corner, lay Jurka Slavik, unconscious and immobilised. He was shaking all over from the damp and cold that had penetrated his weak body, causing fever and dizziness. They had removed his uniform and he was dressed in a garment that resembled a cassock.

"Milo, cover for me!" called the young girl to her friend, as she activated the penetration rays. The iron door collapsed like a cardboard box.

"They're coming!" came the voice of captain Lu-gi who felt the approaching danger. "They're coming! Quick, we go..." repeated the little Black Cloudian.

"Not so fast Lu-gi, not so fast..." replied Milo, pulling the trigger of his multispectral gun. The first group of guards to appear in the semi-darkness was forced to beat an untidy retreat.

"Eat this!" Milo shouted again as a new burst of fire left the barrels of the gun, targeting another group of guards that had appeared from the neighbouring gallery.

Lu-gi ran to Johara who was desperately trying to revive Jurka but with no success.

"Lu-gi help," said the little captain in his bland voice and he pushed the girl aside. Lu-gi placed his hands on Jurka's head and the lights on the triangle on his forehead blinked on and off. As if by a miracle, Jurka Slavik opened his eyes.

"Johara, Lu-gi, where am I?" the young man managed to stammer but there was no time for explanations.

"Johara, quick!"

It was Milo's rough voice, echoing like a sad bell through the cell.

"One minute, just give me a minute!" replied Johara. Then she turned to Jurka. "Don't move!" she ordered and the young man could only watch the girl in bewilderment. Johara pressed a button on her belt and stretched out her hand, pressing the suffering youth on the forehead.

"Close your eyes," she ordered, as she activated the system of transferring electrolytic energy cells to Jurka's body. The girl was actually sending part of her own strength into her friend of the Nectar Brotherhood.

Jurka quivered like a fish for a moment but the next, when he had recovered, he was a different person. His eyes suddenly took on a vitality and freshness, his blood seemed to be flowing through his veins, hot and renewed. Jurka Slavik was back.

"By Grace..." came the voice of little Lu-gi who was hopping up and down nervously in front of the two friends.

"Let's go!" said Johara and she took him by the hand, leading him carefully to the cell door. There, amid dust and flying stones, Milo was fighting his own battle.

"What do we do now?" called out Johara to the dark-skinned student.

"I don't know, I'm busy fighting!" replied Milo. "Give me hand, kiddo, don't just stand there..."

Johara looked around to assess the situation. They appeared to be trapped in the prison area, however well Milo was preventing their enemies from approaching and neutralising them. There was no way out since all the exits had been sealed, while at any moment reinforcements could arrive from Zar-ko and Taka-mura, even from Tao Li.

"Milo, there's only one solution. We get out by the same way as we came in. Where they definitely won't be expecting us..." proposed Johara. "They can't have sealed their own escape route," she added.

"What are you saying? That we go back to the Cig-ants?" objected Milo but Johara was adamant.

"Leave these here to me," she called out, as a new group appeared at the entrance to the cell, taking up battle positions.

The knockout gas worked its miracle once again and the guards, one by one, fell down unconscious like blades of cut grass.

"Oooh, I'm enjoying this!" exclaimed Milo, but Johara had no time for such behaviour. "Come on, let's go!" she called to the others.

"Yes, let's go, OK. We can go but how is Jurka going to go with us?" Milo's question was perfectly reasonable. Jurka could not fly since his precious AETP equipment had been removed.

"Don't worry about that, I can carry him. Jurka's flying with me," answered Johara. "You and Lu-gi, make way for us," she added.

"Hmm, you look a bit small to be carrying our friend..." Milo said but Johara pointed to her back and the jetpack. "This will be carrying us, my boy, this here..." she said and that was the end of it.

Milo went in front, captain Lu-gi took up his position behind, followed by Johara. The girl wrapped her arms tightly around Jurka and once the jet pack began its work she was able to lift him as if he was as light as a feather. The flight to the exit and to safety had begun.

The Cig-ants guarding the fenced inner area did not even see the three bullets speeding among them. The flight down the underground tunnels was a smooth one until they approached the battle area. Things were not so rosy there. The hellish fire was still burning with the same intensity since the Cig-ants, thanks to their enormous strength, were able to resist the unceasing attacks by the swarms of Nectaroids, repelling their swoops without suffering serious or mortal injuries.

The three friends, led by Milo, checked their flight. They needed to assess the situation together before attempting to escape from the mine.

"Hmm, we're at an advantage now," said Milo and Jurka, by now completely recovered, agreed with him. "Yes, I know what you mean. We can hit them from here where they won't expect it," he said.

"Precisely! They'll be caught in crossfire and will be startled. That's when we get away, flying through the tunnel up to the surface... The Nectaroids will cover our escape," Milo explained.

"It's perfect, Milo, perfect..." commented Johara and Jurka nodded in agreement.

"Could captain Lu-gi have a different idea?" Milo asked the little Black Cloudian who answered with a simple "no."

"Right, let's get to work!" murmured Milo, loading up his multispectral gun.

"No, not with that, Milo," said Johara. "Against these monsters it's useless..."

"So what are we going to hit them with? The knockout liquid and gas doesn't affect them either. How?" Milo wondered aloud.

Jurka shrugged his shoulders. "I don't know, guys, I don't know," he said.

Johara sat in silence, racking her brain over what to do, when Lu-gi's voice interrupted her thoughts.

"Lu-gi know!" the little captain exclaimed in his characteristic tone. They all turned to him. What brilliant idea would their Black Cloudian ally come up with this time?

"Lu-gi whistle..." was all he said and the other three looked at him, open-mouthed. What did Lu-gi mean? What was that about?

The little Black Cloudian gestured to them to stand aside and he stepped into the open area of the mine, among the ruins, the shooting and the flames that were falling like rain. He stood motionless as a statue and with both hands covered his huge crescent-shaped ears. Then he stretched his neck, the rings flashed on and off and soon reached full power while the triangle on the youngster's forehead was working overtime.

Then the unexpected happened! From captain Lu-gi's wide open mouth they heard a strange, piercing sound, like an extended alarm signal. The three friends of the Nectar Brotherhood immediately plugged their ears. The piercing sound continued to ring through the mine and when it echoed on the sides of the various walls, the place was transformed into a stage on which it sounded as if dozens of cacophonous orchestras were playing at the same time.

The fire-breathing dragons seemed to have had enough. At first they bellowed in confusion, giving off sparks from their nostrils. Then they looked right and left, seeking the source of he sudden unbearable sound. Immediately afterwards they started beating themselves on all sides, as if possessed. The noise had driven them mad, throwing them into total confusion, and their behaviour resembled that off crazy wind-up toys.

Lu-gi stopped his whistling and turned towards his friends from Earth.

"Ready? Let's go!" he said and without wasting a moment they all flew among the dazed Cig-ants. The Nectaroids set to work once more, showing no mercy as they hit the monstrous creatures which were trying to recover from the sudden misfortune that had struck them.

By the time they had recovered it was too late. Milo carved a path through the tunnel and, without meeting any difficulty or resistance, they soon saw above their heads the dim light of Winter City. The swarms of Nectaroids followed the escapees and soon they were all were treading safely on the surface, safe and sound.

All?

All except one. The harsh cold struck the raggedy-dressed Jurka at once. The young man suddenly began to stagger and his tormented body was again shaking all over. Without the protection of his space suit he was a tiny crumb in a vast white and frozen landscape. They hadn't thought of that...

The light-haired youth felt the polar cold penetrate his body and take it over like an angry hurricane. His nostrils had frozen and his breathing grew hard and heavy. His feet and hands became stiff like those of a wax dummy and he started to tremble all over. It was clear that, in such terrible cold conditions, he would not survive for long...

Milo picked up his sick friend and gestured to the others to make for the familiar cave. Once inside its welcoming walls, Johara proposed to Milo that he activate the flame thrower.

"We need to warm him up with whatever we've got," the young girl murmured to herself.

Milo switched on the flame thrower but it did not seem to make any great difference. The cold was so bitter that something more effective than the flames of a flame thrower was required.

They were in urgent need of a fire to warm Jurka. Milo set the Nectaroids to work, searching inside and outside the cave for branches or anything that they could burn. Nothing! The cursed Winter City had nothing on its surface but endless snow and icebergs...

Jurka looked to be losing the battle. Johara embraced him tightly, trying to transfer as much heat to him as she could from her tiny body. Milo continued with the flame thrower but it appeared to be an unequal fight. Little Lu-gi looked on with his expressionless deep-set eyes, unable to offer any help.

"Lord Salvador of wisdom, by Hahanoff, let's call on Lord Salvador!" Johara exclaimed in desperation. "Milo, our protector is the only one who can help us..."

Milo simply replied "yes, you're right" and began the ritual.

Fortunately their mentor was present.

"What's up now, kids? What is it that makes you keep calling me at the most inconvenient moments?"

Lord Salvador appeared at the entrance of the cave, in a cheerful mood as always. He was dressed up to the nines, in a black dinner jacket and a bow tie, plus a stovepipe hat, white gloves and matching scarf. He was puffing on a huge cigar.

"By Hahanoff, prime minister of the gods, why are you disturbing me? Tell me quickly! I'm in no mood to miss the dwarfs' concert," said the wise lord in a strict voice.

"But Lord Salvador, can't you see what's happening? We're losing Jurka, do something, please..." whined Johara.

Milo, who was holding Jurka's fever-ridden body, tried to murmur something but he began sobbing. The swarthy giant felt that the end was approaching and he burst into tears. Unless, of course, the good lord could perform another of his miracles and save him right now...

Lord Salvador glanced briefly at the young man, delirious with fever. His breath had become heavy, like a snore.

"Jurka kaput!" announced Lord Salvador of wisdom in an official tone.

"What? What did you say, Lord Salvador?" screamed Johara, while Milo broke into loud sobs, as his young friend suddenly stopped moving in his grasp.

"Jurka, finished. That's what I said, young Johara," the wise lord repeated coldly.

"No! No, it's not possible! He can't be! Do something! In the name of Master Hahanoff, do something!" cried the young girl.

"Neither Master Hahanoff nor I can do anything, little girl," replied Lord Salvador with the same bland look, as if nothing had happened. "What can we do? That's life, we all have a beginning and an end. Apart from me, of course..." the lord of wisdom added humbly. He was immortal.

"No! No, it can't be true. Jurka can't be dead..." Milo kept saying, weeping loudly.

Johara was not going to let this go. "You listen to me, Lord Salvador. I'm not putting up with this!" she answered back audaciously. "You, the wizard, you the miracle worker, you who can bring whole back planets from the dead, you can't give Jurka his life back?" the girl shouted.

Lord Salvador gestured apologetically. "Dear Johara, unfortunately I can't..." he murmured. Lord Salvador paused briefly before completing his phrase:

"But you can!"

Johara and Milo were dumbfounded. What was the crafty lord telling them now? At such a tragic moment, surely he couldn't be playing a joke on them?

Johara was fuming with anger and she spoke her mind to the wise lord.

"You should be ashamed of yourself, Lord Salvador. Making fun of our suffering! Don't you at least feel sorry for our friend? You don't respect our feelings and on top of that you're having a laugh?"

"I'm serious, my girl. I can't save him. But you can give him his life back," the wise lord repeated in all seriousness as he puffed out smoke from his cigar like an old steam engine.

"You're not tricking us, Lord Salvador, are you?" Milo managed to say amid his tears.

"Milo, what is life worth without a joke?" replied the wise lord, but he was quick to add: "But, honestly, Johara is the only one who can save Jurka. Only she can bring him back to life..."

"Then tell me how to do it, Lord Salvador. Really, tell me how I can save him. I'm ready to do whatever you say to bring Jurka back!" Johara cried obstinately.

"I'm telling you the truth, my dear, why don't you believe me?" the wise lord replied at once. He then cast a furtive glance at his watch. “Oh dear, I’m late, I’ve got to go now,” he added, provoking new explosions of protest from Johara and Milo.

“Oh all right, I won’t go until we’ve sorted out this business,” Lord Salvador rushed to clarify his position.

“So, tell me what I have to do. And I’ll do it right away, right now!” insisted Johara.

“Yes, yes, tell us Lord Salvador, in the name of Master Hahanoff, tell us...” repeated Milo who was still holding the lifeless body of Jurka Slavik in his arms.

“But it’s so simple, my friends,” said the wise lord. “Johara, you will give him the kiss of life!”

“That’s all?” exclaimed Johara in surprise, while Milo was speechless. How could a dead person be brought back to life with a kiss? Or would the wise lord perform another of his miraculous tricks? He wouldn’t let a member of the Nectar Brotherhood be lost, he couldn’t, thought the dark-skinned giant.

“I told you, it’s so simple. I’m at a loss why you didn’t think of it yourselves,” Lord Salvador told them. “I’m leaving you now and I wish you a fine resurrection,” he added, turning on his heels and preparing to disappear from their sight.

The two friends looked at each other, lost. What were they going to do now? What else but try the solution proposed by their protector and mentor? Johara asked Milo to place Jurka’s lifeless body on the floor of the cave and she bent over his frozen face. She took a deep breath, opened the young man’s mouth and prepared to give him the kiss of life, when she was interrupted by the voice of Lord Salvador who had reappeared.

“Er... sorry my dear, I forgot to mention one small detail,” he said.

“Now what? Why are we wasting time? What detail?” Milo angrily asked the wise lord who was scratching his forehead.

Johara turned her head, bewildered. She was impatiently waiting to hear the detail that Lord Salvador had forgotten to tell her. The wise lord gave a cough. “Ah yes, I forgot to tell you, Johara, that you’ll give life to Jurka with your kiss, but you’ll be giving him some of yours... well, yours, to be precise,” he wise lord clarified and disappeared.

Johara was speechless. Her mind had stopped working and all she could do was gaze at some place in the void. Her tearful eyes glassed over and she could not utter a word. She felt as if she had suddenly been struck by lightning and destroyed. The young girl felt faint and collapsed, like an empty sack, next to Jurka's lifeless body.

Milo was going crazy. As if it wasn't enough that he had lost his friend, now he was in danger of losing Johara too. What a tragedy! What was the hapless boy to do first?

Lu-gi, who al this time had been looking on, silent and expressionless, as the tragic events unfolded, hurried at once to Milo's side.

"You strong. You save friends," he told him, touching him with his fingertip. "Get up, Milo, help Johara," he said and the swarthy giant felt as if an electric current had passed through his body. He felt his strength growing and he leapt up like a wild animal.

"Johara, come back to your senses!" he shouted to the girl and seized her by the shoulders.

"You've got to decide what to do," he told her straight.

The young girl opened her eyes, shook the snow from her short black hair and stood up straight. At Milo's instigation she had regained her senses. Yes. Now she had to decide what to do. Without delay.

She looked Milo in the eye but her friend turned his head away. He could not bear to see the girl's pained expression. Then she looked at Jurka. His lifeless body had turned blue and a light layer of frost appeared to cover his face. Johara wept. Her heart could not bear the sight of her dear friend dead…

Slowly she approached the body and cleared away the frost. She wiped Jurka's face, stroked his light-brown hair with both hands and kissed him gently on both cheeks. Then she placed her lips over his half-open mouth and with a determined movement gave him the longest, bitter-sweet kiss of life.

Milo had turned his back on her, vainly trying to stifle his poignant sobs, so only the imperturbable captain Lu-gi was there to observe the scene.

At first Johara felt a weak heartbeat in Jurka. Straight afterwards she felt his body tremble. Then, through his half-open mouth, she felt him shudder into to life, fighting to emerge from the dark dungeons of Hades.

Jurka Slavik came back to life! And when the light-haired youth opened his eyes, he felt resting on his head a familiar, warm face. It was the serene face of Johara who seemed to be smiling at him, greeting their reunion.

Jurka half-sat up, dizzy and confused.

"What happened to me, Johara? Milo? Where are we?" the young man managed to whisper.

Milo jumped up and down as if receiving an electric shock. "Jurka, you're alive?" screamed the dark-skinned youth, but he received no answer. Jurka stood up, holding Johara in his arms. As if lost, he looked first at the girl, then at Milo, unable to believe that the young girl was dead.

"No, she can't be! I'm dreaming... Milo, tell me this is all a bad dream... A nightmare..." Jurka raved, without receiving any answer.

Only Lu-gi spoke: "True, Jurka. Johara die for you. You live..."

Jurka turned his crazed face towards the little captain and then to Milo. "What's the little guy saying, man? Tell me, don't make me suffer any more..." he managed to stammer.

Milo was in no position to utter a sound, as he was crying inconsolably, grieving for a second time over another member of the Nectar Brotherhood.

Jurka gently placed Johara's body on the frozen floor of the cave and curled up next to her. He was mentally and physically exhausted and on the verge of collapse.

"Lord Salvador of wisdom, I can't take any more..." he murmured.

"Who called me?" came a voice from the mouth of the cave.

The two friends raised their heads and saw the familiar, so welcome face of their mentor and protector smiling broadly at them. He was still dressed in the formal clothes that he had worn to the dwarfs' concert.

"Ahoy there, Jurka Slavik! Welcome back to the land of the living!" said the wise lord.

"Why? What happened? Was I dead?" asked Jurka.

"One hundred per cent!" replied Lord Salvador. "Just as dead as little Johara is right now..." he added.

Milo nodded his head and captain Lu-gi was heard to say simply: "Yes, Jurka, you die."

Jurka was totally confused. "If I was dead, how come I'm alive now? What happened? I was resurrected?" he managed to murmur.

"Of course. Since young Johara agreed to give you life. That's why she took your place among the dead," Lord Salvador explained in such plain terms that there could be no arguing.

"What!" Jurka Slavik cried out and fell to the ground. Milo and Lu-gi ran at once to revive him and get him back on his feet.

"Come on now Jurka, don't be like that. Wouldn't you have done the same for Nefeli? Ooops... for Johara, I mean," the crafty lord corrected himself.

There followed an eternity of silence. The wise lord looked down on the youngsters, waiting for their next move.

Milo broke the silence He lifted up his gigantic body and announced: "Lord Salvador, I request the privilege of resurrecting Johara at any cost. I'm ready!" His voice was breaking with emotion.

"No, Lu-gi turn now..." interrupted the young Black Cloudian. "I resurrect Johara!" added the little captain.

"Stop! Both of you, stop!" Jurka broke in. "I'm first. I'm ready to correct what happened, Lord Salvador of wisdom," Jurka Slavik demanded in a steady voice.

The two friends – and Lu-gi in the middle – were now having a real row. One was asking for permission to sacrifice himself for Johara, while the other insisted on making reparations. Their voices boomed around the hospitable cave as the sound levels rose dangerously.

"Enough! That's enough!" came the wise lord's strict order. "Owww, you're deafening me with your wild shouting. It's enough to make me want to send the lot of you to the other world... so that I can have some peace and quiet once and for all..." he mumbled.

"And captain Lu-gi with them..."said the little Black Cloudian in his bland voice.

Lord Salvador made a funny grimace. He shot a cunning glance at the three friends, shook his head and his stovepipe hat up and down and laughed for all he was worth: "Got you again kids!" he jeered. "Who says that Johara needs your help to come alive, eh?"

Jurka, Milo and Lu-gi looked behind them. There, before their astonished eyes, stood little Johara, alive and well!

"What's up? Why are you looking so upset and miserable? What's wrong with you. You look as if you've seen a ghost," said the young girl and they all responded as one: "Right in one, Johara. We've seen a ghost..."

Calm and tranquillity returned to the Nectar Brotherhood. The Nectaroids, following orders from Lord Salvador, saw that Jurka got his AETP suit back and that damage to the others' outfits was repaired. Lu-gi took care of his own business, informing Ben-azir about everything that had happened and, at the same time, receiving new orders. He would remain with the allies from Earth until further notice.

"All's well that ends well..." said Jurka Slavik to himself as he watched Johara and Milo testing the readiness of the systems in their uniforms.

Johara was first to complete her testing.

"Jurka, I'm ready. What do we do now?" she asked.

"We need to get out of this cursed place as fast as we can, that's what..." replied the light-haired youth who was now completely back to his old self.

"I'm ready too!" declared Milo. "Ready for action. Let's go and get our own back," said the swarthy youth, full of strength and self-confidence. After everything that had happened, the thirst for revenge was very powerful.

"Let's make quick resumé of the situation. We need to clarify our priorities, right now," proposed Jurka and his friends agreed.

The three members of the Nectar Brotherhood sat down together with captain Lu-gi between them. Jurka was first to speak.

"It's clear that we have no business here any more. Consequently, we need to get out, the faster the better. The question is, where shall we go? To the Lake of Youth? Is that where we'll find Nefeli again? Or somewhere else?"

"Jurka, do we really have to chase around after Nefeli?" objected Johara. "Wasn't she the one who led you straight into the hands of the guards and Tao Li? I say we go after Tao Li and his Tigers and we fight the guards with Ben-azir's guerrillas. Let's forget about Nefeli," the girl added.

Jurka looked at her, shocked. "How can we give up on our mission halfway through? How can we break the first rule of the Nectar Brotherhood? 'Honour above all!' No, Johara, we can't abandon our plans. What do you say, Milo?"

The dark-skinned boy raised his eyes and looked pensively at is two friends. "I say that whether we like it or not, we've got to do both. If we go after Tao Li, we'll find Nefeli too. And if we search for Nefeli, I'm sure we're going to come across Tao Li and Taka-mura. So I don't see any reason for you to argue," said Milo. "Unless there are other things involved..." he added, glancing cheekily at Johara.

The young girl blushed and hurried to say that she agreed with Milo's reasoning.

"Very good, that's fixed then," concluded a relieved Jurka. "Now let's look at the other aspect of the situation. Where shall we head to?"

"That depends on what each of us thinks about Nefeli's role," said Johara.

"What do you mean by that, kiddo?" asked Jurka.

"What I mean is that one possibility is that she's cooperating with them, willingly or not... If not, it's completely different. Anyway, whatever the case, I think that Tao Li has got her. So we'll find her when we locate the Tigers," concluded the short-haired girl.

Milo was quick to agree with Johara. "You're right, kiddo. That's what I think too. Tao Li took her, Tao Li must have her. In any case, whether it's like that or not, Nefeli was part of their plans to capture Jurka. We saw that with our own eyes."

"OK, then. We're decided on that. Where do we go? Back, to the Lake of Youth? To Autumn City? Or somewhere else? And if so, where?" Jurka asked again.

At that moment, the triangle on captain Lu-gi's forehead sounded. The little Black Cloudian stood up and touched his large crescent-shaped ears with both hands.

"Lu-gi signal, guerrilla headquarters... Urgent..." he explained in his bland voice.

The others fell silent. What urgent situation required that captain Lu-gi be in contact Ben-azir's headquarters?

Soon afterwards, the little Black Cloudian relayed the message from headquarters to the three friends: Doctor Soc-rat had arrived on the planet. The Council of Elders was holding an emergency meeting in the Dark Palace and all forces on Black Cloud were in a state of alert in the vicinity of the Aerial Fortress. All sectors of the cities had been placed in quarantine and only Spring City, where the Mace-bearers and other members of the privileged class lived, was open to residents and visitors to the planet...

"There's the answer to your question, Jurka Slavik," said Johara, as soon as Lu-gi had completed his report about the urgent message. "Tao Li and the rest of them must be in Spring City, isn't that what we should conclude from what captain Lu-gi has told us?" Johara asked.

"In the circumstances, it most definitely is," Jurka agreed.

"So what are we waiting for? Let's get going!" shouted Milo who stood up and activated his jetpack.

The other two did the same.

"Lu-gi, take us to Spring City!" ordered Jurka and the little captain flew first towards the cave's exit. He was followed by the members of the Nectar Brotherhood and a rearguard of Nectaroids.

Winter City was just as harsh and inhospitable as it had been when they first arrived. The bitter cold froze everything but this time their uniforms made all the difference. Nonetheless, a snowstorm that had blown up made their flight difficult. The strong wind struck them head on, whipping their faces and preventing them from seeing properly. It was a dangerous situation since their enemies could be lying in wait, ready to take full advantage of the adverse weather conditions. Jurka suggested flying at a lower altitude and sent a swarm of Nectaroids ahead with Lu-gi. At the same time, for any eventuality, Johara activated her reconnaissance antenna, even though nothing but an infinite white sheet was visible.

The flight continued with some obstacles – over mountains and glaciers – but with no nasty surprises, until the snow began to disappear and sparse dots of land, which gradually turned into large grey-green strips, began to come into view below them. It was clear that they were on the borders of Spring City. Jurka gave the signal to land. They needed to make a stop before deciding how and where to proceed. What's more, they had to prepare for the possibility of being surprised and to make sure that they didn't fall into their opponents' trap again. Who knows what Master Zar-ko's malicious men and the Tigers would think of this time?

ର

Noise filled the Aerial Fortress. Guards ran here and there carrying out orders, other officers and holograms jostled in the endless corridors, carrying messages and other requests. The Mace-bearers were especially busy, conscientiously carrying out their missions like good senior civil servants, while the Elders of the Council were in continuous session, under the vigilant eye of Doctor Soc-rat. The overlord of Black Cloud had taken over the Dark Palace and was directing everything from within.

In the city itself, locals and visitors were out and about but they were awkward and nervous as they speculated about the reason for the sudden state of alert. What was happening to the planet? Why weren't the state screens providing any information? Who would be the envoy bringing them the orders of the Council? And when would the other cities be open again?

As always happens in such circumstances, a lack of information became the mother of all speculation. Some started talking about an imminent invasion from the distant planet of the Warlord Shades, others insisted that there was a serious crisis in relations between the Council of Elders and Doctor Soc-rat, while those who were better informed spoke of problems with the mining of Cre-matum...

At military headquarters, Master Zar-ko, Taka-mura and Tao Li were examining the data and images that the Om-niscient was transmitting non-stop. They had received details from Winter City about the escape of the accursed members of the Nectar Brotherhood and they were particularly concerned about what would happen next.

Where were they right now? Where were they heading? What were the bold youngsters planning? It was this that concerned them above all.

The Om-niscient gave the first signal. Movement had been detected in sector F on the borders of Spring City.

"Image magnification!" ordered Master Zar-ko once more. "Show indications of thermal activity," he added.

Still nothing.

"Damn Vasi-vuzuk!" cursed the Three Star Commander as the Om-niscient persisted in giving a signal for movement in sector F.

Taka-mura was quick to suggest to the Commander that they send a detachment of armed guards to the area. Tao Li added that he would be particularly pleased to accompany the guards if it turned out to be the hated Earthlings of the Nectar Brotherhood.

"No, not so fast," Master Zar-ko said, quick to interrupt the proposals from his advisors. "Let's first make sure of their precise location and then we'll see..."

The Commander looked anxious. So far, all his efforts to neutralise the Earthly troublemakers of the Nectar Brotherhood had failed. And that was not all. No, he was in danger from Ben-azir's movement which had formed an alliance with them and was helping them. The longed-for Fourth Star now looked to be very far away and this caused him great sorrow. What would happen if he failed? How would Doctor Soc-rat judge him? What if he sent him into retirement as area commander for the accursed Winter City?

This thought alone made Master Zar-ko shudder. No, he had to do something, and it had to be fast and, above all, effective. At any price...

The Om-niscient gave a clearer signal and the picture froze on the borders of Spring City.

"Got you, my little birds!" shouted Taka-mura as the screens zoomed in on the young friends. "A-ha! We've got the Nectaroids too," said the Captain of the guard on seeing how the rounded yellow and black figures of the tiny robots stood out in the picture.

Master Zar-ko interrupted his thoughts and studied the images from Spring City. Things were not looking good at all and he had to take a decision. Suddenly an idea came to him and he turned to Tao Li.

"Right, my dear friend, the time has come for you to show who you are and precisely what you're worth," said Master Zar-ko without beating about the bush with pointless introductions. "Here's the Nectar Brotherhood and here's your opportunity..." he added enigmatically.

Tao Li looked at the Black Cloudian officer with mistrust, clearly confused. What on earth did Zar-ko mean? That he was going to face the dangerous invaders by himself?

The thought running around the brain of the cunning leader of the Tigers was, unfortunately, precisely what Commander Zar-ko had in mind.

"Yes, you'll go with your gang and you'll challenge the enemy to a duel," explained Master Zar-ko. "We'll be observing and, at the right moment, we'll intervene. But first you have to lay him low and defeat the group by getting their leader out of the way," he said.

Tao Li, for all his faults, was no fool. This proposal struck him as curious since, up to now, they had taken on the Nectar Brotherhood jointly, with the guards, and had never manage to succeed completely. So what was this suggestion all about? Why did Zar-ko want him to go with just the Tigers to take on Jurka Slavik and his group? What was the sly Commander up to?

Young Jurka did not concern him. He believed he could win a duel between the two of them. Consequently, there must be something else to Master Zar-ko's proposal and Tao Li decided to use some cunning of his own.

"With great pleasure, Master Zar-ko. Thank you for honouring me with such a mission. Just one thing, I'd like the blessing of the

Council of Elders..." he said. And then, after a moment's silence, he dealt the real blow: "And that of Doctor Soc-rat, of course..."

Master Zar-ko was absolutely enraged, though his huge bald head did not budge. Nor did his deep-set, blank eyes reveal anything. He stood there, like a statue, motionless like all the Black Cloudians and weighed up the situation. "If we go to the Council, forget it," the Commander thought. "It will look as if I'm retreating and the Elders will realise at once what the purpose of this tactic is...Hmm, that will be bad for me. And if this business reaches Doctor Soc-rat, I'll have had it...Hmm... now what do we do?"

The difficult situation was resolved by the senior Councillor who suddenly appeared on the screen.

"Commander Zar-ko," he announced. "The moment has come for you to show us how much we can depend on you. It's time for you to sort things out and bring a final and irrevocable end to this ridiculous story of the youngsters from Earth and their allies here. Their presence is unacceptable in Spring City and, of course, the same goes for the Dark Palace. That would be unthinkable, it would be sacrilege of the highest order!"

The Elder paused to confirm that his message had been given properly. "Bear in mind that we shall be watching you, as will Doctor Soc-rat," he concluded.

"At you service, Elders, give me your orders!" thundered Zar-ko. "By Doctor Soc-rat, I'm ready..."

Making a virtue of necessity, Master Zar-ko was suddenly tied hand and foot. His plan to send Tao Li first had fallen on deaf ears and now he would have to resolve the situation himself...

One bad thing is often followed by many more and when the red colour of absolute priority flashed on the screens and Doctor Soc-rat appeared, the Commander felt that the worst was yet to come.

He was not mistaken. The black-dressed figure of Doctor Soc-rat filled the screens of Spring City. Everyone hung on his lips.

Doctor Soc-rat stroked his beard, the only symbol of superiority that Fate had granted him since the time of the Lost Sun.

"Greetings Doctor Soc-rat!" echoed the cries from the mouths of the subjects of Black Cloud.

Doctor Soc-rat began to speak from the black hole that was his mouth. His voice resounded like a prayer.

"I greet you, o children of Black Cloud... May the Two Suns always illuminate your path..."

There was a pause. Doctor Soc-rat stroked his beard once more, as if wishing to draw wisdom and guidance from it.

"Our planet is in danger..." began the Black Cloud overlord's sermon. "Law and order are in danger... the system is in danger..."

The doctor paused once again.

"The Cre-matum is in danger!" he went on and a wave of shocked and anxious murmuring went through the Black Cloudians.

Then he dropped the bombshell: "Lord Salvador and the White Cloud are here!"

A long drawn-out "oooooohhh" echoed everywhere and the shock became a nightmare.

"Lord Salvador? The White Cloud? How could that be? Where had that accursed individual turned up after so many suns and winters?"

The questions hung, like Vasi-vuzuk and Me-gaera, over the bright sky of Spring City...

"Calm down!" ordered Doctor Soc-rat and everything fell silent. "By the Great Sun, we shall crush him!" he cried out and everyone burst into cheering. Since Doctor Soc-rat had said that they would crush him, there was no reason to worry, The planet's great enemy would be crushed...

The Elders of the Council immediately called Commander Zar-ko and informed him that he had to succeed in the mission with which the overlord had entrusted him. He would wait at Headquarters until they had negotiated with the doctor and then they would announce their decisions and the plan of action.

ᔕ

The last snows had disappeared behind the mountainside and, as the members of the Nectar Brotherhood descended, Spring City unfolded in all its magnificence before their surprised eyes. The green meadow, which spread out as far as the eye could see, resembled a painting. The green colour of the fields blended with the yellow of the chrysanthemums, the red of the poppies and the blue of the cornflowers, while the scent of the pure white lemon blossoms turned the breeze into an invisible reservoir of fragrance.

It was the kingdom of tranquillity...

Jurka took a couple of deep breaths and sighed.

"If you're looking for Paradise, this must be it," he said and Milo was quick to agree. "By Lord Salvador, this isn't a City, it's an enormous flower garden," exclaimed the swarthy giant ecstatically.

"Don't rush to judgement, guys, don't rush. Things aren't always what they seem, right?" interrupted Johara, who was still observing the area with her reconnaissance antenna. "Let's see what we have here..." said the girl, as a curious, huge building appeared on her screen. All around its sides was a transparent grey material like dull glass while along the edges were green climbing plants, giving it the appearance of a greenhouse. At its highest point was a circular dome, in the centre of which a huge disc could be seen revolving, like a vigilant eye.

"Dark Palace, Doctor Soc-rat. Heart of planet," explained captain Lu-gi in his icy voice.

"Hmm, all the indications are that the palace is fully operational," said Johara. Jurka agreed. "Yes, it looks as if you're right, kiddo. That's what the picture shows..."

"Which means, Jurka, that Doctor Soc-rat must be here," concluded Milo.

"Doctor Soc-rat, city," confirmed captain Lu-gi and showed Johara the sign that was flashing on the front gate of the Dark Palace.

"A-ha!" answered the girl. "So we have to present our credentials too. I didn't know that..."

"Do you know what this means, Johara?" asked Jurka and, without waiting for an answer, added: "It means that they've already organised our welcoming committee. If I'm right, it means that they've learned their lesson and won't risk anything with us," the light-haired youth concluded.

"Yes, you're right Jurka... Except that I'm hoping that we've learned our lesson," answered Johara.

"Well, let's be properly prepared, what are we waiting for?" said Milo and ordered his alert systems to become operational. The other two did the same, while Lu-gi stretched his hands high. It was time to communicate with guerrilla headquarters in order to coordinate their movements.

"Let's go!" Jurka gave the signal to move and the group of four slipped down the hillside, stepping carefully through the greenery and shrubbery. The Nectaroids flew low in a semicircular formation, having already checked the territory ahead.

They must have been a few hundred metres from the first houses in Spring City when captain Lu-gi gestured to them to stop. Milo at once armed the multispectral gun while Johara brought the defence mechanism into operation. Jurka ordered the Nectaroids to take up battle stations while he approached the little Black Cloudian. They were all hiding in the bushes.

"What's up, captain Lu-gi?" he asked.

The little captain did not answer. He stood motionless, expressionless and totally absorbed with recording the indications from his sensors. Only when the small triangle on his forehead stopped blinking was he heard to say: "Lu-gi feel danger..."

"Where? From whom?" asked Jurka at once while Johara and Milo glanced hurriedly around. Nothing but trees, bushes, gardens and small houses surrounding them. Peace and quiet reigned everywhere.

The lights on Lu-gi's forehead flickered on and off again. The little Black Cloudian turned and pointed in the direction of the bushes.

"Here, around us!" was all the little captain had a chance to say before the surrounding bushes appeared to come to life. They suddenly spread out their branches like tentacles which they wrapped around the bodies of the four young friends. Milo vainly fired his multispectral gun. The branches were dense and thick and the missiles could not check their tight embrace.

"Nectaroids, help!" shouted Jurka. The tiny yellow and black robots swooped down like hawks, striking the plants and bushes with direct razor-sharp hits. But still it was an unequal fight.

Johara decided that there was no other solution and activated her herbicide gas. The place turned yellow from the successive explosions of herbicide and the three friends were forced to activate their air filters. The gas proved to be their salvation since, within a short time, the deadly branches appeared to be withering and losing their strength, freeing the unfortunate Earthlings and Lu-gi from their fatal embrace.

The three friends and the little captain were checking the damage and trying to recover from the unexpected attack by the plants when Lu-gi again put the group on alert.

"Vision of Grace, Lu-gi see danger!" said the youngster in his annoying, bland voice and pointed in the direction of the orange groves.

"What's that?" Milo shouted out and Jurka joined in: "Master Hahanoff, I don't get it..." Johara, whose antennae were providing a clearer picture, kept a cooler head, while the nano-computer was working non-stop.

"It is swarm of Buzzles" announced Lu-gi.

"And it's obvious that they're attacking us. Take cover!" said Johara as the Buzzles lined up in an arrow formation ready to strike.

"Nectaroids, stop them!" Jurka ordered immediately and the tiny robots took up a shield formation.

The battle did not last long. The Nectaroids repelled the attacking swarms with successive explosions, but the fight was unequal. The Buzzles carried out attacking dives from all sides, from different heights, dropping a sticky liquid which gradually rendered the Nectaroids useless by immobilising them. When the resistance of the yellow and black robots was exhausted, the awful Buzzles regrouped, ready for a decisive strike on the group of four who were vainly trying to assist in the Nectaroids' defensive task. Even when Milo activated the multispectral gun's automatic spray function, the Buzzles looked unbeatable because their attacks were endless.

"Jurka, let's do the trick with the identical copies again!" shouted Johara and the young man agreed at once. They only just managed to start the image reproduction process in time as the Buzzles were already flying in circular formations above their heads.

"What are they doing now? Why aren't they attacking, man?" asked Milo who, to be on the safe side, was firing warning shots at the enemy.

"I don't know. How am I supposed to know?" Jurka answered.

"Look!"

Johara's cry told them that the Buzzles had begun their descent to a lower altitude. When they reached a particular distance, they stopped, regrouped and worked on covering a broader surface. When they took action they resembled deadly machines. They passed in swarms over the heads of the four friends and their identical images and sprayed the horrible thick, sticky liquid over the whole area. It was as if the heavens had opened and a storm had broken out with thick honey falling instead of rain!

Jurka realised in awe that the thick drops of liquid were sticking like leeches to their bodies and their outfits, making their movements almost impossible. Worst of all, when the sticky drops fell on their heads, they covered their eyes and restricted their vision. Neither the defence mechanism, nor their identical copies, nor the use of herbicide, was working. The situation was hopeless...

"Master Hahanoff, what are we going to do?" Jurka cried out in despair as he saw his friends collapsing beneath the weight of the constant shots of the horrible, thick, sticky liquid. He, too, was beginning to stagger like a blind person and to trip over, losing his balance, unable to see properly and to assess the size of the catastrophe. Captain Lu-gi had also been immobilised and he resembled an insect that had suddenly been covered by a huge drop, trapped for eternity. Johara was fighting to escape from the shower of thick liquid which now covered most of her body, while big Milo was having incredible problems with his movements and his multispectral gun had been rendered useless.

Suddenly the Buzzles turned around and began to plan a new deployment. The bombardment with the thick liquid stopped. Jurka could not believe his eyes. He tried to move but, to his horror, discovered that he was trapped and unable to react. He looked around and saw that the others were in the same hopeless situation.

"Now what do we do?" he called out loudly but he received no answer.

"Jurka, look!" Milo's heart-rending cry made him look towards the orange groves. There, he saw the imposing black figures of self-propelling fighters.

"Master Hahanoff, what are those?"

"Those Hor-nets," echoed Lu-gi's voice. "Fighters Doctor Soc-rat," added the young Black Cloudian.

The three friends watched as the black fighters flew towards them, singing Doctor Soc-rat's military march:

"With two smacks on the behind
And two more on the back
We bring order to the place
The Master's whip we crack!
So all can see
Yes all can see
Who's the boss
In Spring Cit-y"

The terrible Hor-nets, Doctor Soc-rat's pride and joy, were coming to finish off the Buzzles' job. That was becoming all the more obvious...

"Master Hahanoff, we need help," repeated Jurka as Milo and Johara began chanting, like a premature requiem, the Hymn of the Brotherhood.

"O Lord Salvador, where are you now that we need you?" shouted Jurka who was now on his knees under the weight of the thick liquid that was pushing him downwards in a slow, torturing manner.

"Present and unshaven!"

Lord Salvador made his appearance among the trees. "Ahoy there, Jurka!" the wise lord called out.

Jurka uttered a cry of desperation: "At last, at last Lord Salvador. We're drowning..."

"Now don't upset my dinner, young man! I can see that you're drowning in that... in that... in honey! Still, it's fun. Who would have said that you'd have such a sweet death?" said the wise lord sarcastically. "Anyway, tell me what it is that you want from me?"

"What do I want? I want you to help us, that's what we all want!" Jurka shouted desperately, the liquid by now having immobilised him on the ground.

"But can't you see that I'm having dinner?" answered the lord of wisdom calmly.

Only then did they notice that he was seated at a large, well-laden table, with a white serviette at his neck, eating lobster and enjoying every mouthful as evidenced by his exclamations of satisfaction.

"Mmmm! Aaaah! Wow!" he said over and over as he devoured the choice dish.

"Lord Salvador, help us!" It was Johara's voice that made him interrupt his enjoyment of the lobster.

"Ah, little one, are you in danger too?" the wise lord asked in an innocent tone.

"There's me and Milo and Jurka and Lu-gi," echoed Johara's desperate cry. "Can't you see, my lord?"

Lord Salvador pretended to survey the scene. Then he stood up slowly and began to sing:

"Observing everything around
With my two sparkling eyes
I see in light, in darkness too
And everybody calls me wise..."

"Lord Salvador, we've had it!" came the heart-rending voice of Jurka Slavik. The young man was stretched out on the ground, weighed down by layers of thick syrup. Johara had almost disappeared beneath the mass of the unknown liquid, while Milo was on his knees, desperately trying not to fall over. Captain Lu-gi had disappeared under a small mountain of the honey-like substance. The Hor-nets had come into firing range and were preparing to pierce their four immobilised and neutralised targets with their razor-sharp noses, burying them for ever under the fatal, thick liquid.

Lord Salvador scratched his head.

"Hmm, we need to do something," said the wise lord.

He then rose, turned his back on them and stood to attention. Without saying a word he dropped his trousers, stuck out his naked, bony backside and started the fart concerto!

First a loud "brrrroom" was heard and the place was filled with an unbearable stink. Then he began to take tiny steps and each time he jumped to one side, his bottom let rip a series of farts: "Brrrrr.... brrrr....brrrr...."

The Hor-nets started to fall, as if struck by Death. Those that managed to get away beat an untidy retreat, flying in panic towards the orange groves to escape the awful volley of farts.

Lord Salvador turned his head and surveyed the battle scene. The ground was scattered with unconscious Hor-nets and Buzzles but his young friends were still trapped beneath the weight of the thick, sticky liquid.

Lord Salvador guffawed: "Hmm, you look like a really nice dessert to help digestion, that's what you are my young friends," he said teasingly as he pulled his trousers back on. "Master Hahanoff, I could swallow you in an mouthful," he murmured.

Then he closed his eyes, grimaced with his mouth and sneezed: "Atchoo!" His allergies were affecting him and he couldn't stop sneezing: "Atchoo... atchoo... atchoo..."

When he eventually stopped, he saw captain Lu-gi and the three friends of the Nectar Brotherhood standing and looking at him with obvious admiration and adoration. The wise lord, their mentor and protector, had again pulled off one of his miracles. The thick, fatal liquid had melted like wax every time the lord of wisdom sneezed until it had disappeared altogether.

The three friends recited in unison the Thanksgiving Ode to their saviour:

"We thank you great, heavenly father
All-knowing one of the visible and invisible,
Everywhere present and fulfilling everything,
O Lord Salvador of wisdom
Accept our gratitude..."

Jurka, Johara and Milo lowered their heads in a gesture of recognition and respect, while little Lu-gi watched the ritual, unmoving and unmoved as always. Lord Salvador performed somersaults to show his satisfaction. Then he disappeared.

CHAPTER 4

Doctor Soc-rat was furious with the hairdresser he had brought with him from planet Green Vegetables. The four-handed barber had made a mess of things by cutting the doctor's thick beard dangerously short and pointed so that it now stuck out slightly at the bottom, making him look like a bald goat.

"I'll cut off two of your hands, you idiot!" shouted the overlord of Black Cloud when he saw his face in the mirror. The symbol of his power and omnipotence, his only legacy from Fate, had been chopped dangerously short and he risked becoming the laughing stock of the galaxy, the courtiers and the Elders.

"Is that what you call a trim where you come from?" screamed the stubby Doctor Soc-rat and the barber from planet Green Vegetables vainly tried to assure him that it was the last word in fashion...

"Honestly, Doctor Soc-rat. Your beard is something else, time-honoured lord. This style will make you look even more imposing..." the barber from Green Vegetables tried to convince him. Doctor Soc-rat's anger finally dissipated when Kolo-Kol, his Chief Secretary, arrived for instructions and began complimenting the overlord, as usual: "What a wonderful trim... what a fine beard... That is remarkable..." Secretary Kolo-kol repeated.

"Very well, where are my invited guests? Where are the representatives of the interplanetary council? What's keeping them?"

The sullen Doctor Soc-rat changed the subject since the shadow of the dome on the Dark Palace indicated that time was getting on...

Kolo-kol skilfully placed a stool next to the throne and the stocky overlord stepped onto it, using it like a stair, and sat surveying everything on the highest level of the massive Conference Hall.

All around, holograms lined up ready to serve the noble guests. Everything was in place and Doctor Soc-rat knocked three times on the floor with his sceptre, giving the signal for the procession into the Dark Palace to begin.

First to take up their places, behind the throne, were the Mace-bearers, ready to observe the conference of the interplanetary directorate and to record each of its decisions on the data transmission devices in the Om-niscient's terminal archives. The screens on the huge circular dome on the roof of the Palace all came on at once and the portrait of the overlord filled them. The hall filled with the sound of the military march of Black Cloud's power-wielding class.

The Elders entered the Dark Palace in a procession and took up their positions on the presidium, to the right of Doctor Soc-rat.

The Commanders, led by Master Zar-ko followed; then Taka-mura's guards entered and, finally, came the group of state employees who monitored and registered the Cre-matum.

When they had all taken their places on the surrounding balconies and down in the stalls, the screens played the international theme music that announced the arrival of the foreign sovereigns of the galaxy. Creatures from every corner of space made their impressive appearance, taking their places in a semi-circle in the first row of the Upper Balconies. Then the music changed to a sweet melody and the Viv-andré came in, swaying provocatively to the music. The representatives of the interplanetary directorate broke into cheering and acclaim:

"Viv-andré, Viv-andré allez!
For a life of sunshine and making hay!"

Last to enter the Dark Palace were the observers from Earth: Tao Li, Nefeli and the members of the Tigers gang who sat behind Taka-mura's guards in the Lower Balconies.

Doctor Soc-rat stood up and played ostentatiously with his beard. All the guests rose to their feet. It was time for the Hymn to the Overlord. Doctor Soc-rat raised his sceptre and the international choir of holograms began to sing with musical accompaniment:

"Hail great doctor, Father Soc-rat
First Elder, Pride of the planet,
Bearer of the sceptre, guardian of the law
By everyone revered

Master of the immortal, yes the immortal,
Master of the immortal beard!
Hail, hail, hail!"

The doctor signalled to them to sit down and they all took up their seats once more. Chief Secretary Kolo-kol sat on a stool at Doctor Soc-rat's feet, while the Viv-andré hung around the throne of the stumpy leader, patting him flirtatiously on his bald head...

"First item on the agenda: Cre-matum production and commerce," announced Kolo-kol in his most official tone.

The Chief Secretary pressed a button on the panel in front of his seat and all the information was translated into the ears of the members of the interplanetary directorate:

"A problem arose with the Cre-matum production but the Cig-ants are working feverishly to correct it. It is absolutely essential that the production lines be reinforced by new workers from elsewhere in the galaxy if the two-winter plan is to be achieved. For this reason," the report concluded,"the Council of Elders proposes the granting of a licence to import labour from distant Earth in exchange for the export of limited amounts of the precious material..."

"Good!" Doctor Soc-rat decided, but there was tension in the Conference Hall. It was clear that there were objections and mumblings of dissent. The delegation from planet Brides asked to speak first.

"With all respect, Doctor Soc-rat," said their spokeswoman, "we submitted a request a long time ago for the market to be opened up to our subjects but no decision was reached. We demand priority. Our delegation cannot return empty-handed because then we'll have a problem, a serious problem..."

"Why? What problem? You'll be without reproduction units? That can be settled at once..." laughed Doctor Soc-rat scornfully and the Mace-bearers at once registered his decision: "The request from Brides is denied."

The spokeswoman from planet Brides persisted and was about to say something when a whistle from the doctor removed her chance to speak. The Bride sat down and the leader of planet Four Satellites addressed the gathering.

"Great doctor, master of the beard! We understand your decision to begin imports from distant Earth. However, I wish to point out that we Satellitians have a great advantage: We are your most loyal allies and we have kept the borders inviolable in the Mad Cow belt. It would be a great honour for us if you were to grant us the licence to export labour to Black Cloud. In exchange, we will give you control of the Satellite of the Winds. It's a fair exchange..." concluded the leader of planet Four Satellites,

"Hmm," murmured Doctor Soc-rat, stroking his beard. "Proposal accepted!" he decided, and the Mace-bearers immediately wrote it down.

Two or three other delegations from regions of the galaxy stood up to speak but Doctor Soc-rat took the wind out of their sails.

"Enough!" he shouted and imposed complete silence. He then asked Chief Secretary Kolo-kol to put the issue to a vote.

"All those in favour?" asked Kolo-kol and on the big screen appeared the numbers: 154 in favour.

"All those against?" Only the delegation from planet Brides insisted on its view. There were no abstentions so the matter was considered resolved. The Mace-bearers dutifully recorded the result.

"Very good! See how impeccably the procedures work?" said Doctor Soc-rat. "The majority decides and the minority follows. The legal system triumphant... Let's move on," he added and Kolo-kol announced the next item.

"Invaders from planet Earth have got through Black Cloud's security barrier and represent a direct threat to law and order on the planet. At the same time they are a threat to the interplanetary cooperation system and an immediate danger to the trade and exploitation of Cre-matum..."

A long-drawn-out "aaaaah!" was heard in the Conference Hall of the Dark Palace, as the delegates expressed their surprise. Chief Secretary Kolo-kol continued undaunted:

"There is credible information from the Om-niscient that none other than Lord Salvador himself is behind the Light conspiracy..."

A new, even more intense wave of concerned exclamations drowned out Kolo-kol's voice.

Lord Salvador himself? Was it possible? How did that happen? How did he get here? The delegates from all corners of the galaxy were worried...

Doctor Soc-rat abruptly cut off the announcer and, forcefully banging his sceptre on the floor, imposed silence.

"Quiet, you cowardly, spineless beings!" he shouted. The Conference Hall fell silent.

"That's better. The matter is receiving my personal care and attention. For this reason, there is no cause for concern..."

Doctor Soc-rat stood up from his throne. "By the power of my beard, I shall crush the enemy! I shall annihilate the trespassers! And I shall make jam of Lord Salvador of wisdom!"

The Presidium screen lit up with words: "Glory to the great Doctor Soc-rat!" and the Mace-bearers, guards and Elders cheered him to the rafters: "Doctor, hail! Doctor, hail! Doctor, hail!"

Doctor Soc-rat's address had given them courage and changed the atmosphere in the Conference Hall. Now, with morale boosted, a general sense of euphoria prevailed and Kolo-kol was obliged to restore order by dealing an acoustic blow to the delegates. Doctor Soc-rat had settled down on his throne and was enjoying every minute of his triumph. The Viv-andré had provided him with zi-van and the overlord, full of contentment, was slowly drinking the thick, black liquid.

When the celebrations had died down, the Chief Secretary, proceeded to complete his report about the raiders from Earth and their protector, Lord Salvador, without omitting to mention that Benazir's Spe-ranto guerrillas were collaborating with them...

"I will not hear of that...that... that disgraceful traitor!" Doctor Soc-rat screamed and at once Kolo-kol ordered a hologram to offer the overlord another shot of choice zi-van. The doctor knocked the intoxicating liquor back in a single gulp and gestured for silence. In the Conference Hall, total silence reigned once more. He then rose from his throne and waved his sceptre in the air.

"And now, dear conference delegates, I would like to announce that before the day is through, the invaders will be arrested and handed over to be judged by the interplanetary directorate, here in the Dark Palace," declared Doctor Soc-rat. "No-one takes me on, no-one!" he added in an imposing tone and everyone in the Conference Hall rose to their feet once more.

The Presidium screen was switched on again as new cheers and shouts of "hail" greeted the overlord's declaration and Kolo-kol vainly attempted to restore order.

Master Zar-ko, at a loss, looked at Taka-mura who shrugged his shoulders. He had no idea how and when the young raiders from Earth would be arrested. Who would carry out the mission? Who would arrest them and bring them to the Palace? Tao Li raised his hands. He knew nothing either...

Master Zar-ko was deep in thought. The personal guard of the overlord, the infamous Hor-nets, had failed so how would a new attempt to arrest them succeed? On the other hand, who could doubt Doctor Soc-rat and his personal assurances?

Master Zar-ko sank quietly into his chair. If the doctor was right, then everything would come to an end but, unfortunately, most probably without him. But here, the Three Star Commander, had reached a false conclusion…

"Master Zar-ko!" The voice of Doctor Soc-rat pierced him like a poisoned nail.

The Commander stood to attention: "At your command," he replied mechanically, while feeling the earth moving beneath his feet.

"Three Star Commander!" the overlord went on, "it has fallen to you to lead the detachment that will accompany the prisoners to the Conference Hall in the Dark Palace. Be prepared!"

"Always prepared!" replied Master Zar-ko and, relieved, settled into his chair. Kolo-kol announced a break and the delegates poured into the adjoining reception rooms of the Dark Palace. It was time for eating and drinking.

The Commander was in no mood for such things. He was thinking about what Doctor Soc-rat was up to when a hologram informed him that he should go at once to the private rooms of the Council of Elders. Still there were Tao Li, Taka-mura and a strange, two-headed being that was introduced as Sky-livdi from the distant planet Upside Down.

Chief Secretary Kolo-kol requested the attention of those present and Doctor Soc-rat entered the private rooms, swaying and bending and with tiny steps. They all greeted him with one voice: Hail Doctor!" and were given permission to sit. Chief Secretary Kolo-kol ordered the holograms to offer zi-van to everyone and called for silence. The overlord made himself comfortable on the divan and asked for their understanding. He would like to lie down for a while and take a nap. The faithful Chief Secretary would give them an analysis of the action plan that he had drawn up. Only then would they wake him and, if they had questions or queries, they would pose them. Everyone wished the overlord a dreamless sleep and turned their attention back to Kolo-kol.

Doctor Soc-rat's plan was a real work of genius. Since all previous attempts to arrest the invaders from Earth and their allies had failed – even the powerful Hor-nets – all that remained was the space-time trick.

“The what?” they all wondered and Kolo-kol explained to them that it was the last word in vigilance and law and order enforcement, seen during his recent trip to Upside Down. As representative of the planet, the esteemed being Sky-livdi, would coordinate and, as the highest lord’s envoy, supervise the whole operation.

What were they going to do? They would simply contact the group of raiders from Earth and attract their attention. That was all. The rest was a matter of technical handling by Sky-livdi. To implement the operational plans, they would use Tao Li and his men with Nefeli, as well as Taka-mura, under the supervision of Master Zar-ko. When the operation was over, the Three Star Commander would have the honour of accompanying the prisoners to the Dark Palace and placing them before the overlord and the representatives of the galaxy.

The being from Upside Down assured them that the trick was simple and flawless. Through visual contact – one head explained – the being would activate the covering hood system which would trap them within an invisible energy field. The second head added that, as a result, while they think that everything is taking place in the same space and time and they believe that they are fighting against Tao Li and the guards to free Nefeli, in reality the invisible energy field, on the orders of Sky-livdi, will transport them to another space-time dimension. Where? Where else? Straight to the Dark Palace before Doctor Soc-rat for the Grand Finale!

∽

The four young friends moved cautiously through the suburbs of Spring City. Everything was so beautiful that, for a moment, they thought they had left all danger behind.

Wrong! As they entered the first green park that they came to, captain Lu-gi stopped them. The youngster again sensed danger and the other three, who by now knew Lu-gi’s warning system inside out, immediately went on the alert. Johara was constantly on the lookout, thanks to her reconnaissance antenna, but saw nothing. Milo swung his multispectral gun right and left, covering his friends, while Jurka approached the little Black Cloudian.

“Well, captain Lu-gi? What do you see?”

The little captain did not reply. He kept his two arms high in the air as his lights blinked on and off continuously, but gave no reply.

"Strange...," murmured Jurka and Lu-gi confirmed it: "Yes, strange..."

But there was nothing strange – just Tao Li's voice echoing from afar.

"Jurka! Jurka Slavik, can you hear me?"

Jurka took a step backwards. His instinct told him that he should take care, but he pricked up his ears to confirm that what he was hearing had nothing to do with ghosts and nightmares.

Tao Li's voice came again, loud and clear: "Hey, clever dicks, can you hear me? Why don't you say something?"

Johara gestured to Jurka that they should first hide and then answer, if they wanted to. Tao Li was not a person to be trusted Milo agreed with her and pointed to a shallow ditch that crossed the garden, close to trees.

"Let's go," said Jurka and they ran to the place that Milo had shown them. Only little Lu-gi remained motionless.

"Let's go, captain Lu-gi!" shouted Jurka but he received no answer. Johara whispered that perhaps it was better that way since the youngster appeared to be in communication with his family. Perhaps he would find out more about the strange situation.

Tao Li's voice rang out again. This time he forced Jurka to pay him some attention.

"Hey, Jurka. Someone wants to talk to you..." shouted the leader of the Tigers and at once Nefeli's distant, heart-rending cry was heard:

"Jurka, help!"

The light-haired youth sprang up. "Did you hear that?" he asked his friends and Milo glanced across at Johara without saying a word. The black-haired girl was still as cold as ice.

"Oh come on, all this again, Jurka?" she said in a strict tone but the young man's attention was still focused on the direction of the voices.

"Jurka Slavik! Help me... Please, Jurka... Help!" came the sound of Nefeli's desperate voice.

Jurka jumped up from the ditch. "Where are you, Nefeli?" he called out as loud as he could. "Tell me where you are."

There followed a moment's silence which was broken by Tao Li's harsh tone.

"Over here. And if you've got the guts, come and get her, if you dare big boy, come on big boy!"

For once Jurka reacted calmly.

"We're not idiots, Tao Li, we're not idiots like you, man!" he answered in a steady voice. "If you're such a big man, you come out. Show your face. Come out with Nefeli. Just you and me!"

Tao Li's loud guffaw could be heard at the other side of the park. Then he appeared in the bushes, holding Nefeli by the hand. The pretty blonde looked awful, which made Jurka's heart beat faster.

"All right big boy? What will you do for this?" Tao Li asked sarcastically, as he dragged Nefeli along like a lamb to the slaughter. The blonde beauty groaned with pain and Jurka took a couple of steps forward.

"Jurka, no!" Lu-gi's bland tone stopped the young man from Earth who turned to him, bewildered. The Black Cloudian captain repeated his warning: "Jurka, no..." he said again and moved slowly to where Milo and Johara were standing.

Jurka stopped short, confused. Why was Lu-gi telling him no?

"Why, captain Lu-gi? Why shouldn't I go?" he shouted but the youngster could not enlighten him. "Don't know," he answered, adding, "Lu-gi say no"

Johara nudged Milo. "Get ready just in case. Something tells me that our friend's going to get himself into trouble again," she whispered. "Jurka, listen to reason this time! Don't go!" the young girl begged her friend.

"Can't you see, Johara? Don't you believe your eyes?"

"Jurka, it could be another trick. Remember what happened at the Lake of Youth..." pleaded the black-haired girl.

Jurka looked at Johara and then at his enemies. Tao Li had grabbed Nefeli by her blonde hair and was whirling her around like a maniac. "See bitch! See how much you-know-who loves you? Eh? He won't so much as move his little finger for you, the shit!" Tao Li shouted and Jurka was beside himself.

"All right, you bum! All right! Let the girl go and we'll work this thing out! Just the two of us..."

Neither Johara's pleas, nor Milo's objections nor even Lu-gi's warnings could stop Jurka.

On the other side of the park some of the Tigers and Taka-mura appeared, who seized Nefeli from Tao Li's hands as he began to walk alone towards Jurka. Johara and Milo jumped up and readied themselves. Only little Lu-gi did not show himself since, confident in what he had sensed, he preferred to retreat to a safe distance.

"How do you want to fight, big boy?" asked Tao Li sarcastically.

Jurka stopped. "Tell them to let Nefeli go. Otherwise, there's no fight," he said and Tao Li at once signalled to Taka-mura and the Tigers to do exactly as Jurka had asked.

Johara nudged Milo.

"I'll tell you why I'm scared, man. Tao Li looks changed... He seems very different to me, very civilised... Something's not right. Something's definitely not right," said the young girl.

Milo merely said, "Hmm, you may be right," and checked his multispectral gun once more.

Nefeli had been freed by Taka-mura and the others and was staggering away from them towards the side of the park. Jurka checked that she was all right and decided to take a few more steps forward. Tao Li did the same, provoking him: "So, baby face, how do you want to fight? With your fists or with one of these?" he shouted, revealing the iron bar that he had concealed in his clothing.

"Fists, stupid, fists!" answered Jurka who was boiling with rage.

The two duellists were within a short distance of each other, somewhere in the middle of the park. They began moving around as if each were measuring the strength of the other with his eyes.

"Lord Salvador of wisdom, give me the strength to beat this bum!" Jurka made his wish and threw himself upon his hated rival. The two wrestled themselves into a tight hold. Tao Li, the taller and bigger of the two, tried to turn Jurka over and throw him down to gain the advantage but the youngster clung on like a screw that wouldn't come loose. As a result they were both turning around as one body, neither able to throw the other...

And then the strangest thing happened!

As the two young fighters turned together, everything else began to whirl around too: the park, Nefeli, Taka-mura's guards, the Tigers, Johara and Milo. Everything! At first they seemed to be moving slowly, as if on a children's roundabout. But then the rotation grew faster until, as if possessed, they were all spinning around like tops until they had lost all sense of space and time...

Everything disappeared from sight and when they opened their eyes, they were suddenly on the ground in a large, enclosed space in which pandemonium reigned. A cacophony of noise, voices, whistles, hymns and cheers filled the place.

Jurka looked around and, in his dazed state, saw dozens of pairs of eyes fixed on them as if they were in the middle of a huge gladiatorial arena. Tao Li was not next to him but was posing, with a broad grin on his face, on the lower level of the huge hall, with the Tigers next to him and, next to them, Nefeli.

Milo managed to stand up and spoke first: "Well, man, I think we've done it again... Or am I mistaken?"

"No, Milo, you're no mistaken. Yet again we've been victims of Goldilocks over there," said Johara, pointing to Nefeli. Then she turned to Jurka. "Are you all right?" he asked and the young man nodded. "And Lu-gi? Where's captain Lu-gi?" wondered the girl, looking around for their comrade.

Lu-gi was not there. He had disappeared, as if the park had swallowed him up. The three friends stood up, leant on one another and, hand in hand, formed their familiar triangle.

"Where are we?" asked Jurka since he had now become aware that they were surrounded not by Black Cloudian guards but by creatures from all over the galaxy. The light-haired youth tried to activate his outfit's defence shield but in vain. Nothing worked, and Milo's multispectral gun had disappeared into thin air. Johara pointed upwards to the imposing dome that covered everything.

"I'll tell you where we are, Jurka. In Doctor Soc-rat's Dark Palace. And from what I can tell, we're not here as honoured guests," the girl added with a touch of irony.

In the middle of Black Cloud's large Conference Hall sat a stubby fellow with an enormous head and beard and the place was shaking from all the cheering.

"Hail Doctor! Hail the Master of the Beard! Hail, Doctor Soc-rat!" echoed around the hall and the three friends realised at once what was going on.

"Hmm, speak of the devil..." murmured Johara and nodded towards the stocky doctor. Around him, like a butterfly, flew the two-headed Viv-andré...

The overlord lifted his sceptre, imposed an immediate silence and gestured to Chief Secretary Kolo-kol to make the requisite announcements. Doctor Soc-rat's slimy collaborator took up a pose and began, parrot fashion, to speak in praise of the omnipotence of the overlord whom no-one dared take on. Whatever he promised he brought to fruition and there, before the interplanetary directorate, incapacitated and humiliated, were the invaders from Earth, the trespassers across the planet's borders. The magic power of Doctor Soc-rat had resolved the issue. Now it was time for punishment.

"Three Star Commander, you have the honour and the privilege to bring the three criminals before Doctor Soc-rat," announced Kolo-kol.

Master Zar-ko leapt up and strutted about like a cockerel: "At your command, great overlord!" He then ordered two guards to follow him as he marched with official steps to the centre of the large Conference Hall and the prisoners. The delegates broke into more cheering, making the hall more like a fight arena.

When he reached them he ordered sharply: "Follow me!" and the three friends of the Nectar Brotherhood, whether they wanted to or not, were obliged to march behind him.

Once lined up in front of the short doctor's throne, they saw a face that was enough to make them laugh. Even for a Black Cloudian, Doctor Soc-rat was a jarring note as his short, pointed beard made him look more like a goat than a normal inhabitant of the planet. The overlord looked at them with annoyance but he pretended not to realise what they were smiling about.

"By Vasi-vuzuk, I'm going to turn that barber into mincemeat!" he thought as the Viv-andré placed a glass of zi-van in his hand.

"Hmm, let's see what we have here..." the stubby doctor murmured with a studied air and Master Zar-ko at once gave his report: "These are the three invaders from Earth, Doctor Soc-rat," he began to explain but the overlord did not require explanations about such an obvious matter.

"Cut the crap, Commander! You think I don't know who's in front of me?" Doctor Soc-rat chastised him and the Three Star Commander was quick to answer: "You know everything, time-honoured master of the beard!"

The doctor paid him no attention and turned to the three youngsters.

"Come closer..." he ordered and leaned his bald head forward so as to examine them more closely. His deep-set, empty eyes fixed first on Milo, then they looked Johara up and down before finally turning to Jurka.

"Hold out your hands!" he ordered. "And now, open your palms."

The procedure was a familiar one and the three youngsters complied immediately.

"A-ha, so you are Jur-ka" he said to the light-haired youth. "And you Mi-lo... you Jo-hara... Right, what are you doing here?" asked the overlord of Black Cloud, more out of academic interest than anything else. They did not have time to open their mouths when Chief Secretary Kolo-kol began to read out the charges against them:

"The three young people are organs of the hated Lord Salvador and they planned the Light conspiracy with him... With his help they illegally entered the territory of the planet and formed an alliance with the local Spe-ranto fighters of the traitor Ben-azir in order to upset law and order... They were involved in vandalism in Square 12 of Sector B in Summer City... They acted, with the enemies of law and order, Ben-azir-s guerrillas, at the Pleasure Baths from where, after battles, they freed prisoners, thus interrupting the process of their moral rehabilitation... They violated the inaccessibility of the Lake of Youth. They attempted to prevent the production of Cre-matum, they entered Winter City, they attacked the Cig-ants and freed convicts... And, finally, they entered Spring City, where they put up armed resistance to an attempt to legally arrest them..."

The gallery was seething with rage and indignation. Wild jeering and whistles of disapproval followed the announcement of each charge. The delegation from Four Satellites in the Mad Cow belt bawled louder than the rest, demanding the immediate and exemplary punishment of the invaders. Their leader jumped up: "Great Doctor! Give us the pleasure of punishing the enemies of interplanetary security. It will be a great honour for us..."

"Sit down you fool!" Doctor Soc-rat cut him short. "I don't need anyone's help and they will certainly be punished on this planet since they have violated our borders and carried out their criminal activity on our territory," he added and that was the end of the matter.

With a gesture, he imposed silence on the Conference Hall and turned towards the three friends.

"Well, you ugly Earthlings, you have heard the charges. What do you have to say?" asked the stubby doctor. The Mace-bearers prepared to record the testimony of the three accused.

Jurka looked at the other two who nodded to him and he decided to speak first.

"Mr Soc-rat..." he began and Kolo-kol interrupted him at once.

"Doctor Soc-rat, doctor!" he clarified, stressing each word.

"Aaah!... Doctor, yes, of course, Doctor Soc-rat," Jurka Slavik repeated. "We are here to carry out a mission that has nothing at all to do with the actions of which you have accused us..." the young man began and looked around. He wanted to see what kind of a reaction his introduction had made but all he could make out was an icy silence. Jurka cleared his throat and continued to explain how they had decided to travel to Black Cloud because Tao Li and his gang, the Tigers, had abducted Nefeli…

"Errrr! Just a minute…" Doctor Soc-rat interrupted him. "You mean to tell me that you're here for an ugly girl from Earth?"

The overlord guffawed and Koko-kol gave the signal. The screen on the Presidium lit up and gave orders: "Ha, ha, ha!" The whole of the Conference Hall rocked with laughter and whistles. The Viv-andré was propelled up to the dome by the power of the laughter.

Jurka grew red with anger and looked at Milo and Johara. But they, too, were trying to stifle their laughter. Jurka could not stop himself: "OK, they're making fun of us, but what are you grinning for? Eh?"

Milo was holding his belly and could not say anything while Johara merely pointed to Doctor Soc-rat. The overlord of the planet had stood up on his throne and was spinning around like a wind-up toy, obviously laughing with all his might at his own joke. Next to him, waving like a reed in the wind, was the Viv-andré and his slimy Chief Secretary, and all around were the Elders of the Council, Master Zar-ko and his guards.

Jurka could no longer bear the sight of the ballet of the shaking creatures and he, too, burst into laughter. Now things grew even more hilarious. The more the Black Cloudians laughed, the more the three friends from Earth rolled around on the floor, creased up with laughter. And the more the Black Cloudians saw them, the more they split their sides.

It was Tao Li who provided a way out of the situation. With the arrogance that had always been his hallmark, he took a step forward and addressed Doctor Soc-rat: "Hey, Doctor!" he shouted. No-one paid him any attention and, having received no answer, he took another two steps forward: "Hey, Doctor Soc-rat, are we going to get some work done or are we going to spend all day giggling?" the impertinent youth called out.

The overlord stopped shaking and rocking.

"What did you say, young and mindless Tao Li?" he screeched.

The Conference Hall froze and Kolo-kol menacingly approached the leader of the Tigers. The great Tao Li, disconcerted, tried to mend the situation: "Well, I was saying that we should continue the trial… get it over with a bit earlier, Doctor Soc-rat… under your guidance, of course," he stammered but the stocky overlord was in no mood for such behaviour. He raised his left hand and clenched his four-fingered fist, blowing lightly in the direction of Tao Li. The young man was lifted into their air like a feather. Now he was the one to be awkwardly shaking his body in the void, vainly searching for something to hold on to. Doctor Soc-rat made a circular motion with his fist and Tao Li began to perform funny somersaults in the air. Before the shocked eyes of the members of the Nectar Brotherhood, the Conference Hall broke into cheering and applause. Doctor Soc-rat's show was a real treat...

The dumpy overlord opened his palm and Tao Li fell to the floor with a thud, like an empty sack.

"That, young man, was to teach you not to put your nose in other people's business. Next time, you request permission to speak before opening that disgusting mouth of yours," murmured Doctor Soc-rat before returning his attention to the three young prisoners.

"So, what were you saying?" he asked.

Jurka was not sure whether he should continue to explain to the overlord of Black Cloud what it was that had made them travel so far. He was afraid of being mocked once more and so he merely said that he had already told him the reason why they had come to the planet.

"Hmm, hmm..." murmured Doctor Soc-rat, stroking his beard. He then turned to the presidium of the Council of Elders: "What do you have to say, Elders?" he asked and they replied as one that they were not interested in internal differences on Earth. "Great master of the beard, these are matters that do not concern us," the senior Councillor said. "What counts for us is the confirmation of the charges," he added and the other Elders nodded their heads in approval.

"Correct," decided Doctor Soc-rat and the Mace-bearers dutifully registered the verdict and sent it to the archives of the Omniscient.

"So, confirm the charges," ordered Doctor Soc-rat and Kolokol clapped his hands twice. On the dome of the Dark Palace, an enormous screen immediately lit up and before the interplanetary directorate, as in a film, appeared scenes from what the Chief Secretary had announced earlier.

"Guilty! Guilty!" screamed the representatives of the planets and Doctor Soc-rat signalled to them to quieten down. "I am curious to see what they will say after all this evidence," the overlord announced. "Let's hear them before passing the required sentences," he added and turned to Jurka. "Well, young man, what can you say following confirmation of the charges?" he asked.

"Everything Jurka's said is true! We've got no differences with you. Ours are with them!"

Johara had managed to speak before her friend in answer to Doctor Soc-rat.

"The girl's right," added Milo. "The Nectar Brotherhood's quarrel is with the Tigers, not you... As for the battles, you started them, not us. We acted in self-defence," added the swarthy giant.

Jurka grew bolder and responded to Doctor Soc-rat: "You were the ones who provided asylum and formed an alliance with those bums. We don't want your Cre-matum or anything. We just want Nefeli!"

Kolo-kol signalled to the Viv-andré to offer the overlord a drink. He was very good at his job and he calculated that the young people's words would have annoyed Doctor Soc-rat. He would certainly be in need of something to refresh him and improve his mood.

"There you are, time-honoured lord, great master of the beard," said the slimy Chief Secretary in a servile tone and the Doctor swallowed the zi-van with pleasure.

"Tao Li, approach!" he ordered as soon as he had downed his drink and the leader of the Tigers shuffled toward shim. "How do you respond to the claims by your compatriots from Earth?" Doctor Soc-rat asked him.

"It's rubbish, great lord of the beard. Total rubbish, don't believe them," Tao Li replied at once. "They're just envious and they don't know what to do. The girl came with me of her own free will. Ask her..." Tao Li added, pointing to Nefeli.

The blonde beauty was sitting to one side, saying nothing at all. The familiar half smile formed on her lips and a shudder passed through Jurka. Johara looked with mistrust at the young woman who, seemingly carefree, was smelling a red rose, while Milo murmured that they were in for an interesting time...

Nefeli responded to Doctor Soc-rat's gesture and, swinging her hips coquettishly, approached her compatriots.

"Go on, babe, tell them!" Tao Li urged her but Nefeli said nothing. She merely turned to Jurka and shot him one of her captivating smiles. The light-haired youth felt himself melting with happiness and Johara grimaced: "Here we are again..." the black haired girl murmured and she turned her jet-black eyes away, looking elsewhere.

"Well, ugly Earth girl, we are hanging on your lips," said Doctor Soc-rat and signalled to her to speak. Nefeli turned towards the throne and curtsied: "My Lord, how is a girl to know if everything happened as Tao Li says or in the way Jurka has described it?" she asked with an innocent air.

"Or how I'm telling you!" added Doctor Soc-rat and he asked her straight: "What you are saying, ugly young woman, is that you cannot tell us if you were abducted by the Tigers or of you went with them voluntarily? How hard can it be to clarify this for us? Which of these ugly mugs from Earth is telling the truth?"

Nefeli did not reply at once. She turned first to Tao Li and looked at him as he, by his expression, urged her to speak. Then she turned to Jurka Slavik and smiled at him. Then, with a look that could kill, she addressed Doctor Soc-rat.

"Great doctor, master of the beard, I can say one thing…" Nefeli began in her divine voice. "I would like Jurka Slavik to be my friend," she said enigmatically and Doctor Soc-rat started to stroke his beard nervously. He was losing his composure and his patience. He considered that, irrespective of the tricks and bickering of the young people from Earth, the charges against the members of the Nectar Brotherhood had been proven and their sentence was a foregone conclusion. Why should they spend any more time on this story and the claims of abduction?

"Ugly, hairy Earth girl, can you tell us whether the claims about you being kidnapped are true or not?" asked the furious overlord.

Nefeli was not frightened by the doctor's expression. "Well, of course Jurka Slavik might have thought that I'd been kidnapped… I told you that, didn't I?" replied the young beauty calmly.

Doctor Soc-rat was beside himself. He rose from his throne and began to revolve, flying up and down, as high as the enormous dome of the Dark Palace. A deathly hush covered the entire Conference Hall as they all awaited his explosion.

And that was what happened! The stocky overlord of all the planets in the galaxy suddenly dived and landed in the midst of the Earthlings who were watching in silence.

When he waved his four-fingered hand, there was pandemonium! Thunder and lightning filled the hall as if the heavens had opened and all the fury of Vasi-vuzuk was being poured down on them. Everyone rushed to hide under their seats or anywhere they could find while the Elders stood up and began chanting the March in honour of Doctor Soc-rat:

"With two strokes on the backside
And three more on the back..."

Even this could not appease the raging, stubby overlord. On the contrary, that was precisely when the worst happened, just what the Elders, the guards and other Black Cloudians had feared: Doctor Soc-rat spun his sceptre high and, amid the thunder and lightning, began blowing furiously as the wind whirled. A hurricane took hold of everything and everyone, throwing them up into the void like toys. Only Doctor Soc-rat and his faithful Chief Secretary stood in the middle of the Conference Hall enjoying the spectacle until the stubby overlord decided that it was time for another thirst-quenching drink. His fist loosened and, as he flew back to his throne, people and creatures, seats and desks, all landed untidily on the ground.

"Ahh, that feels better..." mumbled Doctor Soc-rat as all the members of the interplanetary directorate landed bumpily in their places.

"It's a disgrace! What is this? A disgrace..." Jurka said to himself as the humiliated aliens, dazed and beaten, continued to chant in chorus the military march in honour of the overlord...

The members of the Nectar Brotherhood counted their injuries, as did Tao Li and his Tigers, while Nefeli, her hair wet and tousled, looked more like a wild animal than a dreamlike blonde fairy queen. Strangely, no-one had been hurt, as if an invisible net had been protecting them.

"What on earth...what was that, by Master Hahanoff?" said Milo over and over again, as his stomach was churning and he felt sick. Young Johara fixed her short hair with her hands while Jurka tried to regain his balance after the whirlwind.

When they looked around they could not help laughing. The Black Cloudian guards were staggering like drunks, while the Elders on the Presidium, unable to stand on their feet, lay all over the ground, quivering like carp. The unfortunate Master Zar-ko had lost his precious staff and was desperately searching for it amid the wrecked furniture, bending under the piled-up chairs and desks. Taka-mura was chasing him, trying to help his superior because he knew very well that his fury would eventually be vented on him. "Birds of a feather flock together" as the old saying went. So he needed to show solidarity at all costs, otherwise who could say what punishment awaited him...

The representatives of the other planets were worse off. With no prior knowledge about what happened whenever the overlord's anger burst forth, they were not prepared for being thrown around in hurricane conditions and they paid a high price. Some were still revolving at speed, some were bumping into others as they walked around, unsteady and crumpled, while the delegation from Four Satellites had given up altogether and were doing somersaults in the air like acrobats…

How could the members of the Nectar Brotherhood not forget their own pain?

"You may be laughing, young ugly mugs from Earth, but I'm going to make you cry!" came the echo of Doctor Soc-rat's voice. The three friends were forced to focus their attention of the stocky doctor.

"Shut up!" said the overlord, restoring order, and Chief Secretary Kolo-kol repeated it like an echo: "Shut up! All of you!"

Order was restored to the Conference Hall. It was decision time. Doctor Soc-rat called the Chief Secretary over and whispered something in his enormous crescent-shaped ear. The Mace-bearers stretched their necks and prepared to record the announcement of the sentences. Everyone was intently awaiting the doctor's decision.

"Earthly invaders, stupid transgressors of law and order on planet Black Cloud, be upstanding!" ordered Kolo-kol and the three friends looked at one another. "Be upstanding? How could they stand up if they weren't sitting?" they wondered.

Kolo-kol paid no attention and continued unfazed with the announcement of their conviction.

"The time-honoured great overlord, the only master of the beard, the one and only Doctor Soc-rat, has decided and orders the following: The three intruders from Earth – Jur-ka, Jo-hara and Mi-lo – will be exiled to the deserted planet Ya-ros where they will settle. They will be supervised by the Locusts and every two suns they will report to the headquarters of the Three Star Commander. The Council of Elders will deal with their case, if and when they show practical signs and provide a written statement of their remorse. I, the overlord, the great Doctor Soc-rat by this present…"

Kolo-kol was unable to continue reading out the verdict. A bang was heard in the Conference Hall and from the middle of the dome there suddenly appeared a small white cloud. The cloud proceeded in waves, painfully slowly, towards the centre of the Hall and hung, like a white curse, above their heads. A familiar voice echoed through the Dark Palace.

"Ahoy there, friends!"

"Oooooohhh" went the delegates, while Doctor Soc-rat cursed:

"By Me-gaera! Lord Salvador, by Vasi-vuzuk, it's Lord Salvador!" he exclaimed.

"Present and unshaven!" replied the wise lord, as he stepped out of the little white cloud and was welcomed with enthusiasm by the members of the Nectar Brotherhood.

"Ahoy there, Lord Salvador of wisdom!" Jurka shouted with all his might as Johara added with relief: "Oh, dear lord and protector, you can't imagine how glad we are to see you..."

Milo had turned red with excitement and he started shouting that now it was game on...

Kolo-kol cut short the announcement of the sentence and crept fearfully to the side of his protector, the overlord. The Viv-andré gathered its two heads and hid behind the throne. The Elders stretched their hands in front of their bald heads and began to chant prayers to deliver them from evil, while Master Zar-ko and Taka-mura, in a show of self-defence, immediately placed the guards on alert and started firing at the unwanted visitor. Lord Salvador whistled indifferently and the bullets, as if striking an invisible, impenetrable wall, ricocheted back to where they had come from, causing panic and disorder in the hall.

"Hold your fire, you idiots!" grunted Doctor Soc-rat and Master Zar-ko obeyed at once.

The shocked delegates of the interplanetary directorate looked on with fear and admiration at the famed lord since, despite all the rumours and stories that circulated about him, they had never had the privilege of seeing Lord Salvador in person.

The wise lord was dressed in a sailor suit and, having flown around over their heads, he stood still, like a monument, in the middle of the Conference Hall. He folded his arms across his chest and addressed the gathering from on high.

"Greetings, greetings to the elite of the planetary system! Hail, hail, Doctor of Darkness and appropriator of generations of Black Cloud since the time of the lost Third Sun. Hi to you all..." bantered Lord Salvador. Then he turned to Doctor Soc-rat: "So, shorty, great master of the ridiculous beard, aren't you going to offer me a drink after so many winters?"

"Get out of here! You want me to treat you to a drink? Stop insulting me, you false lord of false wisdom..." Doctor Soc-rat replied haughtily, under the jeers from the crowd. "Anyway, you're the one who's gone against the traditions of our planet. How can I give you a drink when you don't drink zi-van?"

"Listen goat-face, just give me a drink and I'll take care of the rest," Lord Salvador persisted.

A long-drawn-out "aaaaahhh" was heard from the Elders and the other Black Cloudians. How could the hated lord address the great master of the beard in such a disrespectful manner?

"Give it to him, golden-tongued lord!" shouted Milo enthusiastically, while Jurka was enjoying himself tremendously: "Yes!" the young man exclaimed and made a familiar gesture with his fist. Johara was smiling broadly and enjoying the spectacle in silence. Her beautiful big black eyes sparkled with joy and exultation.

Doctor Soc-rat signalled to the Viv-andré to offer the drink that the lord desired. The cup with the zi-van was placed in the wise lord's hands. He looked at it, sniffed and made a grimace of disgust. "Yecchhh, you call this turpentine a drink? You think you're clever, goatface? What shitty drink is this?" Lord Salvador wondered aloud and the Conference Hall again echoed with disapproving voices.

"Well now, false lord! You don't like our drink? Then you can drink our urine! Offer him some urine" shouted the furious overlord and everyone cheered: "Yes, yes! Urine, give him some urine...! Let him drink urine!"

Lord Salvador looked around at the crowd and answered simply:

"Very well, since you want some urine, you can have some of mine!"

Without saying another word, he unzipped his white trousers and began to spray everyone around the Conference Hall with his urine!

"Ooohhh" shouted the delegates who ran to protect themselves from the urine that was soaking them from above like acid rain.

The members of the Nectar Brotherhood were jumping up and down in their enthusiasm and Milo was heartily enjoying himself. "Wow! What a scene! Pee-spray from the air!" he kept saying while Jurka and Johara had joined hands and were encouraging Lord Salvador by shouting rhythmically "Encore! Encore!"

Doctor Soc-rat grew as red as a pepper with anger and shame. "Stop it you mad lord. Cut the crap!" he shouted as he ducked beneath his throne to protect himself from the unwanted rain shower.

"All right! Now have we shown who's boss around here?" shouted Lord Salvador and he zipped up his trousers.

Doctor Soc-rat returned to his throne and imposed silence. "What do you mean? Who's boss around here?" he asked.

"Just a minute, give me a minute to replace my lost fluid... And I'll tell you..." replied the wise lord who continued to hover in the air above their heads. With a theatrical gesture of his hand, he brought the cup of zi-van in front of his nose. Then he sniffed it gently and the cup miraculously filled with a foaming liquid.

"Cheers, idiots! So, hail to you, doctor of darkness!" he said and downed the cup in one. "Ah, if only we had some more champagne Milo, what do you say?" murmured the wise lord and a thunderous belch echoed around the hall. "Ooops, pardon me," said Lord Salvador, looking around apologetically.

Doctor Soc-rat paid no attention and hurried to repeat his question: "What do you mean, false lord of false wisdom? Who do you think is boss around here?"

The overlord did not wait for an answer. His anger had reached its peak and, naturally, he was not ready to accept a public humiliation from his spineless enemy, the hated Lord Salvador. He needed to regain his reputation and his authority. What would all the representatives of the interplanetary directorate say if he did not? An outlet from the questions was provided by the Viv-andré. The two-headed being approached Doctor Soc-rat and, in his ear, whispered the magic formula for dealing with the eternal hated enemy:

"Poppy, great doctor! The ring of the poppy!"

At the same time the lips of the Viv-andré, first one and then the other, blew into the empty wide open mouth of the overlord and retired...

Doctor Soc-rat had a glow in his deep-set empty eyes. With his four fingers he stroked his precious beard and focused on his hated enemy. Two red beams of light fell on the body of the wise lord, making him tremble like a leaf in the wind. Having shaken him enough, he delivered the final blow: From Doctor Soc-rat's wide open mouth began to emerge successive circles of gas, like smoke rings, which encircled the tormented, thin body of the lord of wisdom who was unable to react, imprisoning him in a suffocating ring. Lord

Salvador looked distant, as if drugged… Doctor Soc-rat, with a nod of his bald head, landed Lord Salvador on the floor.

After this, the overlord raised his sceptre and slowly turned it towards the dome. Lord Salvador was taken up from the floor like a balloon and he began to rise and rise, slowly and painfully, incapable of reacting, towards the dome of the Dark Palace.

The Conference Hall rocked with cheers and celebrations. Everyone stood up and started to sing the Hymn to the Overlord:

"Hail great doctor, Father Soc-rat
First Elder, Pride of the planet …"

The three friends of the Nectar Brotherhood watched the sad scene in astonishment, unable to believe their eyes. Was it possible that the wise lord could ever be beaten? Was it possible that he could be humiliated in such a crushing manner?

Jurka was in tears, Johara sobbed and Milo was crying too. They wanted to do something, to help their mentor and protector to escape from this awful situation but, unfortunately, they were powerless. Lord Salvador was heading slowly and painfully for the dome, from where Doctor Soc-rat would throw him into hellfire.

"Hail doctor! Hail doctor!" the delegates shouted in chorus, on the orders of Kolo-kol, while the overlord settled down on his throne and watched the hated lord fly in circles towards the exit. The Vivandré was flirtatiously flying around the throne.

"By Master Hahanoff, do something lord of wisdom!" begged Jurka in a whining voice as he looked the Brotherhood's protector in the eye. Lord Salvador appeared to be lost in the void but when his gaze met Jurka's, he winked at him.

"By Master Hanahoff, the Lord is playing tricks!" exclaimed the young man.

"What? What's that, Jurka?" shouted Johara, while Milo turned in surprise in the direction of his light-haired friend: "Say that again, man, say it again…" murmured the dark-skinned giant and Jurka pointed to the roof: "I said he's playing tricks!" the young man repeated. "Look at him!" he called to his friends, pointing to Lord Salvador.

The wise lord suddenly stopped spinning and appeared to regain his drugged senses. He hung hovering in the air for a while, then his eyes lit up and he fixed them like a blade on the Conference Hall throne and Doctor Soc-rat.

"Coming to get you, shorty, watch out!" shouted the wise lord and he took up a horizontal position in the air. As he was still bound by the smoke rings, he resembled a living torpedo, ready to shoot off towards its target.

Doctor Soc-rat was at a loss. He tried again to perform his magic but neither the nods from his enormous bald head, nor the puffs of smoke, nor the desperate movements of his four-fingered hands and his sceptre had any result. Lord Salvador began to whistle, like a shell, as he began his descent towards the Conference Hall and Doctor Soc-rat ran for cover behind Chief Secretary Kolo-kol who was trembling like a bird, in search of protection. The Viv-andré flew around the throne like a headless satellite, while on the Presidium, the Elders exorcised the evil with psalms. Master Zar-ko resorted to his favourite method of trying to shoot the flying lord but the bullets ricocheted loudly off the walls around without striking their target. Taka-mura and the guards tried to provide cover for Doctor Soc-rat while Tao Li seized the chance to grab Nefeli and hide behind the Elders' desks, ready to make a run for it at the first opportunity. As for the representatives of the interplanetary directorate, they watched dumbfounded as the dramatic events unfolded…

Lord Salvador swooped down like an eagle and seized the throne by the legs, raising it high into the air. Then he began to play with it, kicking it up and down with the tips of his toes until he smashed it to pieces with a single head butt. Immediately afterwards he freed himself from the smoke rings, straightened his crumpled blue striped sailor's vest and landed, rocking and swaying, next to the crouching Doctor Soc-rat.

"You never learn, shorty," he teased. "You never learnt not to count your chickens before they're hatched, did you?" added the wise lord as he jumped about in front of the humiliated and unspeaking overlord. The three friends of the Nectar Brotherhood ran to him, ready to offer whatever assistance they could.

"A mandolin, kids, bring me a mandolin!" ordered the lord of wisdom and without waiting for his bidding to be done, he suddenly had the musical instrument in his hand. A sweet melody filled the Conference Hall and Lord Salvador's voice drowned every other sound:

"My name is Salvador
I am a lord with shining eyes
All day long I drink and drink
And still they call me wise!"

The three friends of the Nectar brotherhood took up the refrain and sang their hearts out on the chorus:

"Oh yes, you're wise, you're wise
In fact you're second to none
You guard the Good, You punish Bad
You're Hahanoff's chosen one
You're loved by rich and poor
You're the omnipotent Salvador!"

The Dark Palace was suddenly transformed into one huge, cheerful music hall, where the dancing and singing of Lord Salvador and the friends of the Nectar Brotherhood replaced the insubstantial and soft performance of the interplanetary directorate. The spectacle was pleasing, so pleasing that the representatives of planet Brides began to sing along with the choir of the wise lord and his friends from Earth. The Brides danced and sang, heartily enjoying the spectacle while the clumsy four-handed barber from planet Green Vegetables imitated then before trying out dance sequences to the melody. The Brides and the barber continued to sing along with the others on the Ballad of Lord Salvador:

"My name is Salvador
A famous lord am I
All day long I eat and shag
And still they call me wise!"

Doctor Soc-rat was beside himself with fury.

"You'll pay for this, you traitors. Yes, traitors! By Vasi-vuzuk, I'll have you all exiled! Yes, exiled to Ya-ros with this lot..." screamed the stocky doctor with the silly pointed beard.

Lord Salvador and his friends paid him no attention. The Black Cloudian officers, the Elders, the guards and the Mace-bearers, stood awkwardly by, as if they had been stricken by thunderbolts, watching the spectacle and waiting for Doctor Soc-rat to get them out of the present impasse. What would the omnipotent overlord do? How would he react to this major act of sacrilege? How would he maintain his own authority and that of everyone else?

The stubby doctor stopped short and called Kolo-kol to him. He whispered something in his ear and the Chief Secretary took up a suitable pose and announced in a thunderous voice:

"In the name of the overlord, the great master of the beard, the one and only Doctor Soc-rat, I call a truce!"

Lord Salvador and his friends paid no heed and carried on singing and dancing.

"Attention, attention! In the name of Doctor Soc-rat, desist! I declare a truce!" repeated Kolo-kol.

This time Lord Salvador stopped the performance.

"On what terms?" he asked, at the same time playing a pretty tune on his mandolin.

"No terms!" replied the Chief Secretary and stepped aside. Onto the stage stepped the crumpled Doctor Soc-rat. He looked around to make sure that he still enjoyed the respect of the members of the interplanetary directorate and ordered the Mace-bearers to switch off the Om-niscient's minute recording devices. "What we say, false lord of false wisdom, will stay between us..." the overlord began but the wise lord interrupted him: "No deal, shorty," he replied. "Everything will be recorded with total transparency. That's how we work in our galaxy, isn't that right, kids?"

"Yes, absolutely," Jurka hurried to confirm. "Anyway, what kind of a truce is it without archives and protocols?" added the young man from Earth.

The Conference Hall was humming: "Minutes, we want minutes!" shouted the delegates of the interplanetary directorate who wanted to be a part of the game.

The overlord of Black Cloud and the planets scratched his bald head and stroked his beard: "Hmm, hmm, very well. Let's keep minutes of what's said," he said and the Mace-bearers immediately activated their machines. The Om-niscient would register everything for the sake of history.

"Now you're talking. Now we can play..." murmured Lord Salvador.

"Very well, then let us proceed," said the stocky, bearded overlord and he called the Elders of the Council and Master Zar-ko to him. "This is my delegation," he said.

"A-ha! Good... One moment while I gather my people together," replied Lord Salvador and he signalled to the members of the Nectar Brotherhood to stand near him. "And now, shorty, we have a surprise for you," he went on. "Since you have your guards with you, we are forced to expand our delegation," he said and turned to the small white cloud that was still hovering high above, near the dome of the Dark Palace.

"Spe-ranto, come out!" ordered the wise lord and from the soft walls of the craft appeared the gallant leader Ben-azir. She was followed by Ti-hon, Ma-ru and captain Lu-gi.

"This is my delegation for the negotiations," he announced to Doctor Soc-rat.

The Conference Hall buzzed with sounds of the representatives' exclamations. How was it possible to negotiate with Ben-azir's fighters?

"Oohhh! This is unacceptable! Remove them at once!" roared Doctor Soc-rat, only to receive an immediate reply from Lord Salvador: "The make-up of our delegation is not negotiable, shorty," he said dryly and the overlord swallowed his tongue.

Ben-azir flew ostentatiously to the centre of the Conference Hall, where her allies stood. The other fighters followed, beneath the gaze of the astonished delegates. Captain Lu-gi went straight to his three friends from Earth and climbed onto the shoulders of Milo who could not have looked more sweet...

"Hail, powerful shorty, master of the ridiculous beard..." said Ben-azir sarcastically. "Aren't you pleased to see me again?" she added.

Doctor Soc-rat was going mad. All he could do was stare stupidly at the leader of the Spe-ranto guerrillas as she stood before him, imposing and provocative, waving the green shawl with the Third Sun, the emblem of the Spe-ranto organisation.

The Elders of the Council hurried to find a way out of the situation. "Let bygones be bygones. Now we have another problem to resolve..." they said and turned to Lord Salvador. "Well, lord, what do you propose?" they asked.

Doctor Soc-rat looked at Ben-azir out of the corner of one empty eye. He waited for her reaction but it was the wise lord who spoke.

"Everything in its own time, Elders. Everything in its own time... First we have to clear up the matter of my friends here," he replied and pointed to the members of the Nectar Brotherhood.

"Their sentence is invalid because it is false!" stressed Lord Salvador to provoke protests from Doctor Soc-rat.

"Invalid? How come? Everything was proven with visual evidence, how can it be invalid?" roared Doctor Soc-rat, possessed of such rage and indignation that he did somersaults in the air to vent his anger.

"The visual picture is evidence that says nothing," replied Lord Salvador coldly. "You were fighting them from the first moment that they came peacefully to your planet. You set the Locusts against them, you removed the Plasticanopy from the time closet, you hunted them down constantly. You never asked why they had undertaken such a long journey from Earth to Black Cloud... Is this justice?" asked Lord Salvador.

This was too much for the stubby doctor. He coughed embarrassedly and Kolo-kol went near him, patting him gently on the back. "Get well soon, o great master of the beard!" the slimy Chief Secretary wished him and helped him to sit on a new throne that holograms had brought there. The two-headed Viv-andré at once offered him some zi-van.

"Drink up, great doctor, drink up, it will do you good," the two heads urged him.

"I don't need a drink, I'm OK," Doctor Soc-rat answered. Then he turned to Lord Salvador, banging his sceptre on the floor. "This is nonsense, do you hear, false lord? Nonsense!" he shouted angrily. "As if we're not allowed to protect our sovereign rights from foreign imposition..."

"And the Cre-matum, and the Cre-matum," rumbled the Elders on the Presidium.

"Yes, that's right, the Cre-matum. What were your friends from earth doing in Winter City? Eh? What were they after at the Lake of Youth? What business did they have in Spring City?"

Doctor Soc-rat was on a roll and he didn't look like stopping until he was cut short by Nefeli's voice.

"Me!" said the blonde beauty loudly.

The Conference Hall froze. All eyes focused on the girl from Earth who had had the audacity to interrupt the great master of the beard, the time-honoured Doctor Soc-rat.

"Bingo!" shouted Lord Salvador. "Well, short master of the pointed beard? What have you got to say?" he asked and performed a somersault. "Speak!"

Doctor Soc-rat's voice was choking with anger and indignation about the desecration of the sacred place by the ugly, hairy Earth girl and, instead of replying, began to emit sparks from his mouth. Kolo-kol ordered that he be given zi-van at once. This time Doctor Soc-rat drank it in a single gulp. Only then was he able to speak.

"Tao Li, come here!" he ordered the young man from Earth. "Tell us, is it true what the ugly young woman is saying?" the stubby doctor asked the leader of the Tigers. "Tell us, is it true or false what's being said about her abduction?" he repeated.

Tao Li took a step forward and, with an air of great authority, replied: "It's all lies, great doctor. She's lying. She came with us willingly. And anyway," the leader of the Tigers added sarcastically, "what would she want with the kid, eh?"

Jurka blushed with anger but Milo restrained him: "Cool it, man, cool it. Leave the wise lord to his game," he whispered. Johara lowered her head and avoided looking at her friends. She didn't want them to see how much she had been affected by what had been said...

"You see, false lord of false wisdom? You see what the truth is? Not all these big words..." said Doctor Soc-rat provocatively.

"Big words or not, Nefeli spoke quite clearly. It's your boy who's spouting lies," replied Lord Salvador, immediately causing a noisy reaction from the members of the Black Cloudian delegation.

The senior Elder of the Council took the floor. "Listen, this quarrel isn't getting us anywhere," he said in a calm voice. Then he turned to the two rowing leaders. "Why don't we resolve the difference in the old-fashioned, traditional way?" he proposed.

"How?" exclaimed the members of the interplanetary directorate who, thus far, had been following the discussions as outsiders. It was the first time that they had heard anything about an old-fashioned, traditional way of resolving disputes.

An equally bewildered Jurka turned to Lord Salvador who gestured to him not to worry.

"Let's see what they have to say first and then we'll see," he told him.

Milo asked captain Lu-gi what they were talking about but he too raised his hands apologetically. He had no idea what they meant. Only Johara looked upset. Her instinct told her that something bad was about to happen, and the girl with the short black hair was not mistaken.

Doctor Soc-rat imposed silence. Then he announced in an official tone the plan to resolve the issue.

"A duel to the death!"

The Conference Hall froze once more. The representatives of the planets tried to digest Doctor Soc-rat's laconic announcement when the Elders of the Council broke out in cheers: "Yes! Yes! A duel here and now!" they chanted rhythmically and the guards and the Mace-bearers followed suit.

A wave of cries broke out in the Conference Hall as all the representatives chanted the same slogan: "A duel here and now!"

Doctor Soc-rat turned to Lord Salvador's delegation.

"Well, false lord, what do you have to say?" he asked, posing haughtily on his new throne as he awaited a reply. If Lord Salvador accepted, everything would go as planned. If he refused, he would be humiliated in front of everyone...

The wise lord made a sign with his hands, asking for time out. Then he gathered the members of his delegation together.

"We've had it, guys," he told them. "A challenge to a duel is a matter of honour and we can't refuse it..."

"But who will fight whom, lord of wisdom?" asked Milo, who wanted to show that he was ready and willing.

"He'll most likely want us," said Ben-azir, but Lord Salvador shook his head. "No, Ben-azir. It's not your turn yet. The duel concerns our friends from Earth. After all, this whole row has been about them..." the wise lord remarked and addressed the members of the Nectar Brotherhood.

"So, who's going to be our fighter?" he asked.

"I am!" came the single reply from all three voices.

Jurka, Johara and Milo were all offering to fight the duel.

"Aaaah! Don't give me a headache now, kids!" said Lord Salvador. "We need one, not three," he added.

"I'll fight, that's it!" declared Milo.

"Anyway, I'm the most suitable, right?"

"No way! I'm going to fight the duel. I'm the most nimble on my feet and that's an advantage, isn't it?" said Johara but Jurka cut her short.

"Kiddo, stay where you are. I'm going to fight the duel because I'm entitled to. It was me who got you mixed up in this business, so let me at least get you out of it," said Jurka coldly. "Anyway, isn't all this fuss over me and Nefeli?," asked the light-haired youth. He received no answer It was obvious that he had the advantage.

"All right, the matter's fixed..." Lord Salvador summed up the situation. "We've found our fighter. Now we need to see what kind of a duel it is," he added enigmatically and turned to the throne.

"Doctor of the ridiculous beard, we accept. Jurka Slavik will duel for the Nectar Brotherhood. Who will be his opponent?" the wise lord was curious to know.

Doctor Soc-rat laughed heartily and his body rocked to a fro on the throne. Next to him Kolo-kol was spinning around while the Viv-andré swayed around in the air, light as a feather.

"Fine, fine!" Doctor Soc-rat managed to say as soon as he had stifled his laughter. "Our fighter is Tao Li, who else?" he announced contentedly and the leader of the Tigers at once shouted out "Hail doctor!" Then he turned to Jurka Slavik: "Get ready to lose one more time, scum!" he exclaimed.

"Dream on, you bum, dream on!" shouted Milo who couldn't stand the provocation. Instead of responding, Tao Li guffawed sarcastically and all the members of the Tigers gang laughed with him. It was crystal clear that the slim and stronger Tao Li would make mincemeat of the light-haired youngster...

Johara sat down, silent and sad. Once again Jurka Slavik had been blinded by his passion for Nefeli, again he was risking everything for her, and he didn't deserve it, the short-haired girl thought and her big black eyes filled with tears from the pain.

Doctor Soc-rat banged his sceptre on the floor three times. "Let the duellists draw near!" he ordered and the two young men from Earth approached the throne. "Elders of the Council, make the draw for the type of duel!" ordered the bearded doctor.

The Elders stood up and on the screen behind the presidium there appeared a series of strange shapes. Each one represented a particular type of duel. The Councillors called Kolo-kol to them and told him to press the button for the draw. The Chief Secretary obeyed and the strange shapes began to flash on and off in a feast of colours and sounds. Not a word could be heard in the Conference Hall as the excitement built up to a climax. What would the draw throw up? Which shape would remain illuminated?

When the piercing, brief sound of the siren sounded, all the lights went out except for one. Kolo-kol pointed with his four fingers to the shape that was still lit up.

"Shark hunt!" he announced in his official voice and the Mace-bearers duly recorded the chance decision.

Lord Salvador turned to Jurka: "My young friend, at least you won't have to put up with being punched," he said in a soft voice. "Now, the only thing to be scared of is being swallowed by the shark," he added, causing Johara to burst into tears. Milo consoled her, saying that Jurka was clever enough to deal with Tao Li and the shark, while the light-haired youth received the news of the draw calmly.

Ben-azir approached Jurka and wished him good luck. So did Ti-hon and Ma-ru, while captain Lu-gi whispered in his ear: "You know, swim?"

Jurka smiled and thanked his Black Cloudian friends before turning to the members of the Nectar Brotherhood.

"Why the long faces, guys?" he asked them. "Don't worry, if I've got you with me, plus the wise lord, everything will be fine... Isn't that right, Lord Salvador of wisdom?"

The wise lord looked Jurka in the eye and the young man felt as if he had been hypnotised.

"Jurka Slavik, you have my blessing. May Master Hahanoff be with you..." Lord Salvador said and then told him in a whisper: "Jurka, remember the White Cloud!"

Their conversation was interrupted by the voice of Doctor Soc-rat.

"Chief Secretary Kolo-kol, announce the rules of the duel," the short, bearded overlord ordered and the Chief Secretary struck a pose: "The two duellists will fight against the sea monster in the Sea of Serenity. Their aim is to destroy the shark and to return safely to the Dark Palace. Whoever fails will be eaten by the beast. If it swallows both fighters, the result will be a draw. The personal amphibious craft will be of their own choice and may be equipped with any type of weapons system," added Kolo-kol. He paused slightly and added:

"All bets to the presidium, please!"

Pandemonium followed.

The representatives of the interplanetary directorate ran like madmen to place their bets in the hope of winning one or two Cre-matum in exchange for the offer of voluntary service in the farthest outposts of the galaxy. The odds on Tao Li were not attractive since he was the favourite – they were two suns and a winter's work to one Cre-matum – while for Jurka Slavik they were much better – one sun's work to two Cre-matum.

The Elders took the bets and the Mace-bearers entered them onto the computer. Doctor Soc-rat was rubbing his four-fingered hands with satisfaction as he saw that he would be killing not one but several birds with one stone. The Viv-andré bet his small change, since its bet counted as two, while slimy Kolo-kol managed to persuade the Captain of the guard, Taka-mura, to bet for him too in exchange for a promotion to One Star Commander. Master Zar-ko did not bet at all since he considered that winning Cre-matum was of no concern to him. After all, he had his own amount stashed away while, with a promotion, he would lead a charmed life. So why take a risk for nothing? The Brides, somewhat paradoxically, all bet on Jurka Slavik, as did the barber from planet Green Vegetables who had nothing to lose since Doctor Soc-rat had mobilised him and took him on all his travels, keeping him far away from his homeland and the pleasures of life.

Master Zar-ko received orders to accompany Tao Li to his amphibious craft. It was a small, versatile, Black Cloud all-weather model, armed with the last word in interplanetary technology. Milo, with little Lu-gi on his back, led Jurka to the little white cloud which was a mini replica of the White Cloud spaceship. The two duellists took their places in their all-weather craft, Doctor Soc-rat imposed silence and raised his sceptre in the air.

"Let it become a sea!" he said and the dome of the Dark Palace filled with enraged waves from the Sea of Serenity.

"Duellists, in position...Go!" the stubby overlord ordered the two duelling pilots and the Conference Hall shook once more with the shouts and cheers as the two craft dived into the stormy sea.

Milo was biting his nails with worry as he tried to see the first pictures of the virtual duel with the terrible shark, while Johara looked on, helpless and teary-eyed. The Spe-ranto fighters formed a small circle and prayed to the vision of Grace to protect their young friend from Earth, Jur-ka. Only Lord Salvador appeared to be indifferent to what was happening – he was squatting on the floor cracking walnuts that he ate after each sip of zi-van, which he looked to be enjoying.

ေ

The deep blue colour of the stormy waters of the Sea of Serenity made it hard to see properly. From its depths rose entire forests of seaweed which prevented the smooth sailing of the amphibious craft and even threatened to ensnare and immobilise them. Deep underwater caves and rocky ravines made up the natural environment of the Sea of Serenity, from which at any moment the terrible, deadly shark might swim out and swallow them up...

Jurka Slavik switched on the craft's all-weather lights on all sides and activated its external protective shield. All the weapons systems were on standby. Tao Li sailed higher than Jurka, which gave him the advantage of being able to monitor not only the area around him but also his opponent's moves. And there was a further advantage: when the dreaded shark attacked the mini White Cloud, the malicious Tao Li would be able to lend a hand to ensure that his enemy was annihilated that much faster...

The monster made its introductions in the inhospitable waters of the Sea of Serenity in grand style. With a roar it warned of its presence, causing submarine vibrations. The stormy waters smashed mercilessly against the two craft, causing them to shake as if they were flimsy nutshells and to crash right and left against the walls of the undersea caves.

Jurka was first to see the two shining beams emerging from behind the rock at the side of the cave's entrance. Then he noticed the light growing stronger and when the huge head of the monster appeared at the cave's opening, he was completely blinded.

"Reverse, top speed!" Jurka ordered and the white cloud swiftly moved backwards.

It was too late... The shark managed to attack the small craft with its sharp, pointed nose and, having pierced it, hurled it away to float uncontrolled and to crash against the rocks. The beast made a circular turn, roared and shook its tail. Tao Li's black craft, which was sailing higher up, was thrust upwards to the surface of the sea like an empty shell. It flew up into the air like a balloon and dived back down with a noisy splash into the waters of the Sea of Serenity.

Tao Li seized the control lever and steadied his ship. The shark was swimming in the water below, ready to strike another blow against his kingdom's invaders.

Jurka's white craft was going backwards and forwards like a ping-pong ball from rock to rock and when his systems finally managed to stop it, the amphibious craft found itself trapped between the rocks. The computer made an automatic report on the damage: "Crack right side, stern... Complete destruction of defensive weapons systems ... Loss of power 30%..."

Jurka Slavik swore through his teeth: "Damn it!"

"Panoramic visuals – now!" the young man ordered and everything seemed to be in perfect working order. "Thank goodness," murmured the young man... However, his thanks turned out to be no more than a turn of phrase because he just had time to see the monster which had located him and was heading, like a torpedo, straight for the white craft.

"Soundshield – now!" he shouted and all around the small craft invisible sound-carrying waves began to leave the craft like breakers. The shark collided with force against them and, with a roar, found itself being turned upside down in the water. It circled once and stopped, motionless, opposite the white craft. Its eyes shone brightly as they fixed themselves on their target. It opened its huge mouth and a thick, greenish-yellow fluid began to spew from between its pointed teeth.

"Oh Master Hahanoff, it's sound dissolvent!" shouted Jurka and at once gave the order for smoke bombs to be fired. The area around the white craft turned as black as pitch and only the two phosphorescent beams of light from the monster's eyes penetrated the darkness. Jurka Slavik realised that it was time for him to make his getaway, shooting as he did so.

"Fire and motion!" he ordered and the white craft's weapons systems began to fire whatever was left in their arsenals. At the same time, the small amphibious craft headed upwards since that was the only way of escape from the tight embrace of the rocks.

Jurka looked behind and was relieved to see the monster palpitating under the continuous fire from his weapons. Now was the moment for a decisive counter-attack, he thought, but he had no chance to do anything. A bang was heard and his craft was rocked to its foundations.

"Oops, sorry kid, my mistake..." the voice of Tao Li boomed through the sound system. Jurka gritted his teeth so as not to swear. As if the monster wasn't enough, he now had Tao Li's craft crashing into him, supposedly by mistake...

The leader of the Tigers laughed loudly in his familiar arrogant manner and turned his attention to the wounded monster.

"Now I'm going to show you, you filthy beast!" Tao Li shouted and armed his torpedoes with knockout liquid. "Right, eat this!" he screamed as he pulled the trigger. Two trenches were formed by the black craft which shot through the dull waters of the Sea of Serenity. When they hit their target, a red lake coloured the depths, covering everything around.

Tao Li celebrated:

"I'm Number One
The winner is me,
I'm on fire
I'm Tao Li!"

Tao Li's triumphant song was brought to a sudden end when, from amid the red darkness, the monster appeared, alive and angry.

"What? What on earth?" exclaimed Tao Li and rushed to order the systems to fire at will. Shells and missiles shot out of the black craft like fireworks but the shark's massive head remained untouched, pointing in Tao Li's direction. The wounded beast roared once more as it wildly attacked the black craft. Tao Li ordered the craft to reverse and beat an untidy retreat. That was his mistake. No-one could get away from the lord of the Sea of Serenity by retreating...

The enormous beast was now playing with the black craft as a cat with a mouse. First it knocked it gently, causing it to spin out of control as if seized by a typhoon. Then it began to strike it with its huge tail, bouncing it like a ball from rock to rock. When it had enjoyed the game for long enough, the shark prepared for the *coup de grace*: It immobilised the craft between rocks and, having swum all around it like a lion sizing up its prey, stopped opposite, ready to pierce it with its nose which stuck out like a double-edged sword from its head.

Tao Li, quivering like a fish caught in nets, was delirious with fear. The monster was there in front of him, ready to finish him off...

Suddenly everything changed! A small flying object, lit up like a Christmas tree, sped through the dull, coloured water like a shining arrow and penetrated the body of the enormous shark. It was Jurka Slavik's white craft rushing to help and it gave the monster a massive electric shock!

The shark started to quiver and shake like a earthquake-stricken building about to collapse. All around was chaos. The waves of the Sea of Serenity grew rough and carried everything away in their stormy wake, lifting Tao Li's ship like a shell. The shark was mad with pain, having been burned, but it had still not been destroyed. The monster proved to be a true survivor and Jurka Slavik quickly steered the white craft into the safety of the first cave he found in front of him.

Tao Li's black craft was not so lucky. The wounded shark, still thrashing about in the water, waving its huge tail right and left, struck it with such force that it was lifted into the air, high above the stormy waves of the Sea of Serenity, and away to the rocks along the coast...

It then turned to the white craft that had electrocuted it. The monster was foaming at the mouth with pain and fury. Emitting a terrible roar, it headed for Jurka Slavik, ready to finish him off.

"Go, go, white cloud!" shouted Jurka and the pursuit began.

The shark approached the small amphibious craft and opened its mouth to swallow it up but Jurka, with skilful movements, got away from it at the last moment, adding more tension. The deadly hunt continued without a break when suddenly Jurka Slavik noticed behind the white craft the strange, transparent grey-white screen undulating like a veil, similar to the one he had seen on the White Cloud spaceship.

Lord Salvador's words came into his mind: "Remember the White Cloud..." Wasn't that what he had said before Jurka climbed into the small white craft?

Then it hit him! Only then did he realise the brilliant construction of the spaceships of the White Cloud's class. It was an incredible, self-reproducing craft that nothing could ever destroy.

Jurka smiled on seeing that the shark was still furiously chasing him. It was now time for the hunted to become the hunter. And instead of hitting it with all the weapons at his disposal, he realised that he needed to act with prudence and cunning.

He knew, at last, that he would have to change from hunter to fisherman. And the white craft would be his bait. Yes, now was the right moment for him to catch the monster...

He armed the explosive systems and activated the automatic explosion timer to one minute. Then he reduced speed, steadied the craft on a straight course and watched the screen where the monster could be seen readying itself to attack and swallow them.

The shark was now just a breath away. Its two shining eyes pierced their target and its enormous mouth opened threateningly. Its razor-sharp, cylindrical teeth came into sight, filling the screen.

"Transfer – now!" ordered Jurka and in one bound he was behind the whitish-grey screen.

A terrifying "hrrrrrappp!" was heard as the shark's powerful mouth closed and its sharp teeth seized hold of the white craft, crushing it as if it were as soft as ice cream. At the same moment, the figure of Jurka Slavik was launched towards the surface, covered by the protective grey-white veil.

The light-haired young man's body was washed up on the shore and the protective garment dissolved immediately. Jurka stood up and turned his eyes back to the water. Several tormenting, anxious moments passed. The Sea of Serenity now looked calm, as if nothing had happened, as if in its depths there had never been the dominant presence of the terrible shark.

The young man started counting: "Five, four, three, two, one!"

The sound of the explosion in the monster's insides was deafening and so strong that huge waves at once blew up. Jurka ran for cover as the waves crashed onto the shore and pieces, large and small, of the sea monster fell all around like withered figs...

Chapter 5

The atmosphere in the Dark Palace was one of rapture. Lord Salvador and his friends had organised a crazy celebration and fireworks were going off noisily in the Conference Hall which had been transformed to resemble an outdoor picnic site. The wise lord's mandolin was performing its miracles and the Brides surrounded the wise Salvador, dancing and singing. The barber from planet Green Vegetables was drunk and, brandishing his scissors, he was chasing Kolo-kol, shouting that he wanted to cut off his unmentionables.

On the presidium, commotion reigned. The Elders were counting the profits and losses from the betting while the Mace-bearers dutifully registered the result of the duel:

"The winner is Jurka Slavik from planet Earth!"

Doctor Soc-rat had taken on the look of a sorrowful virgin. He sank down into his throne, incapable of uttering a word, shamed before the interplanetary directorate whose fury would doubtless be vented on him. They had lost many bets and that was not a good sign. Kolo-kol crept up to the throne like a snail since the shouts and curses of Taka-mura were threatening him directly. As for the Vivandré, its one head kept butting the other since neither of the two would accept responsibility for betting on the wrong duellist...

Jurka emerged victorious and triumphant from the White Cloud and landed on the ground tired but justified. Milo and Johara ran to him and embraced him.

"Well done man, bravo!" the black giant kept repeating, his eyes shining with joy. Johara wiped away tears of happiness and kissed the winner: "You deserve this, Jurka Slavik," she told him. "And I hope that's the end of the business with Goldilocks here..." she added, as Nefeli approached the young man with such light steps she seemed to fly.

"Jurka Slavik, you deserve a caress," declared the blonde beauty and ran her fingers through his light-brown hair. Jurka blushed as red as a beetroot and he became as speechless as a cucumber.

"Th...th...thank you!" he managed to stammer, as he felt his knees giving way.

Nefeli gave him a sweet smile and walked away just as majestically and prettily as she had come. At the other side of the Conference Hall, waiting for her, was Tao Li, ragged and exhausted, with the Tigers consoling him.

Jurka Slavik swore: "Damn you, Tao Li!" he said through his teeth and turned to Johara. "Why, kiddo, why?"

The black-eyed short-haired girl did not answer, except to make a gesture with her hand which touched her heart. Then she lowered her head and made an about turn. She didn't want Jurka to see that she was crying again...

Captain Lu-gi leapt onto Jurka in celebration. Ben-azir and her entourage approached the young victor of the duel.

"Bravo Jur-ka! May the vision of Grace protect you always!" they wished him and the young man replied, "Thanks a lot, guys, and the same to you..."

He could not take his mind off Nefeli. What kind of behaviour was this? What did that caress mean? Why such a sweet smile? And how did she explain going back to Tao Li? Tao Li, who had been beaten and humiliated in front of everyone, from Earth and elsewhere?

Lord Salvador interrupted the young man's thoughts and the questions that were troubling him.

"I see you finally got the message and managed to escape the shark's teeth, young man..." remarked the wise lord and Jurka realised that he had not yet thanked him...

"Lord Salvador of wisdom, please accept my gratitude," he said but the wise lord had other things on his mind.

"Cut the clever talk, Jurka Slavik, you can use that on the others. What's happening with the babe?" he asked, nodding towards Nefeli who was taking care of Tao Li.

'I don't know, my lord, I don't know..." replied Jurka, as if lost, and the wise lord consoled him: "You'll soon find out, my boy, you'll soon find out..."

"How will I find out? Eh, wise lord, tell me, how am I going to find out?" asked Jurka impatiently but Lord Salvador cut him short: "Ooops, stop! You'll see, you'll soon see and you'll learn, yes, you'll learn," repeated Lord Salvador enigmatically and he called his delegation to him.

"It's time to get things straight with shorty," he announced.

"Payback time..."

Ben-azir waved the green shawl with the emblem of the lost Third Sun: "By the Vision of Grace, the Spe-ranto are ready," she said and the other three Black Cloudian fighters nodded in agreement.

"Fine, then. Let me handle the matter of the victory," said Lord Salvador and he turned to the throne and Doctor Soc-rat. The Viv-andré had brought him some zi-van and he was drowning his sorrows with Kolo-kol, flanked by Master Zar-ko and Taka-mura with his guards. The Conference Hall was still seething with rage and things might get out of control. No, no, Doctor Soc-rat was not afraid that the stupid delegates to the interplanetary directorate would bring him to his knees. Those he could take care of with a wave of his little finger. Anyway, what kind of master of the beard was he if he could not manage a crowd of inferior beings, all tied to their dependence on Cre-matum? No, it was the others he feared, the hated Lord Salvador and his company, especially the traitor Ben-azir. By Vasi-vuzuk, he ought to be thinking right now of ways to get rid of them. He needed to use all the cunning that the strength of his unique beard gave him...

"All right, shorty, it's time to talk!"

Lord Salvador's voice rang like a steel thunderclap in the Conference Hall of the Dark Palace. At once all the noise died down and all eyes focused on the presidency.

Doctor Soc-rat stood before his throne, endeavouring to display as much dignity as possible.

"Indeed, indeed, false lord of false wisdom," he replied. "A battle may have been lost on account of this stupid, incapable Tao Li but the war has not yet been lost... There's still everything to play for!" he added and Kolo-kol repeated like an echo: "Everything to play for!"

Lord Salvador burst into laughter.

"Is that so, short and stupid one? There's still everything to play for, is there?" he said. "But of course there is, since we haven't got round to matters concerning Black Cloud or you yet. Only the problem with the Earthlings has been resolved, correct?"

Doctor Soc-rat lost his tongue. The Elders stood up in protest behind their desks on the presidium. Just listen to him! Mixing up Black Cloud business with the Earthlings, and him a foreigner, an outcast and an outsider?

Doctor Soc-rat signalled to them to sit down calmly in their places. He would handle this major issue himself. But first, he would have to negotiate certain things with the hated lord, chiefly the matter of the punishment of the invaders from Earth. The duel had resolved this headache and what remained to be dealt with was the question of what would become of Nefeli.

"False lord of false wisdom, I propose that we move on to a working dinner," Doctor Soc-rat announced. "The representatives of the interplanetary directorate may go to the hall for the reception. And then we'll see..." added the stubby, bearded overlord and Lord Salvador did not waver for a second.

"Oh, that's a wonderful idea. Indeed, it's time for us to enjoy ourselves. We've been dying of hunger in this accursed Dark Palace..." he said and called his delegation to follow him into the official dining room.

The oval table had already been set by holograms. The pitch black tablecloth with its gold embroidered designs of the Two Suns hung down to the floor while , elegant silver knives and forks and gold-plated plates and goblets had been carefully placed on it with great flair. Doctor Soc-rat sat at one end of the oval table and Lord Salvador sat precisely opposite him. The Elders were to the stocky overlord's right while on the left side were Kolo-kol, the Viv-andré, the Three Star Commander, Master Zar-ko, and finally the Captain of the guard, Taka-mura. The Mace-bearers sat on the two opposing sides of the oval table, ready to register everything dictated to them. On either side of Lord Salvador sat the friends from Earth and the Spe-ranto fighters from Black Cloud.

Doctor Soc-rat clapped his hands and the hologram of the Maitre de stated at once: "Present, give your order!"

"Bring us drinks and hors d'oeuvres..." ordered the host and the holograms argued stylishly about which would carry out the orders. Doctor Soc-rat turned to his hated enemy: "What would your false lordship care to try?" the stubby overlord dutifully asked. "Which menu would you prefer? Ours? Earthly? Or Interplanetary?" he added.

"Hmm, hmm... let me see what you've got..." mumbled Lord Salvador and pressed the button on the side of his chair. Like the subtitles of a film, various dishes began to pass in front of him.

"Ah! Nice!" exclaimed Lord Salvador. "I've decided," he said and his personal hologram spoke: "I'm listening..."

"As a starter I'd like some mushroom soup," the wise lord began to give his order. "It will be accompanied by white wine from planet Best. Then I'd like smoked sole with boiled vegetables and a rosé wine... For the main course I'll have two cubes – make a note of that, two cubes – of cutlets à la elastique in a thick pepper sauce with onion stuffing and finely chopped fried potatoes mixed with tomatoes. Red dry wine from planet Borde. And for afters, fruit, plenty of Earth fruit, a tray of mixed home-made sweets and, of course, freshly made coffee with three Suns brandy..." Lord Salvador finished his order.

"As you wish!" the hologram murmured dutifully and made to leave. "And while you're at it... Bring us some champagne, lots of champagne... to start with!" the wise lord completed his order and settled into his seat, smiling with satisfaction. Soon he would be enjoying his favourite menu.

The Black Cloud delegation did not bother with ordering since they all followed Doctor Soc-rat's selection. First they would drink zi-van with three dollops of hors d'oeuvres, then zi-van with two dollops of main course and finally zi-van with a dollop tasting of sweet and fruit. As a digestive they would have a shot of so-ki to sober up.

Ben-azir, Ti-hon, Ma-ru and Lu-gi proved to be light eaters since they ordered just one dollop per course, the first tasting of soup, the next of macaroni for the main course and then a honey-flavoured sweet. They would drink only power juice from the Eternal Tree. The three friends of the Nectar Brotherhood decided to order the cubes from menu 14 which had a starter tasting of sausage and a chicken-flavoured main course. For a sweet they would eat cheese and accompany their meal with fresh grape-flavoured juice.

The champagne flowed freely at the table and Lord Salvador lost no time. He started drinking glass after glass, making inarticulate noises of satisfaction and contentment: "Whooo! Owwww!"

Doctor Soc-rat watched, angry but expressionless, as his hated enemy downed the bottles of champagne one after another and, every so often, called out, "Cheers, shorty, may you burn in hellfire"

The doctor did not remain silent and returned the compliments. The zi-van had literally revived him and his Black Cloudian blood was boiling in his veins, while you would have thought that his bald dome of a head was ready to burst from the pressure.

"Your health, false lord of false wisdom... May you burn with Vasi-vuzuk..." he wished him...

After the starters, accompanied by plenty of white wine, came the other dishes and it was not until they had reached the sweet and the Three Suns brandy that they began discussing the issues that concerned them. Doctor Soc-rat conceded that the victory of the young Earthling, Jurka, though a major surprise, was completely deserved.

"You may now consider that your conviction is no longer valid," he said and the Mace-bearers dutifully informed the Om-niscient of this.

"Now you can take the ugly, hairy Nefeli and get back to where you came from," he added, addressing the three friends of the Nectar Brotherhood. "As for Tao Li, take him with you too, I couldn't care less," Doctor Soc-rat concluded and sipped at another cup of zi-van.

"Yippee! We won!" cheered Lord Salvador and downed his brandy in one.

Jurka looked at him with concern and nudged Milo and Johara. "Guys, our good lord is sozzled again," he whispered. Indeed, Lord Salvador was out of it, that was more and more obvious as he staggered about dangerously, muttering incomprehensibly...

Doctor Soc-rat hurried to order so-ki so as to sober up. It was one thing having to deal with a crafty, omnipotent lord but another altogether when that lord was drunk, thought the overlord...

Lord Salvador understood nothing. He had staggered to his feet and embraced a hologram, while trying to execute dance steps. The result was painful, since with every step he stumbled out of control and on the second step he fell over, apologising as he did so: "Pardon!" he stammered and began the same nonsense again.

Jurka and Milo got up and tried to sort him out and sit him on his chair but the crazy lord slipped like an eel and continued to display his dance skills with new somersaults.

The Spe-ranto delegation was speechless. The situation was tragic and with Lord Salvador out of control, they would be helpless at the hands of Doctor Soc-rat and his men. What kind of negotiations could they hold? What resistance could they offer in the enemy's lair?

Doctor Soc-rat decided that it was time to get the situation under control. He banged his sceptre on the floor three times and imposed silence. Lord Salvador was lying on the floor, waving his arms in their air as if he wanted to hold onto something in order to stand up. In vain! All he could raise was a mocking laugh from Doctor Soc-rat and the members of his delegation.

"Chief Secretary Kolo-kol," said the overlord in an official tone, "prepare the agenda for the negotiations," he ordered.

Kolo-kol ran to his notebooks at one end of the dining room and returned with a red dossier under his arm.

"Here you are, time-honoured lord of the beard. It's all here. Ready!" declared the Chief Secretary showily and stood upright, like a pillar, at Doctor Soc-rat's side.

"Item one: Invasion of Black Cloud by Earthlings..." the overlord began to read and then he swore at Kolo-kol. "We've already finished with that, you idiot of a secretary! Why have you brought it back to me? To give me a hard time for no reason?" grunted Doctor Soc-rat and Kolo-kol bent double in apology. "Forgive me, great doctor, forgive me, it was a mistake... It was registered in error..." Kolo-kol said over and over, shamed in front of the Elders and the other negotiators.

"Two strokes on the backside for the mistake!" ordered the stocky overlord and Master Zar-ko immediately carried out the order. The Chief Secretary said, "Thank you my lord," and that was the end of the matter.

"Let's continue, then, why are we delaying?" shouted Doctor Soc-rat and Kolo-kol began to read the second item.

"Conspiracy by the Spe-ranto guerrillas against interplanetary order in general and of the state of the Two Suns in particular. Violation of the legal status and omnipotence of Cre-matum. Undermining of the highest authority, the time-honoured lord of the beard," concluded Kolo-kol.

"There's more..." shouted the side of the Council of Elders and Master Zar-ko confirmed this: "Yes, great lord of the beard, there are more illegal acts..."

"Stop!" ordered Doctor Soc-rat. "These are enough for us to send them to spend their lives in the company of Me-gaera," whispered the overlord and called upon the wise lord's delegation to speak. "What do you have to say, traitors of the nation and the people?" he asked. Ben-azir rose from her seat. She was furious. She stretched her four-fingered hand towards Doctor Soc-rat and replied in a voice throbbing with anger.

"How dare you read out such false accusations? How dare you threaten us with annihilation before hearing our views? How dare you, eh? How dare you?"

The dining room froze. The reaction of the leader of the Speranto fighters was so abrupt that they all restrained themselves from reacting. But not the powerful doctor. Since Lord Salvador was still rolling around on the floor trying, unsuccessfully, to stand on his feet, the situation was still under his complete control. What could a handful of weak opponents do to him?

"Shut up, traitor!" he roared and his thunderous voice echoed around the dining room. "That's all we need, you giving us a sermon in our own house..." he added and waved his sceptre about. A roar was heard in the room as plates, glasses and other items flew like feathers into its four corners.

Ben-azir was not fazed by Doctor Soc-rat's violent reaction. She banged her fist on the table and ordered the members of the delegation to prepare to withdraw from the negotiations.

"My friends, take Lord Salvador too," she ordered the members of the Nectar Brotherhood and they stood up to obey.

"Just a minute! Who gave you permission to withdraw, eh?" Doctor Soc-rat shouted and, at once, Master Zar-ko and Taka-mura took up positions to restrain them.

Ben-azir gave Master Zar-ko a cold look. "Get out of my way, trash! You were always a nobody!" she told him. Immediately afterwards she addressed Doctor Soc-rat. "And you were always an insolent coward..." she said to his face and the overlord exploded with rage.

"You'll see who's insolent and an coward! I'll show you! By Megaera, I'll rip you to pieces..." he exclaimed and prepared to attack the leader of the Spe-ranto.

Ti-hon, Ma-ru and Lu-gi stood in front of her. "Go on, try!" they said in unison.

Doctor Soc-rat opened his empty mouth and let forth a roar like that of a wounded lion.

The three Black Cloudian guerrillas spread out like feathers on the wind. Ben-azir did not move from her position. Doctor Soc-rat blew again but once more the guerrilla leader stood firm as a rock.

"Curses!" shouted the overlord. "What's going on?" he asked and Ben-azir replied coldly: "This!" and she blew back. Now it was Doctor Soc-rat who was performing a spectacular somersault in the air as the strength of the Spe-ranto leader propelled him backwards. In the dining room there was a drawn-out "aaahhhh!" while Jurka, Johara and Milo were jubilant, breaking into applause and cheering.

Doctor Soc-rat managed to find his feet at once. The Viv-andré was near him, with Kolo-kol, ready to provide assistance, but the stubby overlord dismissed them.

"Get out of here! Leave me in peace..." ordered the crumpled doctor and turned his attention back to Ben-azir. "Now I'm going to show you who's boss around here, you disgusting traitor!" he said through his teeth and stretched both hands in Ben-azir's direction.

"By the force of the Two Suns, by the power of the immortal beard, surrender to me!" declared Doctor Soc-rat and, as if by a miracle, Ben-azir froze like a statue. Then she moved, as if hypnotised, and began to take small, steady steps towards Doctor Soc-rat. Everyone in the hall was speechless...

Everyone, that is, except one! The drunken Lord Salvador suddenly stood up, stumbled once or twice and looked as if he was about to fall down again. He looked at Ben-azir who was a breath away from Doctor Soc-rat's outstretched hands which were ready to grab her by the throat. Lord Salvador stopped him.

"Shorty, hey, shorty... By Master Hahanoff, I'm going to pluck that ridiculous beard of yours!" and Ben-azir started, as if waking from a deep sleep.

"Now give him one, Ben-azir!" came the wise lord's voice and two punches landed on the round cheeks of the time-honoured lord of the beard.

"Aaaahhh!"

The familiar war-cry drowned out the dining room as the Elders and the Mace-bearers, Master Zar-ko and Taka-mura, the Viv-andré and Kolo-kol covered their eyes in shame. The time-honoured lord of the beard had received so many slaps that he shot into the air and crash landed on the floor...

"And now let us return to our places and our business," said Lord Salvador as if nothing had happened.

Lu-gi flew onto the shoulders of Milo who was jumping for joy. Jurka and Johara ran happily to their mentor and protector.

"We thought you'd been drinking and..." Jurka started to say but Lord Salvador did not let him finish.

"Shame on you, Jurka Slavik! How could you get such an idea into your head?"

"But my lord, you were rolling drunk," the young man protested and Johara supported him: "It's true, Lord Salvador. You were completely sozzled, you couldn't stand up, you were crawling around," said the black-eyed girl and the wise lord chastised her: "What are you talking about, my girl? So I had one little drink… Look at me now. Sober as a judge!" he said, and to prove the truth of what he was saying he performed a backward somersault.

"Owwww!" the wise lord groaned as he landed untidily on the floor.

Johara shook her head: "That's enough my lord, get serious now, we've still got a lot of work," she whispered to him as she helped him up.

They again took up their places and the Chief Secretary was ordered by the crumpled Doctor Soc-rat to re-read the accusations against the Spe-ranto.

Lord Salvador listened patiently and when Kolo-kol had finished, he stood up and declared in an official tone: "And now, ladies and gentlemen, bums and scum, let's listen to what our side has to say," he announced. "Ben-azir, the floor is yours," added the wise lord. The guerrilla leader stood up and, without a second thought, denied all the charges.

"The Spe-ranto are fighting for the return of harmony to planet Black Cloud," she said. "The Spe-ranto are aiming to restore the rule of law on our planet and the healthy principles of interplanetary cooperation. Our aim is the liberation of all races and beings from their dependence on Cre-matum…"

"Silence! Stop!" interrupted Doctor Soc-rat, banging his sceptre hard on the floor. "What is this that we are hearing?" he asked rhetorically and immediately answered: "Guerillas preaching disobedience and an uprising against legality, that's what!"

The Elders nodded their heads in agreement while Master Zar-ko, for some reason, had gone a deep red and was seething with rage. Kolo-kol signalled to the Mace-bearers to record everything while the Viv-andré rushed to offer a little so-ki to the overlord. Doctor Soc-rat addressed the auditorium with a condescending air.

"There you are, Elders and representatives, there is your admittance of guilt! What more do we need to hear to be convinced that they are guilty of conspiracy and rebellion against the state? I ask you, tell me…" Doctor Soc-rat challenged them.

"Rubbish! Everything you've said is nonsense, nothing more and nothing less…" replied Ben-azir and returned her attention to the perspiring Master Zar-ko. "As for you, I didn't expect any other reaction," she said enigmatically and fell silent.

The Spe-ranto leader had answered the charges and said what she had to say. Now it was the turn of Lord Salvador to speak. The wise lord rose ostentatiously and lit up a huge cigar, blowing the smoke in Doctor Soc-rat's face. The overlord coughed as the smoke made him choke and Kolo-kol at once ordered the holograms to give the overlord some air and to clean the atmosphere.

In vain! Lord Salvador continued to puff smoke and soon the round, ring-like clouds had filled the dining room, forming a white hole in the air, like a screen in a pitch black frame.

Lord Salvador apologised: "I beg your pardon, dear friends, but I have a weakness for screens. You see, I'm a visual type and I prefer to speak with the language of pictures rather than words," he murmured.

Silence reigned in the room. Everyone was anxious about Lord Salvador's peculiar behaviour. What was the crafty lord up to now? What was that screen all about? And what was he going to show to the negotiating teams?

"Ready?" he asked, as if nothing was going on. No-one answered and Lord Salvador sat down comfortably in his armchair.

"Action!" he ordered, as if directing a film and the white screen began to darken and to gradually fill with images.

At first it showed a panoramic view of Black Cloud and as the invisible, unknown camera performed its slow guided tour, one sun could be clearly seen after the other. First the bright great Sun filled the screen which covered most of the surface. Then, on the other side of the planet, appeared the small Sun and suddenly – by Master Hahanoff! – there appeared on the far horizon a third Sun...

"Aaaahhh!" exclaimed the Spe-ranto and bowed.

"The Third Sun! By the vision of Grace, it's the Third Sun!" they all said as one and Ben-azir reverently waved the green shawl with the emblem of the Third Sun...

"Curses!" shouted the Elders and Doctor Soc-rat swore together.

"By my beard, what in Vasi-vuzuk is this?"

Kolo-kol leaned over to his master's ear and whispered that it was a faked scene.

"This is not acceptable as evidence," protested the Chief Secretary and Doctor Soc-rat, parrot-fashion, repeated Kolo-kol's declaration.

"We'll see about that later," responded Lord Salvador and the Elders decided: "Very well, let's move on... What else are we going to see..." they said aloud so that everyone could hear.

Doctor Soc-rat was fretting and fuming but the Elders' decision was final. Master Zar-ko looked anxious and was fidgeting nervously in his chair. Next to him, Taka-mura was worried too...

"Very well then, let's proceed..." said Lord Salvador. The camera zoomed in and the Aerial Fortress was seen hovering imposingly in the void. The invisible camera penetrated further inside and was soon showing the private apartments of Master Zar-ko in the observatory...

The room was buzzing with the murmuring of those present when the familiar face of Master Zar-ko appeared on the screen in the uniform of Two Star Commander.

Doctor Soc-rat, speechless, watched the scenes as his deep-set empty eyes glanced towards the Elders of the Council. Master Zar-ko nervously waved his staff. He was sweating and every so often would wipe his bald head, trying in vain to appear cool and calm. It was the same with Taka-mura...

The camera was merciless! And when Master Zar-ko's wife appeared onscreen, a long-drawn-out "aaaaahhh!" filled the dining room. It was Ben-azir! The woman was holding a tray of drinks and cubes, ready to lay the table for dinner. Her uniform revealed the rank of One Star Commander, a fact that caused exclamations of surprise around the room. The two of them sat down at the table and began their meal while appearing to be discussing something but there was no sound. The Elders protested. How could they judge fairly if the screen was taking them back to the era of silent films?

Lord Salvador gestured to them to calm down. Everything would be made clear, all in good time, he assured them...

Ben-azir rose from her seat and pointed at the screen with her four-fingered hand. "Now watch this, Elders, all of you, watch!" she shouted and Lord Salvador gestured to her to sit down. The best was yet to come, he whispered to her...

The Elders cleared their throats and the eyes of all turned to them.

"Very well," said the Elders. "Let's continue..."

The scene on the screen changed. It now showed the Dark Palace and Doctor Soc-rat with a longer and heavier beard sitting on his throne. The ever-present and ever-obliging Chief Secretary Kolo-kol stood at one side and, at the other, the Viv-andré was running around and doing the bidding of the time-honoured lord of the beard.

Doctor Soc-rat whispered something in the Chief Secretary's ear and he called the Mace-bearers. When they entered the throne room, Doctor Soc-rat signalled to them to sit down and witness some revealing information that the Om-niscient was going to transmit.

Then he gave the order: "Om-niscient, reveal what Master Zarko is reporting!"

The Om-niscient began its transmission. First it showed the same scene of dinner with the two married Commanders. Then, it appeared that Ben-azir was discussing with her husband, the Two Star Commander.

The One Star Commander was gesturing vividly and quarrelling with him. From her open and empty mouth, their conversation could now be heard clearly. The dialogue was interesting…

"…And for how long is an idiot going to be determining how we live?" Ben-azir was heard to say.

"Don't! What are you saying about the great master of the beard, stupid Ben-azir?"

"What I'm saying is only a little. Listen to him, wanting to have a monopoly of Cre-matum. When are we going to enjoy some? When are we going to travel to magic, dreamlike worlds, eh? When?

"This is blasphemy, Ben-azir. It's not our turn… Doctor Soc-rat is a just man, he knows when to reward us…"

"Just? Who, that dumpy creature? What a joke…"

Ben-azir's figure appeared to rock uncontrollably…

"Stop!" came Master Zar-ko's cry. "You're a sinner! You're… you're unacceptable, yes, by the great doctor of the beard, unacceptable. I won't put up with this rebellion any longer!"

"So, what good news is this film bringing us?" Lord Salvador of wisdom asked calmly. Doctor Soc-rat sprang up: "By the Two Suns, are you mad, false lord? What better proof of the conspiracy, of blasphemy and rebellion against authority can there be than in the document that you've just shown us?

"Yes, yes, we agree with that!" repeated the Elders in chorus as they looked bewildered at Lord Salvador. What was he, after all – the guerillas' defence counsel or the undertaker who would be fitting their tombstone?

"Don't be in such a hurry, mindless Elders! And you, shorty, don't cross your bridges until you come to them! You've seen what you've seen, goatface. Now take a look at this," said Lord Salvador and once again the screen showed the dinner scene.

The married Commanders' meal was over and master Zar-ko was heard to ask for permission to go to Headquarters on urgent business. Ben-azir patted him on the shoulder in a tender farewell gesture and the camera followed Commander Zar-ko's path outside his private apartments. A guard on the corner met him and they marched together to Headquarters. When the camera changed angle, the face of the guard was seen to be that of none other than Taka-mura, Master Zar-ko's guard, faithful as a dog to his master... The two of them were seen entering Headquarters and locking the door behind them, with Taka-mura standing there as a vigilant guard.

Master Zar-ko approached the Om-niscient and inserted a memory coin into the device. Then, the two of them left unseen, just as they had come...

Master Zar-ko was furious.

"All this is an attempt to discredit us!" the Three Star Commander shouted and Taka-mura repeated the cry, "yes, yes, to discredit us..."

The Elders gestured to them to quieten down. Then they turned to the wise lord, bewildered. "And what does that prove?" they asked but Lord Salvador remained silent.

Doctor Soc-rat said nothing but he whispered something in Kolo-kol's ear. The Chief Secretary set off for the exit but Lord Salvador stopped him. "No-one is to leave this room!" he ordered and they all froze.

The Council of Elders was in agreement with him.

"The Council considers the deposition of the film to be extremely important and declares that, for the sake of justice, no-one will leave the room until the final verdict is handed down," they announced and Kolo-kol was obliged to return and perch next to his lord.

Then Lord Salvador spoke.

"The scene that I have shown you, you stupid representatives of the planet's ruling class, shows quite clearly how the ones who conspired and trapped Commander Ben-azir were none other than her husband Master Zar-ko and Taka-mura! They fixed the voice on the film so as to make Ben-azir look guilty!" the wise Lord declared in an icy tone. Then he turned to Doctor Soc-rat: "I accuse you of being an accomplice by allowing all this to happen with your full knowledge and approval, dumpy overlord..."

Doctor Soc-rat jumped up in anger. This was a very serious charge and he would not accept such humiliation in his own Palace at the hands of a rebellious adventurer like the false lord.

"You are a liar and a crook!" he shouted. "You're a charlatan selling favours! You're an enemy of the people of Black Cloud and our galaxy! Why would I take part, as you're insinuating, false lord, in an alleged conspiracy and in the entrapment of the traitor Ben-azir?"

"Because Ben-azir had uncovered the great Cre-matum fraud!" replied the wise lord coldly.

The Elders turned to Doctor Soc-rat. "Well, we are listening, great doctor of the beard. What do you have to say?" they asked.

The stocky overlord was scared.

"But didn't you hear? Didn't you see? That's the truth. All the rest is the work of the devil..."

The voice of the overlord was choked with rage and he began to bang his sceptre right and left. Kolo-kol helped him to sit down and the Viv-andré at once offered him a drink of zi-van while the hologram seized a fan and created a draught of air for the lord of the beard.

Lord Salvador burst into laughter and, to everyone's surprise, started to sing.

"Cool it, cool it, no charlatan am I
Cool it, cool it, I'm not an apple pie
I'm just the one who brings the message
A poor old penniless sausage..."

The three friends of the Nectar Brotherhood were thrilled and they continued the song together:

"No Lord Salvador
You're no charlatan
Nor even apple pie
You're just a magician
A poor old penniless guy..."

The cheerful atmosphere in the dining room turned out to be infectious and soon prevailed everywhere. A great celebration began with everyone in Lord Salvador's delegation standing up, dancing and jumping onto the table, turning the place into a party. The doors were opened wide and the joyful atmosphere was transferred lightning-fast to the Conference Hall and the representatives of the interplanetary directorate. It was now the turn of the delegations from around the galaxy and the Dark Palace was soon humming to the song of the mixed choir:

"We're not tramps and we're not spies
We're brave fighters with a sparkle in our eyes...
We say no to misery, to begging on the streets
No to the dictators, and no to all the cheats!"

Lord Salvador was leaping around joyfully while Doctor Soc-rat and his men were obliged to keep a low profile. They knew perfectly well that their troubles were behind them...

When the song had finished and the cheering died down, the wise lord addressed the delegates in the Great Hall.

"And now, dear representatives of the intergalactic directorate and you, people of Black Cloud, the time has come for you to learn the truth. Yes, now the truth will be revealed. The whole truth and nothing but the truth... About everyone and everything!"

Lord Salvador called the Mace-bearers to activate the transmitters which sent out the highest priority messages to the residents of the planet and screens on all public buildings and Universal Arcades, in homes and workplaces, sounded the alert. Everyone would see the important new message that was about to be broadcast...

First to appear on the screens was One Star Commander Ben-azir, carrying out a routine inspection of the Cre-matum mines. Then her conversation with the official in charge was heard.

"I want to check the Cre-matum processing data. You need to give me the disc..." said Ben-azir and the employee requested the authority of the Council of Elders. Ben-azir showed him her papers and the Black Cloudian official gave her the disc containing the data. Ben-azir took the disc, said "thank you" and left...

The next scene again showed One Star Commander Ben-azir but this time she was in the data processing laboratory in the Aerial Fortress working on the macroanalyst. Ben-azir activated the rays of the Third Sun which proved to be miracle-working and, with their help, succeeded in decoding the top secret data on the disc. The scene showed quite clearly how Ben-azir was continuously making notes of certain data and, by the time she had finished, just how upset she was. She removed the disc from the computer and hurried to her private apartments.

Waiting for her there was her husband, the Two Star Commander, Master Zar-ko. Ben-azir prepared the meal and the two Commanders sat down at the round table, facing each other. The following dialogue took place between them…

Ben-azir spoke first.

"Commander Zar-ko, my suspicions have unfortunately been proved entirely correct. The Cre-matum processing is illegal and has gone beyond the guidelines of the Council of Elders. Instead of producing an intergalactic product for the prosperity of the planets and their inhabitants, it is being turned into vehicle for their total dependence…"

"You're not serious? What are you talking about, Commander Ben-azir?"

"I'm serious. I wouldn't joke about such an important matter. Luckily the rays of the Third Sun helped me to decode everything…"

"What have you discovered? And what's the illegality?"

"The most immoral thing of all! I've discovered a huge fraud. Because now the Cre-matum is planned for other people's purposes, to enslave the minds and feelings of the users. It offers them a fake world, one where hallucinations bloom and everything can be seen as a vision… And in the end the user becomes completely addicted to a fake world of fantasy, a slave to Cre-matum and his bosses… The most precious thing we have – interplanetary harmony – is collapsing!"

"But if your claims are true, then everything is illegal and Doctor Soc-rat is violating the Code…"

"Yes, that's what I'm claiming!"

"Then you must report it to the Council of Elders… But are you sure? Do you have evidence to prove him guilty? Do you have sufficient proof?"

"Yes, it's all here on the disc. And I do consider it my duty to report him. Because, Commander Zar-ko, if we enslave people's minds, if we sell them fake happiness, then, by the vision of Grace, how free and happy will we be? Eh?"

"Correct! So I say: Report this to the Council. I'm with you…"

Ben-azir caressed her husband and left. The scene dissolved and on the screens Master Zar-ko and Taka-mura were seen entering the Dark Palace and heading towards the throne of Doctor Soc-rat who was waiting for them. There followed this dialogue:

"So, what has happened to the traitor Ben-azir?"

"We caught her red-handed, great lord. I have the audio and video evidence here, thanks to Taka-mura..."

"Hand it over!"

Doctor Soc-rat inserted the disc into the transmitter and the scene of the dialogue between Master Zar-ko and his wife Ben-azir was repeated.

"The disgraceful woman! The traitor!" roared Doctor Soc-rat and Master Zar-ko repeated the same words, like a machine...

"Very good! Very good! Now we know what she has discovered and what she plans to do..." murmured the overlord and turned to the two spies.

"Excellent work, Three Star Commander. Well done to you too, Captain of the guard Taka-mura," he said.

"Great doctor, thank you for the promotion!" said the informers.

"And now, get to work. You know what to do..."

"Yes, Doctor Soc-rat. We know..."

Next on the screens came the scene with the faked dialogue between the married couple and then it switched to the presidium of the Council of Elders.

Before them stood Ben-azir in chains and Doctor Soc-rat read out the charges of insulting the leader of the planet, taking a stand against the authorities and conspiracy to commit high treason, and demanded her dismissal from the ranks and eternal exile.

The Council of Elders took delivery of the fabricated evidence from the tape and called as the first witness for the prosecution her husband, the newly promoted Three Star Commander Zar-ko. The Commander confirmed the facts and expressed his sorrow and indignation for living with a Commander who had been taken over by Vasi-vuzuk...

Taka-mura then gave his evidence, which was a eulogy to Commander Zar-ko for his unwavering dedication to legality and the exemplary law-abiding behaviour that he had shown... Yes, the Commander had confided in him about the problem and had entrusted him with monitoring and recording the conversation, which he had carried out, loyal to the legal authorities and the system...

Ben-azir did not speak, except to accuse Doctor Soc-rat of being the brains behind the conspiracy to cook the books and fool the Council and by sacrificing her... No, unfortunately, evidence and proof of what she claimed did not exist. The disc with the information had disappeared... Nonetheless, she called on the Elders to investigate her accusations of illegal Cre-matum processing in violation of the Council's guidelines...

All in vain! The Elders' verdict was overwhelming and unanimous: In the light of the evidence produced, the accused was condemned to a life of exile and dismissal from all her ranks...

The last scene was thrilling, as it showed how Ben-azir managed to escape from the hands of Taka-mura's guards and to find refuge in the darkness of the Old City.

There she organised the Spe-ranto and led the fight for justice and the restoration of law and order and harmony on the planet and throughout the galaxy...

There was now a state of great agitation in the Dark Palace. The delegates of the interplanetary directorate were protesting loudly and shouting, demanding explanations from the overlord and his cronies. Lord Salvador whistled loudly to impose silence once again...

"Stumpy doctor of the beard, what have you got to say?" asked the wise lord.

Doctor Soc-rat had turned a deep red with anger over his public humiliation and he was constantly waving his sceptre up and down, embarrassedly stroking his ridiculous beard.

"It's all lies!" he shouted. "It's faked evidence to slander us and stab us in the back... This is the work of Vasi-vuzuk!"

Doctor Soc-rat got into his stride and attempted to alter the situation which was against him. Lord Salvador listened patiently without uttering a word. When, however, the stocky overlord had finished, he spoke again.

"Elders of the Council! Honourable delegates of the interplanetary directorate, citizens of Black Cloud. Prepare yourselves now for the Grand Finale. It is now time for light to reign in the darkness that the conspirators brought upon you..."

Lord Salvador turned to Doctor Soc-rat and looked him straight in the eye.

"Now, dumpy goatface, your greatest crime is going to be revealed..."

Lord Salvador stopped for a moment. Then he declared triumphantly:

"You and your collaborators blocked the Third Sun!"

The Dark Palace was ready to explode from shocked voices of the delegates, as Lord Salvador explained...

"Yes, Doctor Soc-rat used the Om-niscient and the Silver Curtain to block the rays of the Third Sun and to wipe it from the horizon. Why? Because only the Third Sun could uncover the Cre-matum fraud!"

The Conference Hall was seething and the panicking overlord was forced to hide behind his throne. Kolo-kol huddled there with him while the Viv-andré vainly searched for a way out. Master Zar-ko and Taka-mura were trembling like wingless birds...

"What do you have to say about all this, great master of the beard?" asked the most senior Elder.

"Lies! Lies!... It's all lies..." was all Doctor Soc-rat could stammer and Kolo-kol rushed to add that pictures did not constitute admissible evidence.

"Foolish Chief Secretary, if all that we have seen and heard does constitute admissible evidence, allow me to present the evidence for the charges against goatface here in a live performance!" declared the wide lord with all the pomp of a victor.

The Dark Palace grew quiet again. The whole of planet Black Cloud was now hanging on Lord Salvador's lips.

The wise lord approached the Mace-bearers and ordered them to connect him to the Om-niscient. Once connected, Lord Salvador gave the order: "Om-niscient, in the name of the vision of Grace and Master Hahanoff, prime minister of the Gods, I order you to remove the Silver Curtain from the Third Sun!"

The eyes of all were fixed on the dome of the Dark Palace. The waiting took a few seconds, which felt like an eternity. At first no-one was aware of anything new. But, as the moments passed painfully slowly, everyone saw with their own eyes how the light from the rays of the Third Sun was gradually growing stronger and would shortly spread throughout the sky above the planet.

"Om-niscient, show us the horizon in circular motion!" ordered Lord Salvador and on the great screen of the Dark Palace appeared the first, then the second and – by the vision of Grace, a miracle! – the lost Third Sun.

Lord Salvador, puffed up like a cockerel, requested a bottle of champagne to celebrate the event. In the Conference Hall, anger against Doctor Soc-rat now prevailed, together with admiration for the wise lord.

"So what did you think, shorty? That I'd let you do to Ben-azir what you did to me before the disappearance of the Third Sun? Did you think that I'd put up with exile and accept to wander around in space and the galaxies, as if cursed for eternity?" Lord Salvador drank another mouthful of champagne and was preparing to continue his speech when a commotion, growing louder and coming closer, made everyone look through the grey-black windows down onto the outer fence of the Dark Palace. An army of Black Cloudians and angry beings from other planets was heading for the Dark Palace with violent intentions.

Doctor Soc-rat was at a loss as to what he should do but Chief Secretary Kolo-kol kept his composure.

"Great lord, master of the beard, order an assault to stop them... They'll lynch us!" the experienced aide whispered into the doctor's huge ear.

"Hmm, yes... Master Zar-ko, lead the charge!" the doctor ordered the Three Star Commander but the latter was out of his skull. He had managed to down two or three shots of zi-van and was blind drunk.

"Here's to your good health... and good wine!" the drunken Commander kept repeating.

Taka-mura attempted to mobilise the Hor-nets but the Elders cut him short.

"Stay where you are, Captain of the guard!" they ordered and Taka-mura backed down, tail between his legs.

The mob was now banging on the grey-black doors of the Dark Palace and demanding to be let in. Lord Salvador was forced to take charge of the situation.

"Quiet! Quiet in the auditorium!" he shouted like a good judge and the roar of the crowd subsided. "There will be a public trial. A fair trial..." he announced and the Conference Hall shook with the cheers from the delegates: "Yes, yes, a trial, here and now!" they shouted.

The Elders of the Council conferred on the presidium and announced their unanimous decision: "Yes, there will be a trial. Here and now!"

Lord Salvador downed the last drops of champagne and took on the air of a public prosecutor.

"Doctor Soc-rat, doctor of conspiracy and violator of legality! You are accused of everything that has come to light in this Palace, before the Council of Elders, the foreign delegates and the residents of Black Cloud. What do you plead? Guilty or not guilty?"

Kolo-kol got there before his master and, experienced advocate that he was, requested permission to confer with the accused.

"You have permission," said Lord Salvador. "Until I've emptied another bottle of champagne," the wise lord added and asked for another glass.

"Great lord of the beard, what is your desire?" asked the servile Kolo-kol but Doctor Soc-rat was in no state to utter a word. He had been seized by melancholy and was drowning his sorrows with zivan, with the Viv-andré next to him offering consolation. The overlord was at a complete loss...

"Hmm, things are looking bad," murmured the Chief Secretary, scratching his head. What were the possible alternatives?

First, they could plead guilty, in which case they would certainly receive the heaviest sentence: Doctor Soc-rat would be sentenced to the ultimate punishment, being burnt in hellfire or, in the best case, they would remove him from the galaxy. Not a good choice...

Second, they could plead not guilty, in which case there would be a trial. What evidence and testimony did they have against the undeniable revelation of the crime with the Third Sun? None! So the end result would be the same...

Third choice: They could use the defence of diminished responsibility due to temporary insanity! Hmm, that might work and, as a result the accused would avoid the worst, perhaps being sent into exile. But on the other hand, Kolo-kol himself would pay the price since Doctor Soc-rat would cut off his privates if he made that choice... No, no!

Kolo-kol decided to go for broke. Doctor Soc-rat would be willing to plea bargain in exchange for a reduced sentence. Yes, that was it, that was the best solution!

"We request permission to negotiate with this honourable court!" said the overlord's defence counsel and the Elders gave Kolo-kol and Lord Salvador permission to approach the presidium.

"Respected Elders, we are ready to plead guilty, provided that the prosecutor assures us that he will not demand the ultimate punishment..." the Chief Secretary proposed.

Lord Salvador belched loudly. "Pardon!" he said, and added: "Accepted. The taxpayers won't have to pay the costs..."

The Elders of the Council conferred amongst themselves and quickly decided: "The request is granted!"

No-one wanted to draw out this business. When they had all taken their places again, Kolo-kol made the official announcement:

"We plead guilty to the charges!"

The Conference Hall seethed as the doors on all sides began to shudder beneath the banging of the mob.

"Hellfire! Hellfire!" they shouted rhythmically, demanding that Doctor Soc-rat be sentenced to the ultimate punishment.

"Silence! Silence in the auditorium!" shouted the Elders and Lord Salvador was obliged to whistle as loud as he could to restore order.

Eventually everything grew quiet once more. The most senior Councillor of the presidium asked Lord Salvador to address the court on the issue of the sentence.

"Elders, dimwits and toothless ones..." the wise lord began his address but he immediately apologised. "I beg your pardon, I had mixed up the courts, that's another address... I thought I was on another planet...", Lord Salvador stammered out his apology. "I shall not say very much, since time is Cre-matum," he said before declaring: "I request that the guilty Doctor Soc-rat receive an exemplary punishment. I request that he be given the proper sentence..."

"And what is that sentence?" asked the Elders.

"To be shaved by the barber from planet Green Vegetables!" Lord Salvador declared triumphantly.

Chaos reigned in the Conference Hall. The barber from planet Green Vegetables was jumping for joy and showing off his massive pair of scissors, opening and closing the blades in a display of his skill. The other delegates chanted:

"Barber, come on
Scissors out, beard gone!"

The whole city echoed with the slogan:

"Barber, come on
Scissors out, beard gone!"

The Elders of the Council conferred once more on the presidium, imposed silence and announced their decision: "The punishment is accepted..."

"And to be exiled on planet Brides!" Lord Salvador completed his demand. "That's all..." he said and sat down.

What happened next is hardly describable!

The Brides were celebrating wildly and a great party began since, at last, they would have a permanent male presence on their planet, while the others began chanting the slogan:

"Doctor, don't lose it
It's time for you to use it!"

Poor Doctor Soc-rat, drunk as he was, attempted to prevent the sentence from being carried out, desperately shouting, "No, no! I'd rather have Hellfire!" but who was listening now?

Kolo-kol tried to persuade him that this decision was the best, under the circumstances, but all he received for his trouble was a series of smacks on his behind from the overlord's sceptre. The Viv-andré was rushing around nervously, knowing that its turn would come, while Master Zar-ko fell at Ben-azir's feet and begged her forgiveness, placing all the blame on Doctor Soc-rat. Taka-mura remained rooted to the spot, unable to believe what was going on before his eyes…

The Elders of the Council needed no more than a few minutes to announce their decisions, which the Mace-bearers duly relayed to the Om-niscient's data archive.

"First, the sentences are confirmed and they will be carried out immediately.

"Second, Ben-azir is reinstated to the rank of Commander and she is made an honorary Three Star Commander.

"Third, a general amnesty is announced for all the Spe-ranto fighters.

"Fourth, the original formula for the production and processing of Cre-matum is reinstated.

"Finally, Lord Salvador is made an honorary Ambassador of the Third Sun, with duties throughout the galaxy."

The Elders' decisions set off a new wave of enthusiasm and cheering, but the trial process was not yet over…

"Lord Salvador, what is to become of the rest of the accused?" asked the most senior Councillor.

The wise lord shot them a sideways glance and said simply: "Ah, for them I propose a particularly harsh punishment…"

Everyone hung on Lord Salvador's lips.

"Make them drink cod-liver oil!"

"Cod-liver oil! No, please, not cod-liver oil!" Master Zar-ko begged the wise lord but he was adamant.

"Cod-liver oil, give the lot of them cod-liver oil!" the lord repeated and the Conference Hall again shook from the chants of the crowd:

"Just one spoonful every day
It's a real sensation
It cleans you out and soon you'll say
Goodbye to constipation!"

Lord Salvador grabbed his mandolin and began to play a samba rhythm. Everyone in the Hall was singing and dancing and suddenly an enormous line of beings from all the planets was formed. The chain of dancers jumped about and snaked its way through the whole Conference Hall while in the surrounding streets, people were cheering and singing the Ancient Ode to the Crazy Lord:

"To the wise lord, glory be
To the many coloured one, glory be
To this planet, glory be
To the crazy one, glory be..."

Lord Salvador was having the time of his life with the three members of the Nectar Brotherhood and their Black Cloudian friends when, suddenly, he remembered that there was still one more pending matter to be dealt with...

"Nefeli, come here!" Lord Salvador ordered.

Into the Dark Palace, which was now brightly illuminated by the rays of the Third Sun, came the lithe figure of the blonde beauty from planet Earth.

Nefeli took a few steps in that light walking style of hers, causing Lord Salvador to sigh. She was dressed in a white, flower-embroidered dress which hung on her divine young body like a velvet caress.

"Present..." said the girl and looked at the wise lord with her pretty blue eyes.

"Jurka Slavik, get yourself over here!" continued the wise lord and the light-haired young man took a couple of hesitant steps forward. Milo murmured something about some action while a blushing Johara was trembling with anger.

"Excellent!" said Lord Salvador. "My dear young friends, you've exasperated us for long enough. Now you're face to face. It's time to resolve the Gordian knot that is your relationship. And it's time for those of us who can't work it out to find out who's who in all this... and who wants whom. So you can get on with it with my blessing," said Lord Salvador, stepping to one side where Milo and Johara stood.

The swarthy youth was about to give Jurka a word of advice but his lips stuck together and he was unable to utter a word. The young girl with the short black hair watched Jurka with tearful eyes as he moved towards Nefeli. She felt a lump in her throat and her heart began to beat like a mad bell...

Jurka stared at Nefeli. He had the impression that the blonde beauty was standing in the middle of a heavenly garden, among jasmine and roses, chrysanthemums and carnations, lilies and lemon blossom. He looked into her eyes and, as she shot him that half-smile, he felt his knees giving way. Nefeli looked at him, still with the provocative half-smile, and reached out her hand to the young man.

"Come on!" she whispered and it was as if Jurka had been hypnotised. He took a couple of steps forward and stretched out his hand, but he could not reach the outstretched hand of his goddess.

'What on earth?" he wondered amid the dizziness and took another two steps forward. Nefeli's hand continued to invite him and to pull him like a magnet but, again, he could not touch her...

"Come on, Jurka, come to me!" the beautiful girl whispered to him and Jurka felt breathless. Was all this real? Was he truly so close to realising his dream?

The young man moved two more steps forward, trying to touch Nefeli's outstretched hand. Nothing! He was so close that he could feel it stroking his, but still nothing... He couldn't touch it... There stood Nefeli, in the middle of heavenly garden, with a half-smile on her lips, a provocative look in her eyes and a hand that was inviting his to join with it. Jurka made to move towards Nefeli but it was if he was frozen. What was this nightmare unfolding before him?

Nefeli stood so close and yet, once more, she was so inaccessible. She was there, like a divine vision, but one that retreated further and further away into the depths of the endless garden, smelling the beautiful flowers one after the other...

What was happening? Why was Nefeli walking away? Why was she slowly growing ugly? Why had that half-smile frozen on her tight lips? Why had her beautiful face become spoilt as wrinkles made their way across her rosy cheeks? Why did her white, flowery dress now look more like a bunch of rags, and why was her outstretched hand shaking? Why had she shrunk so much that she now looked like a hundred-year-old woman? Why was she disappearing from the garden?

"Oh my God!"

Jurka Slavik's cry pierced the atmosphere. Milo and Johara rushed to him at once while the wise Lord Salvador paid no heed as he enjoyed his Five Star brandy and smoked his favourite cigar.

"What's the matter, Jurka? You look as if you've seen a ghost," asked his swarthy friend anxiously. "Man, you're sweating like a sponge," he added and Johara at once wiped Jurka's face.

"Did... did you see it?" stammered the frightened youth as he looked at his friends. "Did you see...?" he repeated in a lifeless voice.

"It doesn't matter what we saw, Jurka. What matters is what you saw," answered Milo who was endeavouring to lift him to his feet. The light-haired youth was trembling and his legs had given way before the unexpected sight. He did not know what to do or how to behave and all he could do was repeat, like an old gramophone record, "What happened? Eh? What did I see? God, I don't believe it..."

"Believe it, man, just believe it..." Milo said as, with Johara's help, he sat him on the first chair he found in front of him.

"Jurka Slavik, come to your senses my boy! The lesson's over!"

It was the voice of Lord Salvador that rang out like a command. The three friends turned to him but the wise lord was already bidding them goodbye, waggling his backside, like a goose, as he walked away with quick, small steps.

"I've got other things to do..." they heard him say before he disappeared.

Jurka jumped up. First he looked at Lord Salvador who was disappearing into the distance and then he turned to his two friends of the Nectar Brotherhood. His eyes were shining and it was clear that he had suddenly found himself.

"Milo, my man, what got into me?" Jurka asked with sincerity in his voice.

"It was nothing, man. You mean, what happened to you? Well, how can I put it..." Milo hesitated for a moment, "well, your eyes have been opened!" the dark-skinned giant replied ambiguously and shot him a broad smile.

"You reckon?" replied Jurka and he turned to Johara. Her big black eyes were fixed on him and Jurka suddenly realised how pretty she was. The young girl smiled at him and the boy felt a sweet, lovely feeling wash over his whole being... He stretched out his hand and touched the girl, running his fingers through her short black hair. Johara lowered her gaze and shook her head awkwardly. Now Jurka was caressing her cheek. Then he bent down and without a word gave her a kiss.

"Jurka..." whispered the girl but he closed her mouth.

"Shhhh! Don't say anything, Johara..." he whispered. Then he took her face in his two hands and turned it so as to look straight into her eyes.

"Forgive me, Johara, please... Forgive me for being blind. How blind I've been, kiddo, how blind..."

The black haired girl freed her head and said simply:

"Come on, Jurka!" and took him by the hand. Milo grabbed the light-haired youth's other hand and the three friends stood to attention.

It was time to go back...

Jurka gave the order.

"Beam us up now!"

The three members of the Nectar Brotherhood were on the White Cloud.

"And now, Nec-Tar 1, take us back home!